INTRODUCTION

Love Notes by Mary Davis
Laurel Rivers has just lost her father in a bank robbery of his own scheming. Ashamed of his behavior, Laurel finds her only solace in a sheet of music she discovers propped up on the piano in the church. Each week, a new line of music or lyrics appears, drawing her closer to the writer. But can she bear the truth when his identity is revealed?

Cookie Schemes by Kathleen E. Kovach
Prudie Burke is a headstrong twenty-year-old college graduate who rebels against the 1950s conservative expectation of settling down to raise a family and instead moves in with friends. Alex Prescott is the heir to a Chinese/American restaurant corporation and must find a wife within the year or forfeit all rights to the family-run business. Alex tries wooing Prudie with fortune cookies and slips special scripture verses inside, but is there enough time?

Posted Dreams by Sally Laity
No stranger to loneliness, twenty-year-old Bethany Prescott must provide for her ailing mother. Working at John Granger's real estate office and with no outlet to express her private hopes and dreams, she begins leaving anonymous sticky notes around town—bits of poetry, slices of her dreams, honest feelings she can't tell anyone but God. But someone guesses her identity. Could there truly be someone who'd find her worthy of. . .love?

eBay Encounter by Jeri Odell
Jonica Granger is an inexperienced eBay buyer who hopes to open her own antique store. Houston James already runs an antique store—and everywhere he turns she's in his way, running the prices up. He e-mails Jonica out of frustration, beginning communication that leads from griping about her methods to getting to know her innermost dreams. Where could online romance lead?

Love Letters

*Four Generations of Couples
Changed by Expressions of the Heart*

Mary Davis / Kathleen E. Kovach
Sally Laity / Jeri Odell

BARBOUR
PUBLISHING

Published by Barbour Publishing, Inc., P.O. Box 719, Uhrichsville, OH 44683, www.barbourbooks.com

Our mission is to publish and distribute inspirational products offering exceptional value and biblical encouragement to the masses.

ecpa Member of the
Evangelical Christian
Publishers Association

Printed in the United States of America.
5 4 3 2 1

Love Notes

by Mary Davis

Dedication

To my hubby, Chip, who has given me
a greater appreciation for the musical note.
And to JoDee for sparking an idea in me.

*And the King shall answer and say unto them,
Verily I say unto you, Inasmuch as ye have done it
unto one of the least of these my brethren,
ye have done it unto me.*
MATTHEW 25:40

Chapter 1

Texas 1910

*B*ang! Bang!
Laurel jumped up from the edge of the hotel bed and rushed to the open window.

Several people ran in the dusty street toward the bank next door. "Jonathan Rivers tried to rob the bank!" one of them shouted.

"Pa?" She gasped and stumbled over the packed carpetbags at the end of the bed on her way to the door. Holding up her skirt, she ran out of the hotel and to the bank. The crowd packed outside made it impossible to see inside. "Excuse me." She wedged her way between shoulders, excusing repeatedly, then finally spilling inside the bank entrance.

A man lay stretched out on the floor, his head covered with a gray coat, his clothes familiar. "Pa." Someone touched her arm, and she spun, looking into the sheriff's ruddy face.

"I'm sorry, miss."

"No, no." Tears fell as she dropped to her knees and reached a shaky hand toward the coat that covered the dead man.

"Laurel, don't." Ethan sat against the counter, Doc Benson tending to his bloody arm.

She lifted the wool fabric from the face. "Oh, Pa."

He'd said to pack and wait for him. They were leaving today. She smoothed the hair off his forehead. The worry lines that had deepened the longer Pa had stayed in Hollow Springs were all but erased.

She had prayed for Pa to turn back to the love and acceptance the Lord Jesus was waiting to give him and to find peace in Ma's death. Had he died before he found it?

Covering her face, she wept.

❧

The strain of the past two days lay heavy on Laurel's shoulders as the pungent smell of the disturbed earth filled her nostrils. She stood with only the minister and the sheriff for company beside Pa's freshly turned grave, tears cascading down her cheeks. She dabbed them away with Ma's lavender embroidered handkerchief, but they were quickly replaced. The sheriff brooded under his bushy red eyebrows, his squinting eyes almost hidden. Had he come to see for himself that Pa was no longer trouble for him? Or did he wonder if she would be trouble, as well?

She turned the events of what must have happened that day over in her mind as she had done many times in the past forty-eight hours. Pa had told her to pack, knowing what he was about to do. He'd gone to the bank and pulled out a gun. Where in the world had Pa gotten a gun? She shook her head.

Then the sheriff must have shot him, but not before Pa had wounded Ethan.

The breeze tousled Minister Howard's sandy hair as he spoke his final words and closed his Bible. "I'm terribly sorry for your loss." He hesitated as though he wanted to say more, then gave her a nod and left with the sheriff.

She didn't blame the residents of Hollow Springs for not wanting to share her sorrow. Why would they want to show support to the daughter of a bank robber?

I'm just seventeen. What am I to do? She dropped to her knees, sobbing. "Why, Pa?" He'd caused a great deal of trouble for a lot of people and now left her alone. She set a small bouquet of blue wildflowers on top of the raw dirt, then looked away.

Ethan Burke, in a suit and bowler, stood outside the cemetery's low, wooden border fence, one arm cradled in a sling. Even he didn't want to be near her. She averted her gaze, too ashamed to look at him after what Pa had done. She used to steal glances and catch him looking back. He would give her a smile or tip his hat, and when Pa wasn't looking, she would smile back.

Since Pa had given up going to church after they'd left Maryland, Laurel went by herself with Pa's blessing, because Ma would have wanted her to continue attending church. Pa felt that if one of them went, it was as good as both.

From the first Sunday, Ethan Burke took to walking her back to the hotel. They walked slowly. And last Sunday, he'd been waiting for her outside the hotel before church. Pa didn't know until three days ago when Ethan insisted on asking Pa to court her. Pa wouldn't talk about their conversation, but the next day. . . She closed her eyes in regret. Now all she saw when she looked at Ethan were the glaring results of Pa's bad judgment. She peeked again, but Ethan was gone. She stood and looked around. He was nowhere to be seen.

What had Pa been thinking? Robbing a bank? She shouldn't have asked to stay in Hollow Springs; Pa had been agitated by her request. But she'd felt comfortable in this rustic little town—she hadn't wanted to leave and had hoped hard to stay. Now she had no hope. And no choice. People in town wouldn't talk to her or even look at her, yet she had no means to leave or live.

She still didn't understand Pa's drive to get to California. Ma had wanted to live there, and Pa had kept promising, but they'd never made the move. Not until after Ma died did he get a bee in his britches about it. She'd lost Pa, too, the day Ma died. Her true Pa. He'd become a stranger almost overnight. The day after Ma's funeral, he'd started selling everything they owned, then bought a broken-down Ford. It hadn't even made it to the first town on their trek to the opposite coast. Pa hadn't been the same since.

Now she was left to wrestle with her own conflicting emotions. She was sad that Pa was gone but also happy his suffering was over. Did that make her a terrible daughter? She hoped not. Maybe *happy* wasn't the right word. Content? She'd wanted to stay in Hollow Springs; now she longed for California. If the anguish and pity in Ethan's cobalt blue eyes were any indication, there was nothing left for her here.

She trudged along the boardwalk to the hotel where she and Pa had been staying. She pulled out her room key as she headed for the staircase.

"Miss Rivers?"

She turned to the desk clerk. "Yes."

"May I speak with you a minute?"

All she wanted to do was collapse on her bed and cry, but she walked to the desk.

Mr. Gonzales dipped his head, and she could see his balding crown. "I hate to do this in your time of sorrow, but unless you can pay your father's outstanding bill, I'm going to need your key back."

Outstanding bill? She set her handbag on the counter. "How much?"

"Fifteen dollars."

She gasped. "I don't have that much money."

"I'm really sorry, miss. I can't let you stay unless you can pay."

"Of course not." She pulled three dollars and six bits from her handbag. "This is all I have."

He held out a hand. "I'll take what you've got."

She set the money on the guest registry. "I'll pay you the rest of what my pa owes, Mr. Gonzales, somehow. Do you happen to have any positions open? I could work in the dining room or clean rooms."

"I'm sorry. I don't need a girl right now."

She nodded. "Do you know of any jobs in town?"

He shook his head. "Sorry."

"When I find work, I'll pay the rest of my pa's debt."

He gave her a sad smile and tipped his head to her.

She kept her back straight as she ascended the stairs. When she reached the room, the carpetbags she'd packed the day Pa had robbed the bank were waiting for her by the bed. Two days they'd sat untouched. Pa had said he'd be back soon.

Tears coursed down her face, and she fell to her knees. "Sweet Lord Jesus, what am I to do? I have nowhere to go."

She couldn't remain here at the hotel, so where was she to go? She could sleep outside. The late-spring Texas nights weren't nearly as cool as they had been when they'd arrived in town a month ago. She did not relish the thought of sleeping outdoors, but she and Pa had done it a few times since they'd left Maryland.

Poor Pa. This past year, it was as though he'd been looking out of a dark cave and all he could see was California, as though making it to California would somehow make Ma less dead. Now he was dead, too—and in debt. As his heir, she was responsible for clearing his accounts. That meant she needed to find employment.

⚬⚬

Ethan Burke adjusted the sling on his left arm as he stood in front of the barbershop across the street from the Starlight Hotel. Laurel had seemed so alone at her pa's grave site. Even the way she'd walked, slowly and wearily, showed her lonesomeness. He ached for her. Not one soul from town had shown up at the funeral. How could the whole town blame her for what her father had done? He would have been right next to her if it weren't for what he'd done; at twenty-three, he'd killed a man. Ethan shook his head. It was an awful feeling deep in the pit of his stomach, like a burning coal.

He kicked the post holding up the awning, but instead of the satisfaction he expected, all he got was a bruised toe. If he'd learned how to shoot a gun, Laurel wouldn't have a reason for her tears. He'd only aimed to wound the man. But he was a bad aim, really bad.

In church, Laurel would close her eyes and raise her voice up in song. The serene, ethereal look on her face as she sang to the Lord told him all he needed to know about her faith. And his heart had gone out to her. Now, his heart lay battered in the corner of his soul, fearful to make any attempt at contact.

Though Laurel and her father were drifters heading west, he had hoped they would make Hollow Springs their home, but Mr. Rivers had been dead set on California. So Ethan, too, had begun to set his heart on California, if Laurel would be a part of it for him.

The day before the robbery, he'd asked Mr. Rivers if he could court Laurel. Mr. Rivers had given him a gruff no and walked away. Laurel had been right when she said her pa wouldn't take it well. He should have suggested that he could help with travel expenses. Had he pushed Mr. Rivers into making that fatal decision?

Ethan jerked forward at the familiar slap on his back, though not as hard as usual. He had his wounded arm to thank for that. "*Hola*, Alonzo."

"*Mi amigo*, looking tired. You rest."

He tore his gaze from the hotel. "I'm fine."

Alonzo's dark eyes widened. "To the funeral, you went?"

He'd wanted to. He'd wanted to be right beside Laurel to comfort her in her grief. "I kept my distance."

"You no talk to her? And your *grande* shoulder, you didn't give it to her?"

He looked up at his six-foot friend. "Mine is the last shoulder she'd want for comfort."

"She not give you smiles like honey when her *padre* not look?"

His mouth pulled up at the thought. How could one young lady so captivate him with her guileless smile and soft, quiet voice that caressed his heart like a gentle melody? "She does have a nice smile."

"And eyes that sparkle like green cactus, and hair that is silky and the color of cinnamon, and all perfect things about her," Alonzo recited like a child mimicking a parent. "I know sure she likes you."

"Maybe. Before I killed her pa."

"So on purpose you shot him?"

"No."

"And the padre of the woman you love, why you shot him?"

"Because he was trying to rob the bank."

"The money, you let him take it, not yours anyway."

He pictured Mr. Rivers's shaking hand and the way his gaze had darted about the room. "He was edgy. I was afraid any little thing would spook him. I didn't want him to hurt an innocent person."

"So an accident it was."

"No. I killed her pa."

"She can see that not on purpose you did it."

He had made a grave miscalculation that morning. If he could go back, he would have aimed for the man's shoulder instead of his hand. Or his leg. No. He wouldn't have reached into the drawer for the bank's gun at all. Then maybe no one would have gotten hurt. But then what? Mr. Rivers would have just given up? Not likely. Let Mr. Rivers get away with the robbery? Then Laurel would be a fugitive on the run. What if Mr. Rivers were subdued and went to jail? He shook his head. Once Jonathan Rivers decided to rob the bank and pulled out his gun, there could be no good outcome.

He shrugged. "It doesn't change anything."

"I *comprendo* why you be here in this place to breathe air that is fresh for your *pulmones*." Alonzo pointed across the street. "Your *señorita* of perfection."

He stood up straighter. What was Laurel doing coming back out of the hotel? And with her luggage?

"You will talk to her, yes?"

He wanted to. "It's too soon."

"I talk to her for you?"

"No. Promise you won't say anything to her about me. I'll talk to her when I'm ready. And when I think she's ready."

Alonzo put his hand over his heart and gave a quick nod. "No wait very long." He stepped off the boardwalk.

"Where are you going?"

"I think to talk to a beautiful señorita."

"Alonzo, no. You promised."

Alonzo turned around and walked backward. "I no mention you."

Ethan doubted that. How could he pull him back? "What about Rosita?"

"You no talk to her about this."

Alonzo disappeared into the mercantile after Laurel. He should go, too—accidentally bump into Alonzo, then he could see for himself how she was. He stepped off the boardwalk.

"*Señor* Burke."

He turned. Rosita Menendez sashayed toward him in a brightly colored dress. He glanced at the mercantile then back to Rosita. "Señorita Menendez."

"Hola. I. . .look. . .for Alonzo." Rosita's English wasn't nearly as good as Alonzo's, but she worked hard at it.

If Ethan told her where he was, Alonzo could be in trouble if he was talking to Laurel. Rosita had a fiery jealous streak where Alonzo was concerned. Alonzo wasn't ready to settle down, but when he did, it would be with Rosita. Until then he'd keep Rosita just interested enough that she didn't go off and marry someone else, but not so close she was begging to set a wedding date. If he were Alonzo and had a chance to marry the woman he loved, he wouldn't waste a day. Not one day.

Chapter 2

Laurel looked around the inside of the mercantile. Mrs. Jones stood behind the counter ringing up a man's purchase. She looked at a rack of ready-made dresses while she waited. She'd never had a ready-made dress. Ma had made all her clothes. She hadn't had a new dress since Ma died. Pa had told her to pack light for quick travel. They'd get new things in California. But she'd packed a few small keepsakes—and Ma's wedding dress.

The man at the counter left, and she walked up. "I'm looking for employment and was wondering if you could use a salesgirl."

Mrs. Jones's gray topknot wobbled as she shook her head. "I'm sorry. Some days we barely have enough business for the two of us."

Laurel nodded, and her stomach growled. It had been two days since she'd eaten. "I'd like to get a pickle." She dug in her handbag and then remembered she'd given all she had to Mr. Gonzales.

"I'm sorry. I can't add any more to your pa's bill."

She looked up sharply. "Pa owed money here, too? How much?" She sighed at the amount. "When I find work, I'll pay my pa's outstanding debt."

"Señorita Rivers." Alonzo Chavez filled the doorway. As he came forward, he doffed his hat and put it over his heart, bowing slightly. "Very sorry about the death."

Tears welled in her eyes. He was the first person besides the minister to offer condolences. The surprising thing was, Alonzo was Ethan's best friend. She wouldn't think he would want to talk to her. "Thank you." She blinked back the blur.

"You are doing well, yes?"

How was she supposed to respond to that? *I have no place to live, no family, no money, but I'm well.* "I'll make do."

Ethan Burke was suddenly at Alonzo's side. She froze and stared at his sling. She was not ready to speak to him yet. It was too much for one day.

"Excuse me, Miss Rivers. I need to speak to Alonzo."

She nodded and looked at the floor. She didn't want to see the pity in his blue eyes.

Ethan and Alonzo moved to the corner of the store, spoke a few words, then hurried out the door. Her gaze followed them. She should have at least inquired about his arm. Said hello. Or something. But she was too raw from Pa's death and the current trouble that he had caused. She was not up for a confrontation with the man who obviously didn't want to speak to her. The way he'd hurried Alonzo out of there told her all she needed to know about how he felt. He didn't even want his friend to speak to her.

She picked up her carpetbags and walked outside, where

Mr. Jones stood stacking produce.

"Miss Rivers." Mr. Jones plucked an orange from one of the produce boxes in front of the store and held it out to her. "Got some in fresh."

She shook her head. "I can't pay for it."

He took the orange back. "Sorry."

As the sun began its western descent, she was still without a job. She walked past the bank as one of the employees flipped the closed sign and latched the door. She gazed a moment through the window where Pa had fallen from grace. *Oh, Pa. Why couldn't you have been happy here? What was so almighty important in California?*

She had wanted to stay in Hollow Springs. She'd dreamed of Ethan Burke courting her and asking her to marry him, making a home here. Now she just wanted to leave this town as soon as she was able. And now she, too, could feel the pull of California. Was it her duty to finish the trip her parents had begun?

She noticed Ethan looking at her from behind the bank counter and quickly hurried on her way—then stopped. On her way to where? She had nowhere to go. *Lord?* Fresh tears threatened to spill. She blinked them back. People would hardly look her in the eyes. She sensed that people had positions but didn't want her to fill them. Everyone was ashamed of her. And instead of finding a job, she'd discovered outstanding bills Pa owed.

She must leave town as soon as she was able and start fresh somewhere else, someplace where no one knew what Pa had done. California was as good a place as any. But she would need money to get there. And first she needed employment to pay Pa's debts.

"Miss Rivers."

She turned at her name.

Minister Thomas Howard crossed the rutted dirt road toward her. "Again, I'm sorry for your loss. Have you thought about what you are going to do?"

She tucked her chin. "I've just learned my pa owed money all over town. I had to move out of the hotel, and I must find a job to pay his debts."

"You could go back to family."

"Except for the Lord, I am alone in the world." She felt the loneliness deep within.

"Fortunate for me." He stepped up onto the boardwalk. "My wife needs help around the house and with the little one. Doc Benson has told her to rest more or she could lose the baby. I can only offer you a place to stay and three meals a day for your assistance."

A roof over her head and food in her stomach. It would keep her from sleeping under the starry sky tonight. "I'd be glad to do it, but I'll also need to find a paying position to take care of Pa's accounts."

"If my memory serves me right, when you first came to town, you offered to play piano for Sunday services."

"That's right."

"With Mrs. Howard having a difficult time with this baby, I don't want her overexerting herself. Would you be willing to play for us?"

"Most certainly." Her fingers were aching for the ivory keys.

"The church can only pay a small stipend."

She wanted to tell him she would do it for free, but she needed the money. "I'd be most grateful." The Lord was supplying a roof, food, *and* a way to pay off Pa's debts. *Thank You, Lord, for Your abundant provisions.*

Laurel stood in the doorway of the Howards' bedroom. Mrs. Howard looked half asleep while her two-year-old son sat next to her lifting her hand and letting it fall. Mrs. Howard tucked her arm under the double wedding ring quilt. When the boy dug it out, she moaned.

Minister Howard held out his arms to his son. Little Tommy dropped his ma's arm again and stepped on her leg to get to his pa.

Mrs. Howard rolled her head and sighed. "You're back."

"I'm sorry I took so long." The minister leaned over and kissed her forehead.

Mrs. Howard's gaze darted to Laurel, her eyes widening before looking back to her husband. "What is she doing here?"

The minister adjusted his son in his arms. "Miss Rivers is going to help you with the house and look after Tommy so you can rest."

"I don't need help."

"Doc said for you to rest. We don't want to lose this one, too."

She sighed and nodded.

Laurel swallowed hard. "Mrs. Howard, I appreciate you taking me in like this. Anything I can do to make you more comfortable, just let me know."

Mrs. Howard turned away. "I'm tired."

Minister Howard turned to her. "Maybe you could start supper."

∽⃝ঌ

After supper, Laurel bathed Tommy and carried him upstairs to say good night to his ma. At the voices coming through the Howards' open bedroom door, she stopped.

"I just don't trust someone whose parent could do such a thing," Mrs. Howard said. "She has bad blood in her."

Laurel caught her breath.

"Miss Rivers is no more a threat to you or Tommy than I am. Mr. Rivers made some bad choices, but they have no reflection on her. The Good Book tells us to care for those in need. 'But whoso hath this world's good, and seeth his brother have need, and shutteth up his bowels *of compassion* from him, how dwelleth the love of God in him?'"

The minister was giving her charity. She wished she weren't in such desperate need of it.

"I wish I had your confidence," Mrs. Howard said.

"Should I not trust you because of your brother's behavior?"

Tommy wiggled out of her arms, and before she could catch him, he ran into his parents' bedroom. She stepped to the doorway. "Tommy wanted to say good night before I put him to bed."

Minister Howard scooped him up. "Thank you, Miss Rivers. I'll tuck him in."

She nodded, hoping they couldn't see her distress. "I'll

straighten up the kitchen."

As she wiped crumbs from the table, Minister Howard entered the room. "Please don't take my wife's words to heart."

"Pardon?"

"By the look on your face, I guess you were standing out in the hall just long enough."

She felt the blood drain from her face. "I never meant to listen in. I promise."

He smiled a sad sort of smile. "I know. I'm just sorry you had to hear anything at all. My wife has lost seven babies early on. She's afraid to lose this one now that her time is so close. So please don't fret over her words, Miss Rivers. She gets cross with me, too, these days." He sighed. "You should know that something happens in her mind when she is pregnant. She's not herself. Her condition will only get worse the closer her time gets. All we can do is make her as comfortable as possible and ride out the storm."

Poor Mrs. Howard—to lose so many children before they even had a chance in this world. And then to have her mental condition on top of that. She understood all too well about a loved one no longer being the person he or she once was. Such a cross to bear. "How long until the baby is due?"

"About eight weeks or so. I've been praying powerfully hard for this child. I fear Mrs. Howard might not be able to handle losing another." He turned and left the room.

But she'd caught the sheen in his eyes that he'd tried to blink away. A loss would likely be as hard on him. She sat down at the table and prayed for grace and mercy to blanket the minister, Mrs. Howard, the unborn babe, and little Tommy.

Once she finished in the kitchen, Laurel climbed the stairs to the room she would be sharing with little Tommy. Her heart ached for family, but she'd lost everyone. She desperately wanted to belong but had no one. The loneliness seeped deep inside as she unpacked her traveling bag. She opened Pa's pocket watch, and the photograph of Ma and Pa on their wedding day blurred before her. Once she cleared her vision, she pulled the picture free. A small lock of Pa's ashen hair lay with Ma's cinnamon curl. "I'll take you both to California. It's where you wanted to be."

She dressed and curled up in bed, wishing she were seven again in Pa's lap, crying into his chest over the cruel words of the other schoolchildren. He would stroke her long cinnamon hair and promise her that everything was going to be all right, that Jesus would make everything better. That was the pa she lost the day Ma died. Then it was no longer Pa she imagined, holding her, comforting her, but Jesus. She sobbed silently in the darkness until she fell asleep in her Savior's arms.

Chapter 3

Laurel confiscated the last piece of bread and jam with which Tommy was painting the table—and himself. "I think you're done with that." She ruffled the boy's hair, then dumped the mashed bread into the slop pail. As she came back with a cloth to wipe Tommy's face, Minister Howard entered the kitchen.

"Mrs. Howard hasn't finished with the tray you brought up, so I left it. I'll be out all day but back for supper."

"I'll have it ready."

"Thank you. Could you choose four hymns, three for the beginning of the service and one to close? Mrs. Howard always did that. Whatever you pick will be fine. I'll be speaking on forgiveness." He kissed Tommy on the top of his head and walked to the doorway, then turned. "I can't tell you the amount of comfort it gives me knowing you are here for my wife."

She wished poor Mrs. Howard could feel the same.

"She's just going through a difficult time right now."

Mrs. Howard wasn't the only one. But Laurel couldn't dwell on her own hardships, or she'd be stuck in that muddy place

Pa had been for nearly a year. She couldn't think too long on being orphaned in an unwelcoming town in a strange part of the country where she knew next to no one and had no place to go, no home.

"In every thing give thanks: for this is the will of God in Christ Jesus concerning you."

She had to focus on her blessings, though she couldn't think of any at the moment. But then she looked up and saw the roof over her head, felt the food in her stomach and the clothes on her back. Next to the Lord, wasn't that all she really *needed*?

She cleaned up Tommy, set him on the floor with his blocks, and headed up the stairs to retrieve the tray. She had put off long enough facing Mrs. Howard without the minister there. Knocking softly on the door, she opened it. Mrs. Howard lay on her side with her back to the door. *Please let her be asleep.*

Laurel tiptoed in and took the teacup off the nightstand, setting it on the tray on the floor, but left the glass of water. She lifted the tray. On top was a sheet of paper labeled HYMNS FOR SUNDAY. How thoughtful. Maybe Mrs. Howard was warming to her after all.

Laurel finished up her chores in the kitchen, then took little Tommy for a walk to tire him out before she stopped at the church to practice for Sunday service, two days away. The songs Mrs. Howard had chosen were some of the hardest she'd ever tried; she must be far more proficient. Not having played in a long time, Laurel chose easier, more familiar hymns, hoping Mrs. Howard wouldn't mind.

When she finished, she still felt alone and wrapped her arms around herself. She needed a great big bear hug from

Pa, but the closest she could hope for was a hug from Tommy. She went over to where he lay sleeping on her ma's granny square shawl and scooped him up. "Time to go," she whispered. She dreaded returning to a place she wasn't completely welcome, but she had nowhere else to go. Even so, she really was grateful for the Howards' generosity.

☙

Laurel's stomach was all aflutter as she sat on the piano bench. The small rustic clapboard church was so different from the church with stained-glass windows and padded pews she'd come from in Maryland. She waited for the minister's signal to start. She hadn't played in front of anyone in so long and with so little practice. She had wanted to come over early and practice before anyone arrived, but taking care of Tommy and making sure Minister Howard had a filling breakfast had consumed all her time. Now she had to make do and trust in the Lord.

Shoe soles scuffled on the worn wood floor. People looked her way, then whispered to those close to them. They would be scrutinizing everything she did, every mistake she made. She knew they could pressure the minister to have her removed. But she needed this job. She would show them that God could still use her. *Dear Lord, help me play for You and to forget about all these people waiting for me to make a mistake.*

She swung her gaze to the minister, who was talking to Mr. Jones at the side of the pews. She let her gaze travel the room, and it froze on Ethan Burke. When he looked at her, she looked away. He was the reason she'd wanted to stay in town. Now she couldn't even look at him for the shame she harbored inside. She needed to ask his forgiveness on behalf of Pa, but how could she if she couldn't bring herself to face him?

Had someone just spoken to her? She turned and found Minister Howard staring at her.

"You may begin."

"Oh." She put her fingers to the keys and took a deep breath. *Please let me play well.*

She made it through the first line but stumbled over a note in the second. People were singing, so she hoped no one noticed. Being in front of the town was harder than she'd thought. She usually loved being in church, but today she couldn't wait for it to be over so she could leave.

🕉

Ethan ached for Laurel as she missed another note. She was so tense. It didn't help that people had come in whispering behind her back like circling vultures. He hadn't expected to see her here today. Her presence here took all the courage and inner strength that he heard in her playing.

She played the notes with all her heart and soul. The music had emotion. Mrs. Howard's playing was technically perfect, but there was no life in it. Laurel put her whole being into it.

Minister Howard spoke on forgiveness. He could tell that the minister was wanting the people of Hollow Springs to forgive Mr. Rivers for what he'd done and, in kind, forgive Laurel. He noticed a great deal of shifting and slouching in the congregation as the minister spoke about removing the log from your own eye before removing the speck in your brother's, and about forgiving others so God can forgive you. But forgiveness was slow in coming in this town—if it came at all. Like the time Kenneth Kline was drunk and accidentally shot Widow Olson's goat thinking it was a deer. Kenneth eventually moved away.

Then the minister seemed to speak to him, though he never looked directly at him, and discussed forgiving one's self. How could he do that? He'd killed a man, and the townspeople hailed him as a hero. He was no hero, just the unfortunate soul who'd had the misfortune to pull the trigger.

After the service while the congregation filed out the door, Laurel played softly through the final hymn again. He let the melody wash over him. He would wait until she was finished to approach her.

As the last note hung in the air, Laurel closed the lid to the keys. Here was his chance. He headed toward the front, but she scooped up her shawl and slipped out the side door at the back.

He scrambled to the front and followed her out, but she was already almost to the minister's house. He watched her long hair pat her back as she hurried away. It was clear that she hated him. He'd suspected it, but now he knew.

෯ඊ

After preaching on Sunday, Minister Howard took Monday off, leaving Laurel free to run her errands without little Tommy along. With her handbag clutched tightly, she hurried to the hotel. At the door she stopped and took a deep breath. She hoped Mr. Gonzales wouldn't be offended at her small offering toward Pa's account. She opened the door and walked to the counter. Mr. Gonzales was registering a man and his young daughter. She stared at the little girl clinging to her pa's side. Sorrow lodged in Laurel's throat. The man handed the room key to his daughter and picked up the two larger suitcases. He looked down proudly at his daughter taking charge of the smaller bag and headed up the stairs. Longing ached deep inside Laurel.

"Miss Rivers, is there something I can do for you?"

She took a small amount of money from her handbag. "I've come to make a payment on my pa's bill. I know it's not much. I can even pay a little more if you need me to." She'd wanted to make a small payment on each of Pa's debts, but if Mr. Gonzales wanted more, she'd give him the whole sum and pay on the others next week.

He pushed her money back across the counter to her. "You don't owe me anything."

"But my pa did."

He shook his head. "You don't understand. Your bill has been cleared."

Cleared? "Someone paid it for me?"

"Yes, miss."

"Who?"

"I can't rightly say."

"I want to thank them. Let them know I'll pay them back."

"The person doesn't want to be paid back. And I think he knows you are grateful."

"But who would do such a thing for me?"

He just shook his head.

Obviously Mr. Gonzales had been sworn to secrecy, and she wouldn't push him any further. "Mr. Gonzales, the next time you see my benefactor, would you tell him thank you from me?" She turned to leave but stopped. "And tell him I'd like to meet him and thank him in person."

Well, that would make paying off her other two obligations go faster. She walked to the mercantile. Mrs. Jones looked down her long, narrow nose at the money Laurel set on the counter. "I know it's not much, but—"

Mr. Jones stepped over. "You don't owe us anything. Your account here has been settled."

Again? "By whom?"

"We are not at liberty to say."

Who was clearing her debts? "Will you tell the kind person thank you for me? And that if I knew who he was, I'd thank him in person?" In spite of their frowns, her spirit buoyed. She couldn't think of one person in town who would do this for her. Everyone avoided her and looked away as though ashamed and appalled. Just as the Lord Jesus had paid the price for her sins, someone was paying Pa's. *Thank You, Lord, for the kindness of a stranger.*

She headed across the street to the barbershop and bath-house. "Mr. Adams, do I still have a bill here?"

He ran the straight edge of the razor up Mayor Vance's neck, then wiped it on a towel before looking up at her. "Four bucks."

So her benefactor hadn't found her last debt. She was glad in a way. It would give her a chance to show the citizens of Hollow Springs that she was not the bad person they thought she was. And maybe a certain bank clerk would see it, too. "Here is a small part of what my pa owed you. As I earn it, I'll pay the rest." It shouldn't take her more than a month to settle this account. Then she could start saving to purchase a stage-coach ticket and move on to a town where the people didn't know her story. There she could earn money for a train ticket to the West Coast.

Mr. Adams took her coins and put them in his pocket. "I appreciate that."

"I hear Hank over at the saloon is always looking for pretty girls," Mr. Toole said, waiting for his turn for a shave.

She felt her cheeks warm. She would let them lock her up in jail before she'd work there.

"We don't need any of that, Silas." Mayor Vance shot him a stern look.

She didn't know what to say after that, so she hurried out the open door and crashed into Ethan Burke.

Ethan gripped his wounded arm and sucked in a breath through his teeth.

Laurel gasped, her eyes widening. "I'm so sorry."

He nodded.

"Are you hurt?"

He straightened and took his hand from his arm. "I'm fine."

His hard-set jaw told her he was trying to hide the pain she'd inflicted. Or was he still angry with her over what Pa had done to him? "I didn't mean to hurt you."

"I said I'm fine," he hissed through gritted teeth, a grimace on his face.

She backed away. "I'm really sorry." It was bad enough that Pa had shot him; she didn't have to hurt him, too.

Ethan held his breath as Laurel walked away at a brisk pace. He wanted to call her back and tell her he was fine, but the truth of the matter was, he wasn't fine. The pain that shot through his arm had caused sweat to bead on his lip and forehead. He'd probably popped stitches again. It had happened the second night when he had the nightmare that had haunted him every night since.

He walked to Doc Benson's office and slumped into a chair.

Doc came out of the examination room and shook his head. "What happened this time? You didn't roll over on that arm again, did you?"

"No. Just a little accident. I got clumsy. I may have pulled a few stitches out." He took his hand from his arm. Crimson tinged his shirt.

"That you did. Come on in."

The pungent medicinal odors in the room stung his nostrils. He held his breath for a moment but was then forced to breathe in the smells.

"Sit."

He sat on the table.

Doc helped him remove the sling, rolled up his sleeve, and slowly unwound the dressing. "Looks like all you did was tear her open. I don't see any signs of infection."

The bullet had barely missed the bone but had ripped his flesh wide open. He thanked God again that his wound was minor and that there was still no infection. Mr. Rivers hadn't been so fortunate.

"Is the laudanum helping with the pain?"

He hesitated. "I haven't been taking it."

"Why on earth not? Do you miraculously have no pain?"

"No. It makes me lethargic." He didn't like feeling tired and in a semi-dream state. The stuff tasted awful, to boot. And what ached more than his arm, the laudanum wouldn't help.

"Well, I'll offer it anyway. You want laudanum before I clean this and stitch you back up?"

"I'll pass."

❦

Laurel fell to her knees at the front pew. "Please, Lord, heal Ethan's arm. Don't let him be in much pain. And please let him know I didn't mean to run into him and hurt him." She knelt there for a long while pleading for Ethan Burke and crying.

When she'd exhausted her heart, soul, and mind, she stood and walked to the piano bench. A single sheet of music stood on the music stand, a carefully hand-drawn staff, with notes only on the first line. She picked out the tune in her head, then opened the lid to the keys and played the notes. She played it again and let it wash over her until it was embedded in her heart. The notes caressed her and wrapped around her like a toasty warm hug on a chilly night. It was a natural tune, flowing and simple but with a depth in the chords. The piece, however short, ministered to her soul, as well as to her aching heart.

She looked for an author, but there was no signature.

"Thank You, Lord, for this small blessing in the midst of my trials."

Chapter 4

Ethan saw the glint of the Colt .45 and pulled the bank's .45 out of the drawer behind the counter, coiling his finger around the trigger. He raised it up and fired a moment after a flash exploded from the end of the other gun. Burned gunpowder accosted his nostrils. Through the haze of smoke he could see red soak through the front of the bank robber's shirt as he fell to the ground. He wanted to go to the man, but his legs wouldn't take him there. Then suddenly he was at the dying man's side and putting his hand on his chest. The bleeding wouldn't stop.

Mr. Rivers grasped Ethan's shirtfront with a bloodstained hand. "Laurel will never love you now."

He sat up with a start and moaned, tossing back the covers with his right arm, the sling holding his left arm to his chest. A cold sweat dampened his body. *Oh, Laurel.* He scrubbed his face, then stared at his free hand. He rubbed it down the side of his nightshirt, then went to the washbasin and poured some water. Though the only physical blood on his hands that day was his own, he could feel Jonathan Rivers's blood in every line and crack. He'd scrubbed and scrubbed, but the feeling would never go away.

His nightmare was different in another way. In reality, Mr. Rivers hadn't mentioned love. He'd looked at the hole in his tan shirt grow red with blood, then he'd looked at Ethan with the utmost sorrow, as though he'd come back to his senses, out of some crazed delusion, and realized what he'd done. He'd looked directly at Ethan and said, "I'm sorry." Then dropped to his knees.

Ethan had dropped his gun and come out from behind the caged counter, gripping his left arm and kneeling beside him. "I only meant to shoot the gun out of your hand."

Pain contorted the dying man's face as someone eased him to the floor. His gaze locked with Ethan's. "Tell. . .Laurel. . ."

He waited. "Tell Laurel what?" He wanted to tell Mr. Rivers not to die but knew the request would be futile. "Tell Laurel what?" Tears pooled.

The pain seemed to leave, and a smile touched Jonathan Rivers's mouth. A peace settled on his face as he whispered, "Katherine," then closed his eyes.

In life, he had never looked as peaceful as he did at the moment of his death.

Ethan splashed cool water on his face and stared into the mirror on the wall even though he could see only a dim outline of who he was in the dark. It was better that way. He didn't want to look a killer in the eyes. He put his wet hand on his aching left arm and looked down at the bottle of laudanum the doctor had given him. He'd stopped taking it, so if his reccurring nightmare didn't disturb his sleep, the persistent ache in his arm did.

Would it comfort Laurel to know that at the end her pa was at peace? Would she want to hear it from him? Or had Ethan imagined the peace to ease his own conscience? If death brought peace to Mr. Rivers, did that make his own misdeed less atrocious?

He'd relived that day over and over and always came to the same conclusion. If he hadn't fired, Mr. Rivers might have killed an innocent person in his agitated state before coming to his senses. Mrs. Turner had been in the bank with her three children.

Ethan had done the right thing. He just wished he had been accurate—for the first time in his life. *Lord, help me put this all behind me. Show me I did the right thing. And please help Laurel to see that, too, and to forgive me.*

He sat down at his upright piano, lifted the lid, and caressed the keys. *Did she enjoy her song?* He looked up at the blank sheet of paper propped on the piano and freed his left arm. Doc had told him not to use it at all for at least a week, but he couldn't help it. He didn't need the written music. It was committed to heart, so he played the notes softly in the dark. When he got to the last one, he continued playing, adding a new line. He lit a lamp and wrote it down. Why couldn't he have done that before he'd left the song for Laurel? He'd tried to figure out another line, but nothing had come; he'd decided that was all there was and had left the sheet of music for her on the piano in the church.

After writing in the second line, he filled in the first. A drop of ink fell on the edge of the sheet. He blotted it with his finger, smearing it slightly.

Ethan put his fingers to the keys again and played through the first two lines, hoping to continue. He tried several things, but nothing sounded right with the beginning. He tried to force the notes to cooperate. He struggled the remainder of the night to add to the melody. Nothing came. It was done, then.

First thing in the morning, before work, he would rush the new sheet of music over to the church. Hopefully Laurel hadn't seen the other one yet.

At daybreak, he walked to the church and crept inside. He came early to avoid the risk of anyone catching him, especially Laurel. His music was set on top of the piano. Had she seen it? She must have. He'd left it right on the stand. She had to have moved it. Had she bothered to play it? Or had she simply cast it aside as unimportant?

He put the new sheet in the center of the music stand. She couldn't miss it.

Lord, please let this song touch her in some way. Let her know I care.

❦

Laurel hummed the song that had become dear to her heart as she wiped crumbs from the cutting board after supper. Two more lines of music had been added on separate days this week. The song soothed her aching soul and allowed the healing to come gently. She could feel it. *Thank You, Lord.*

"That's a lovely tune." Minister Howard stood in the doorway, holding the supper tray. "I don't recognize it. What is it?"

Minister Howard had taken a tray up with plates for his family, since Mrs. Howard missed eating with them. Laurel didn't blame her. If Laurel were her, she would want to eat with her family, too, but she had no family. That left her to eat by herself, but she didn't feel lonely doing so. She had the song playing in her heart for company. It surprised her how comforting it had become. The song was her own special gift from the Lord. "It doesn't have a title yet."

"Did you compose it?"

She shook her head. "It's a tune I committed to memory."

"Who did compose it?" He set the tray on the counter.

Should she tell him that someone was sneaking into the church and leaving it? No harm was being done. "I don't know."

He seemed satisfied with that. "Thank you for supper. It was delicious. You will make someone a fine wife."

Ethan's face immediately popped into her head. She mentally shook it away. "You're welcome." She hoped she got the chance to be someone's wife one day. "Minister Howard, can I ask you something?" He nodded. "The piano at the church, does anyone else play it?"

He squinted his eyes in thought. "Not that I know of. Why do you ask? Is something wrong with it?"

"No, nothing wrong. I was just wondering."

He headed for the door. "Tommy fell asleep, so I put him in bed."

"Thank you."

"No, thank you. Your being here is a godsend."

She didn't want to say it out loud, but she had to. "Minister Howard, you should know that Mrs. Howard still doesn't want me here. If you want me to leave, I will." There. She'd said it.

"Nonsense. I've noticed a marked improvement in Mrs.

Howard's health since you arrived. She has more color in her face. She's just not used to sitting back while someone else does her work."

That was a relief. She'd felt like a stowaway all week, knowing how Mrs. Howard felt. But Mrs. Howard's contention toward her was a result of more than just her inability to do her daily chores.

∞

On Pa's grave, a single dried firewheel flower lay next to her own dried bundle of bluebonnets from the funeral a week ago. Who else had been there? And why? She looked around, but she was alone.

She discarded the dry bundle but left the single dried firewheel. Someone had cared enough to leave it. But who? It didn't seem right for her to be the one to take it away, so she laid down her fresh, colorful bouquet of rose vervain, winecup, foxglove, and butterfly weed. The sweet fragrance settled around her.

"Pa, I'm sorry for not coming back sooner. I've been busy since. . .you left. I'm staying with the minister and his wife. Mrs. Howard hasn't been able to keep up with her chores in her condition, so I've been doing a lot of catching up for her. It's awful hard work, but I don't mind so much. It keeps my mind off things." She thought of it as her duty.

"To be honest, Pa, I've been avoiding you because of my guilt, not over your shooting Ethan—I mean Mr. Burke—but over not mourning you as I feel I should." Tears filled her eyes. "I miss you so much it aches, but I'm not sad at your passing." She drew in a shuddered breath. "I know it sounds mixed up, but you went away inside yourself so long ago." She wiped her cheeks with her ma's old embroidered handkerchief. "I'm going to California as soon as I pay the debts just like you promised Ma." She fingered Pa's watch in her pocket. "I love you, Pa."

Pa's struggles in this life were over after nearly a year of fighting with his sorrow, but she would see him again in heaven. Jesus had left the ninety-nine sheep to come rescue her pa from his pain. His suffering was finally over, and he was in a far better place.

She opened the church door, the cool, dark interior a peaceful solace. Propped up on the music stand was the hymn in progress with another line of notes. She rubbed her finger on a smudge of ink on the side and smiled. There were two different sheets of music after all. The one with the smudge and the one without. When the smudged one had disappeared, she'd thought the composer had made a fresh copy and discarded the other. But he was using both.

Whoever was writing this song was writing it at another piano or in his or her head. Should she write something back? *My longing heart has found solace.* As she had hoped Pa had found at last in death. The Lord had given her a measure of serenity in this simple piece of music. But why was the composer adding such small chunks? Why not write the whole thing and then leave it? Why leave it here at all? She didn't really care why. She was just grateful to have it.

Once she had bathed in the song, she turned to the hymnal. The music Mrs. Howard had chosen was once again some of the most difficult she'd tried. Someday she might be as good as Mrs. Howard, but today was not that day.

❦

Laurel hated what she was about to do. But was it any worse than finding out what Pa had done? She took a deep breath and steeled herself as she entered the mercantile.

She stood at the counter with Tommy on her hip. Mrs. Jones eyed her sideways as she measured out red gingham yard goods for a woman. She'd always wanted a dress of red or green gingham. Maybe in California.

She would rather Mr. Jones helped her. He seemed a touch more compassionate toward her plight, but he didn't seem to be nearby. Mrs. Jones was probably hoping she would go away. Well, she wasn't, so she waited.

After helping two other customers, Mrs. Jones turned to her. "You'd best have money if you're wanting something, even a pickle. I don't run a charity."

There would be no pickle today. "I have money."

Mrs. Jones squinted her eyes as though not believing.

"I'm here on Mrs. Howard's behalf."

"How is Roberta doing?" Mrs. Jones's sneer softened.

"As well as can be expected, now that she's able to rest."

"It's a wonder."

Laurel bit her tongue to keep from making a snide remark back. "Mrs. Howard made out a shopping list. She asked if you would mind putting the prices and total on the list for her." She handed the list and money to Mrs. Jones as instructed.

Giving a knowing nod, Mrs. Jones went about filling the order.

Laurel also knew the reason for the prices and total. She

hated the distrust. She'd always been an honest person, and she would prove herself trustworthy to the citizens of Hollow Springs. *This is a lot to bear, Lord. How much more before I break?*

Mrs. Jones made the notations on the list, then handed it back with the change. "I've noted the money Roberta should receive."

How humiliating. "I'll see that she gets every penny." She grasped the handle of her shopping basket and left.

Ethan stopped her outside. "Laurel."

She liked the way her name sounded on his lips. It soothed her ire. Maybe he didn't hold Pa's actions against her after all, but still she could do little but stare at his arm cradled in the white sling, a stark reminder against his dark suit. "Mr. Burke, I hope you are healing well." It wasn't exactly the apology she knew he deserved, but at least he knew she held concern for him.

"It's feeling better." He touched his arm but didn't linger over it. "I've been meaning to talk to you."

Tommy wiggled out of her arms. She held his hand as he stood next to her.

"Bug." Tommy pulled his hand free and sat on the board-walk to watch the ant crawling along the wood.

"I was there that day in the bank. . .with your pa."

She riveted her gaze back to Ethan's sling. As if she wasn't already painfully aware of that fact. "Yes, I know."

"I was beside him when he. . .died."

Tears welled in her eyes thinking of Pa and the way he died—from a plan of his own making. Were things so bad he had to resort to robbery and violence?

"Just before. . ." Ethan looked to the ground then back up to her. "The pain. . ." He seemed unsure of what to say.

If tears hadn't closed her throat, she would have spared him from going on.

". . .seemed to disappear, and he had a look of pure peace on his face. He whispered, 'Katherine,' then just closed his eyes."

Pa had thought of Ma. The thought warmed her. At peace, and with Jesus and Ma. Her prayer answered.

"I just thought you should know."

Tommy screamed.

She spun to see him on his hands and knees in the dirt just off the boardwalk. She set her shopping basket down, lifted him up, and put him on the edge of the boardwalk. Tiny rocks and dirt were embedded in his chubby hands and knees.

Ethan wetted his handkerchief in the watering trough and handed it to her.

She tried to wipe Tommy's small hands, but he just reached out to her and gripped her around the neck. She lifted him, and he whimpered near her ear. His tears and slobber soaked her neck. "I should get him home." She held out the handkerchief to Ethan.

Ethan held up a hand. "You may need it later." He picked up her shopping basket. "Do you need some help?"

She took the basket. "It's not far. I can manage." She'd caused him enough pain and misery, or rather Pa had. Besides, he shouldn't be lifting or carrying things with a bullet wound.

She was halfway to the minister's house when she realized she hadn't thanked Ethan for telling her what he had. *Next time, Lord.*

Chapter 5

Laurel pulled her shawl tighter as the wind whipped her hair around her face. She wouldn't have gone out at all if she hadn't been anxious to see if the mystery composer had added any more to the hymn. Two new lines had been added last week and one on Monday. She also needed to practice more before Sunday.

As she reached for the handle on the church door, someone called her name. Alonzo Chavez came toward her with a brown paper-wrapped bundle under one arm. "Señorita Rivers, these shirts you can fix." He handed her the package.

"You want me to mend some shirts?"

"*Sí.* One shirt needs buttons. One shirt needs new cuffs."

"Shouldn't you have Miss Menendez do that for you?"

"You do this. I pay you." He started to walk away.

"But—"

He held out his hands as he walked backward. *"Por favor."*

"Are the buttons in here?"

He nodded. "The old shirt there, you use parts of it." He turned and hurried off as the first drops of rain began to splatter; the dry, thirsty earth swallowed them with hardly a trace on the surface.

She scurried inside. That was odd. Was Rosita Menendez not skilled with a needle and thread?

She set her shawl and the package on the front pew and went to the piano, hoping for another line of music. Not one but two lines. Her heart danced, then suddenly stopped. Bittersweet. Since the staffs were all full, the melody was finished now; there would be no new lines to look forward to. But still the author had not signed it or titled it.

Would the composer take the music away now that it was complete?

Why would someone write this song elsewhere and leave it here? If the composer didn't play here and no one else played here except her. . . Someone was going to a lot of trouble to make sure she found it. Was the song truly meant for her? Was someone writing her a song? Was it the Lord Himself? She shook her head. He wouldn't need two separate sheets. "Lord, I care not from whence this music comes, but I thank You." She raised her hands to the keys and played the first four lines by heart, then plucked through the last two lines several times until she had them perfect.

⊚♂

Ethan settled into the second pew from the front on the piano side, close to the outside edge. He'd discovered this seat gave him the best view of Laurel without making it obvious that he was watching her. The piano bench sat empty, and the pews were filling. Where was she? It had to be about time.

Laurel walked in the side door. As she took off her shawl, Minister Howard spoke to her. She nodded and sat, then stopped suddenly as she looked up at the music stand. She quickly tucked the sheet of music behind the hymnal.

Does she like the new addition? Did she read it? As with the melody, he'd been given only one line of lyrics, but at least he knew others would come. He understood the Lord's pattern now.

He felt the worship to his innermost being with Laurel's playing. Something he'd never felt with Mrs. Howard's. But then, he wasn't in love with Mrs. Howard.

As soon as the opening three hymns were through, Laurel gave a nod to the minister, scooped up her shawl, and slipped back out the door.

She wasn't staying? Disappointment settled in his gut like a hot coal. Mrs. Howard must need her. Would she come back this afternoon to play the song? Did she ever play it? Did she care?

Yes, he believed she did play it; otherwise, why would the Lord be having him write it for her? He was sure she would be back to play it. He waited outside the church all afternoon so that when she did come back and play it, he could hear her.

She never came.

⧬

Laurel lay awake, disappointed and exhausted. Tommy had been sick. The poor tyke just wanted the comfort of his ma, but Minister Howard didn't want to risk Mrs. Howard's health or the welfare of the baby. Laurel had had her hands full all day and hadn't been able to go back over to the church to play the piano.

She'd desperately wanted to know what the line said. She'd been too stunned to read it and in too much of a rush. At least she knew the music wouldn't be taken away. . .just yet.

The sooner she slept the sooner she could go back to the church, so she let the exhaustion consume her.

In the morning, Tommy behaved as though he hadn't been sick yesterday, running around and eating a larger than normal breakfast. Minister Howard was staying home today, so Laurel left the breakfast tray upstairs. She wanted to run into town before Mrs. Howard started loading her down with additional chores.

She knew she should run her errands first so that she could sit and enjoy the music and study the words, but she couldn't wait that long. She hurried up to the piano. The words were still there. " 'I am here for you through everything,' " she read aloud. She held the sheet to her chest and closed her eyes. No matter her circumstances, the Lord was with her.

Thank You, Lord, for this reminder.

It didn't take much to memorize the words. "I'll be back." She set the music back on the stand and walked into town.

Laurel looked through the bank window. Ethan Burke was talking to the sheriff. She would run her other errand first. She went to the barbershop and paid Mr. Adams what she'd been given from playing piano and went back to the bank. Thankfully, the sheriff was gone. She took a deep breath, then opened the door. She hadn't been in the bank since Pa had died there.

She stared at the floor where he'd fallen. Her lungs shrank.

"Miss Rivers, may I help you?"

She looked up at Ethan Burke and scooted around the spot on the floor that was scrubbed cleaner than the rest. "I'm—" She croaked and cleared her throat. "I'm looking for Alonzo Chavez. I have his mending completed." Would he give her the information? She didn't know who else to ask. And Mr. Chavez hadn't told her how to get his shirts back to him.

The bank manager eyed her from the corner. Did he think she, too, was here to rob him?

"He's not in town today. I can give them to him the next time he's in."

She handed him the package. Was the air thinner in here? She imagined Pa pointing a gun at Ethan and the bank manager.

He took out his billfold and handed her three dollars. "To pay for the mending."

"What? No. That's too much." Her shrunken lungs now refused to take in air.

"Take it. I'll settle up with Alonzo."

Her hand reached out and took the money, then her feet expedited her escape. Once outside, she dragged in a gulp of air as though she'd been submerged under water and had just come up.

"I am here for you through everything."

She breathed more easily. "Yes, Lord. Thank You." She looked at the money in her hand. With this she would be able to finish paying off Mr. Adams and have some left over to put toward a stagecoach ticket out of town. She hurried off to the barbershop and bathhouse. "Mr. Adams, here is the rest of what I owe you."

He squinted his bulging brown eyes at the money. "You just gived me all you said you had. Where did you get more?"

"I was just over at the bank—"

"And they just gave you money?"

"No." Was he insinuating she stole it? "Mr. Burke paid me for some mending I did. If you don't believe me, you can ask him yourself."

He took the money. "I might just do that."

California had to be better than this. She didn't want all that Pa had done in trying to get there to be for naught.

She returned to the church and hammered out the song, letting the words soak into her soul. *I am here for you through everything.* At least the Lord always loved and accepted her.

Chapter 6

Laurel tiptoed into the bedroom to retrieve Mrs. Howard's lunch tray. The cup rattled slightly against the plate as she picked it up.

Mrs. Howard rolled over. "I thought you would have been up before now."

"I was dusting the mantel as you asked." *And I was hoping you would be asleep.*

"I need you to mop the kitchen."

"I did that two days ago."

"Well, it needs it again. I used to mop it every day."

Laurel bit back a retort. "I'll mop it before I go to the church to practice."

"I also need you to beat the living room rug."

She had done that three days ago. . .at Mrs. Howard's request. Dare she remind the woman?

"The house has to be clean for the new baby. And I'm in no condition to do it."

"Can I beat the rug tomorrow? I haven't had a chance to practice any hymns yet."

"Fine." Mrs. Howard waved a hand in her direction. "Go practice. You ignore what I tell you anyway. Don't be long."

Ignore? She knew she should hold her tongue, but she just couldn't. She was too tired from the woman's demands. "I have done everything you have asked of me."

Mrs. Howard narrowed her eyes. "You haven't played one hymn I have recommended."

How did she know that? "The hymns you chose were too difficult for me."

"I can play them." Mrs. Howard's mouth turned up in a joyless smile.

Laurel finally got it. Mrs. Howard was trying to make the hymns difficult for her. "If you would choose simpler hymns—"

"It's not so easy replacing me, is it?"

"What?"

"Don't be coy with me." Mrs. Howard adjusted the covers over her swollen belly. "I know what you are up to."

"Exactly what is it you think I'm up to?"

"Taking my place."

"I'm not trying to take your place." Why would she want to?

"I've seen the way you look at Mr. Howard. He'll always love me. He'll never love you."

She never looked at Minister Howard in a *way*. "Mrs. Howard, I am not trying to steal your husband."

"But if I die giving life to this child—"

"Don't even think that way."

"You would be right here to take over. You would have a ready-made family."

"I don't want your family," she shot back. "As soon as I have enough money, I'm heading to California. I don't want to stay in a town where everyone hates me."

"Can you blame them?"

No.

"You are only here by the grace of Mr. Howard."

"I know that. But I only want to help you."

"Humph. Leave Tommy with me."

"You need your rest."

"I'll not have him calling you Mama before you leave this house."

Laurel scurried out of the room as she fought back tears. She had to keep in mind Mrs. Howard's physical and emotional conditions. And her mental one, as well. Still, the words stung. Minister Howard had said it would get worse, but she never imagined such atrocious accusations.

∞

Laurel sat on the top step of the front porch in the cool evening air. The Howards were all in bed. This was her time of quiet. She let the hymn drift through her. She'd found another line of lyrics today. *"I am here for you through everything; In the wind and rain, I am here."*

She carried the words in her heart, wherever she went, whatever she was doing. The song was her secret. Not even the composer knew what it meant to her. What a treasure it was to her.

She wanted to write a thank-you note, let the composer know how much he had helped her. She ran inside to get pencil and paper and sat back in the moonlight, bright enough to write by. She tapped the pencil on her lips.

Dear Hymn Author. . . No, that sounded too austere. *Dear Sir*—too formal. She felt as though she knew this person's heart, and the author could be a woman. *Dear Person*—too general. *To Whom It May Concern*—too cold.

She would skip the salutation, just get to the heart of the matter.

> *I can't begin to tell you what your hymn has meant to me these past weeks. My life has been fraught with trouble, and your hymn has brought healing to my wounded heart and battered spirit. Thank you for sharing your heart with me even if it was unintentional. I feel as though I know you through your music. Besides God, it has been the one respite in my current difficult circumstances.*

She stopped. *Sincerely, Miss Rivers?* She wanted to give a warmer regard than "Sincerely," but she'd never met this person. And if she signed her name, the person could take offense because of who she was.

Thank you from the bottom of my heart, she wrote, then folded the letter twice.

☙

Laurel stepped out of the mercantile with her shopping basket full. Across the street, Ethan held out a brown paper package to Mr. Chavez. This must be the first chance in four days for Ethan to return Mr. Chavez's shirts. The package seemed a bit larger than she remembered. Mr. Chavez kept his hands in his pockets and shook his head, but eventually he took the package.

"Excuse me, miss," a man said, trying to get past her into the mercantile.

"Pardon me." She moved. How rude of her to be watching them unaware. She hurried on her way.

Once inside the church, she could breathe more easily. She hated going into town. She felt as though people were watching her, scrutinizing her. But Sundays were worse. Even though the whispers had stopped, she knew the citizens of Hollow Springs would never embrace her as one of their own. She had to move on. She wanted to move on.

She set the thank-you note on the piano with the sheet of music, but what if he or she got upset she had been playing the song and took it away? She needed this music right now in her life. She slipped the note back into her pocket. She would leave it when the song had been completed and she had it committed to memory.

A third line of lyrics had been added to the sheet. The sheet with the ink smudge. *"Through good and bad, call on me."* Such a sweet reminder. *Thank You, Lord.* She committed the line to memory and quickly ran through the selections for Sunday. Mrs. Howard was more and more nervous about being alone lately. When she finished and returned to the house, she went straight upstairs to Mrs. Howard. "Is there anything I can get for you?"

"The curtains in the kitchen need to be washed, and the ones in the front room. Beat all of the rugs and clean out the fireplace; don't just sweep it, but give it a good scrubbing. And scrub the kitchen floor—make sure you get all the corners."

She wanted to tell her that the kitchen floor didn't *need* scrubbing again today and that she *had* gotten the corners. But she held her tongue. The woman must be miserably scared of losing this baby.

Later, on her hands and knees in the fireplace with a scrub brush in hand, Laurel sighed at the knock on the door. The last thing she wanted to do was wash out the fireplace, but she shouldn't complain; it could be worse.

She struggled to her feet and dried her hands on her way to the door. She widened her eyes at the visitor. "Mr. Chavez."

He thrust a brown paper package at her. "They both need hemming and one a torn seam and a button gone." He started to walk away.

"Mr. Chavez?"

He turned around but continued walking backward with his hands out from his sides. "Por favor."

He almost seemed desperate in his plea.

And he walked away.

She finished scrubbing the fireplace and fixed supper. Everyone had gone to bed by the time she could get back to the package Mr. Chavez had dropped off. It appeared to be the same one she'd seen Ethan with earlier. She opened it and found two pair of dress slacks. She'd never seen Mr. Chavez in britches like these. She held them up. A little short for Mr. Chavez, too.

Her hands fisted around the fabric. These weren't Mr. Chavez's clothes, and she guessed the shirts weren't, either. Why was Ethan Burke giving his clothes to someone else for her to mend? Was her guilt not enough? Did he pity her that much?

Poor orphan girl of the bank robber. She has no family or home. She would rather have the town's hatred than Ethan's pity.

What had she read this morning in Romans 12? She went quietly upstairs, retrieved her mother's worn Bible, and set it on the table in the circle of candlelight. She ran her finger down the page to verses 20 and 21: "Therefore if thine enemy hunger, feed him; if he thirst, give him drink: for in so doing thou shalt heap coals of fire on his head. Be not overcome of evil, but overcome evil with good." Did Ethan think her his enemy? Was he trying to heap coals of guilt on her head? Too late; she'd heaped them on herself. Was he trying to overcome Pa's evil with good deeds toward her?

Or did he think her evil? Either way, there wasn't much hope of forgiveness from him. She would leave town as soon as Mrs. Howard had her baby, even if she had to walk. If she didn't feel the minister's desperation, she'd leave now.

She sat up by candlelight in the kitchen until she'd repaired the pants and pressed them. Right after breakfast in the morning, she would return them.

❦

Laurel had left the house later than she'd intended. The sun was already straight overhead and hot. She walked into the bank, purposely trying to keep what had happened there from her mind. Ethan was not at his window.

"May I help you?" the bank manager asked.

"I'm looking for Mr. Burke."

"He's gone out to lunch. He'll be back soon."

"Thank you." She stepped back outside to think. Maybe

he ate his lunch at the hotel restaurant. Or had he gone home? Since she didn't know where he lived, she decided to check the hotel.

"Mr. Gonzales, has Mr. Burke come in for lunch?"

"I'm sorry, no."

She went back outside and looked up the street in both directions. Alonzo Chavez leaned on the awning post outside the mercantile with his long legs stretched out across the opening to the steps. Rosita Menendez was telling him something in Spanish, evidently about his rudeness in blocking her path. He had a cocky grin on his face.

"Mr. Chavez. Miss Menendez."

Mr. Chavez stiffened and stood up straight as a board. "Hola—I mean hello." His jaw was set, and his gaze flickered from her face to the package she clutched to her chest. Miss Menendez looped her hands around his arm.

"I'm looking for Mr. Burke. Do you know where I might find him?"

His Adam's apple bobbed as he swallowed hard. "He was posting a letter."

"Thank you." As she turned to leave, Rosita Menendez gave her a sweet smile, but Mr. Chavez still looked uneasy. Did he think she was going to let his sweetheart know she was mending for him? Even if these were his clothes, she was smarter than that.

❦

Ethan stepped out of the small clapboard post office. His brother, Charles, would get the letter soon, and Ethan hoped he would reply quickly. Laurel was striding toward him. "Miss Rivers."

"Mr. Burke." She handed him the package. "These are repaired."

He pulled his brows together. "Shall I give them to Alonzo?"

"Mr. Burke, I saw you give him this package yesterday. These are no more Mr. Chavez's britches than they are mine. They are far too short. No offense."

"No offense taken. Let me pay you." He hadn't thought about how easy it would be for her to discern the difference.

She held up her hand. "You overpaid me for the shirts. We'll call it even."

He was only trying to help.

She lowered her lashes and said something too soft to make out.

"What was that? I couldn't quite hear you."

When she looked back up, tears rimmed her green eyes. "I can't do this anymore. I need to wash you from my heart." She turned to leave.

"Laurel, please wait."

"I have to go. I left Tommy with Mrs. Howard. She gets more and more agitated each day." She hurried away from him as though he'd hurt her.

He wanted to call her back, but it was obvious she didn't want anything to do with him. He looked down at the package. *Lord, how am I to help her if she won't accept my help?* Maybe he shouldn't have done it in secret. Would she also be mad at him for paying the hotel and mercantile bills? He only wanted to help. He would do anything for her.

Chapter 7

Ethan counted the money in his drawer and turned in the cash and receipts to Mr. Yearwood.

Mr. Yearwood took them. "You all healed up?"

He automatically touched his wound. "My arm still aches and is stiff, but I don't have to worry about ripping it open again." And he'd left his sling at home. He didn't like the way Laurel always glared at it. Was it a reminder to her of what he'd done to her pa? If he could help her get past the tragedy, then maybe she could forgive him. He wasn't looking for her sympathy.

"I sent word to the bank's investors about your bravery. Maybe they will give you a small reward for your heroics."

"I wish you hadn't done that. I'm no hero."

Mr. Yearwood clamped his hand on Ethan's shoulder. "It's never easy when you are forced to kill a man. Mr. Rivers was out of control. Think of the lives you saved. I believe he would have killed someone had you not reacted so quickly."

He knew that. But why couldn't someone else have grabbed the gun from the drawer? Anyone else. Then he could have been the one at Laurel's side to comfort her instead of avoiding her. "If you don't need me any longer, I'm going to leave."

"Go. Have a good weekend."

Outside, Alonzo was leaning against the storefront.

He went over to Alonzo and inclined his head down the street. "Starlight Hotel Restaurant?"

Alonzo nodded and pushed away from the building. "Your señorita, she looked for you."

He wished Laurel were his. "Unfortunately, she found me." Not that it would have made any difference if she hadn't found him. She would still hate him.

Alonzo held the door to the hotel open. "You almost put me in big problems with Rosita."

"How? I haven't seen her all day."

"Señorita Rivers, she brought me the mending, and Rosita, she was there."

Oops. "I'll talk to Rosita."

The hostess showed them to a table. "We have a great pot roast tonight with potatoes and carrots."

They both agreed, but he didn't feel much like eating.

Alonzo continued. "No need. Your señorita asked for you; she not give me package."

"I'm glad it all worked out." He'd ruined enough lives. He didn't need to add to the damage.

"This time. I not do it again."

"No need. She knows they were my clothes." He shook his head. "She hates me more now than ever."

"And you love her more, *mucho mas* than before."

He sighed. "I can't control my heart."

A waitress came with coffee for them both.

"Mi amigo, I very afraid for you."

"Why?"

"You fall too hard with love."

Love was the most painful thing he had ever experienced, more painful than a bullet. And he'd do it again for a chance to love Laurel and to have her love him back. "Just as she lost her father, I lost her that day in the bank."

"You not know that. Speak to her. Say everything to her."

He stirred his coffee. "What's there to tell her? She already knows everything."

"Say you are very sorry and you love her. She know that, yes?"

He set the spoon down and took a drink. Too bitter. Hadn't he added sugar? He did so and stirred again. "Why would she listen to me?"

"Maybe she love you also."

He laughed at that. The chances of Laurel loving him were nonexistent.

After supper, he walked home and sat at his piano. He played through Laurel's song. The next line came to him as all the others had. One at a time.

☙

A muzzle flash. Mr. Rivers looked down at his bloodstained shirt. When Mr. Rivers raised his head, Ethan saw Laurel's sorrow-filled face. "Nooo!" Ethan rushed around the counter to where she fell and held her in his arms.

Her gaze found his face. "Why?"

A deep ache ripped him open inside. "I'm sorry. Forgive me." He willed her not to die but could feel her life slipping away.

He sat there for a long time with her lifeless body in his arms. Then he was beside her open grave, still holding her. They wanted to put her in the cold, uncaring earth, but he wouldn't let them.

He woke to find his arms tightly wrapped around his pillow and tears on his face. "Laurel," he whispered in the dark. "Forgive me."

He stayed huddled with the pillow until dawn broke over the horizon and began to light the room. His dream was quite clear. He would never have peace until he asked Laurel's forgiveness for what he had done. He'd told her he was sorry, but forgiveness was different. Anyone could be sorry for her loss, but asking forgiveness acknowledged responsibility. Would she forgive him?

He set his pillow aside and reluctantly climbed out of bed.

Chapter 8

Laurel closed the church door and headed for the cemetery. The fourth line of lyrics had been waiting for her. The second line had been there on Monday when she went to practice and the third on Thursday. It had taken two weeks for the music to appear one line at a time, but four out of the six lines of lyrics had rushed in during one week. The continual anticipation was exciting, but she knew it would soon be over. She both looked forward to the end and dreaded it. She wanted this blessing to last. If she could stop time, she would right now, here, with this song. Would the author title it once he or she was through? She would call it "I Am Here."

She hummed the tune and let the words play in her mind.

I am here for you through everything;
In the wind and rain, I am here.
Through good and bad, call on me;
My love for you is true and faithful.

She stopped at the edge of the cemetery and stared. Ethan

Burke was kneeling beside Pa's grave. He was the last person she would expect there. Had he come to unleash pent-up anger on Pa? She wanted to leave but found herself walking closer. It was time she faced up to what Pa had done and begged for Ethan's forgiveness.

As she came to the grave, she could hear Ethan murmuring softly, pleading. But for what? A fresh red and yellow firewheel lay on Pa's grave. It had been Ethan? A twig cracked under her foot. Ethan jerked around, then stood. His eyes were red, but no tears streaked his cheeks.

He blinked. "Laurel. I mean Miss Rivers." He seemed flustered. "I'm sorry for intruding." He pointed to Pa's grave.

"I'm glad you're here, Mr. Burke. I've needed to speak to you for a long time now." She took a deep breath.

"Please call me Ethan."

Would it be right to be so familiar? "I wanted to tell you how deeply sorry I am."

He knit his brow. "You have nothing to be sorry for."

"What my pa did to you. . ." She stared at his injured arm now out of the sling. "You are a good and kind man. I beseech you on behalf of my pa to find it in your heart to forgive him."

His eyes widened. "I'm the one who needs to beg your forgiveness. I did far worse to your pa than he did to me."

She couldn't imagine what. "Pa shot you."

"His bullet only injured. Mine. . ." The words choked off, and he stared down at his splayed hands, then back up to her with fresh tears in his cobalt blue eyes.

She stared at him a moment and pictured Ethan with a gun in his hand pointed at Pa, then a flash. She gasped. Pa fell, and then there was red. "You?"

He nodded.

"But the sheriff—I always thought the sheriff. . ."

"The sheriff arrived later. I was only trying to wound your pa. I never meant to—to kill him." He looked down at his shaking hands.

Poor Ethan, forced to kill to protect others. What torment he must be fighting within. She couldn't even imagine. She looked to Pa's grave. Poor Pa. So desperate, and Ethan was unfortunate enough to get in the way.

"If I could go back, I'd change it all. Please forgive me." Ethan blinked to focus his vision, to see Laurel more clearly.

"I am so sorry he put you in that position. Of course I forgive you. For a long time he was not the father who raised me. Believe me, he had been a good Christian man. He changed the day Ma died. He died inside, too."

Her forgiveness washed over him, soothing his soul. "Was your ma's name Katherine?"

She nodded.

"I think he saw her just before he passed on—or thought he saw her."

Tears pooled in her green eyes. "I would like to believe so. He would have liked that."

He reached out and took Laurel's hand. "I'm going to see to it you make it to California."

"What?"

"It's what your pa wanted."

She blinked several times, and the glisten in her eyes receded. "You are a very sweet man, but I don't want to burden you any further."

"You are not a burden. Everything I did was to help you."

"Everything? You mean the mending?"

He stared at her a moment. He already knew that giving her work in secret had been a mistake. How would she feel about the rest? "The mending."

She squinted at him. "Was it you? Did you pay Pa's debts at the hotel and the mercantile?"

He was reluctant to answer, but he knew he couldn't deny it. He nodded.

"Why would you do that for me?"

He saw something in her upturned face. Was it hope? "I feel responsible for you—because I took your pa away."

Laurel's shoulders drooped slightly. "The one responsible is my pa. I absolve you from any responsibility you feel you owe." Her voice had become flat and lifeless. "Please let go of your guilt. I don't hold your actions against you. Thank you for all you have done for me."

He sensed he'd hurt her in some new way but didn't know how. Was she further from his reach than ever?

◑◐

Laurel wiped the crumbs from the table and dumped them into the slop pail. Everything she thought was good about Hollow Springs wasn't, except the song. She longed to go play its soothing notes.

Ethan didn't think of her as anything more than a burden

that needed to be taken care of, then forgotten. She didn't want to be anybody's burden. She blinked back tears. *Responsible.* No word could have dashed her hopes faster. She'd cried after her encounter with Ethan yesterday and later cried herself to sleep. She hadn't realized how deep her feelings for Ethan were. Her emotions were all mixed up inside her. She couldn't tell if her tears were because of her poor circumstances or because she now knew that there was no future for her and Ethan.

Minister Howard came into the kitchen with the tray. "Mrs. Howard wasn't hungry this morning." He set the tray on the counter, the food untouched. "I asked her if she wanted you to stay here this morning."

No. She wanted out of this house for a little while.

"She said she's just going to sleep, so you can go, but I'd appreciate it if you would come back as soon as the service is over." His kind eyes looked tired.

Relief washed over her. "I was wondering if I could go over to the church now. I need to practice a little more before the service starts."

He nodded. "I'll be over in a little while."

She escaped out the door before he could change his mind. She breathed in the sweet scent of wildflowers as she walked to the church. She would play the mystery song first, then practice the hymns; that way she wouldn't be playing the unnamed hymn when people started arriving. She didn't want the composer catching her. But first. . .

She knelt at the first pew and opened her heart to God. This was what she needed most, to be alone with God. When she had purged and felt cleansed, she moved over to the piano.

She noticed that the sheets of music had been switched just since yesterday. She scanned to the bottom. The fifth line of words was there: *"Believe in me, I believe in you."*

Yes, Lord, I do believe.

She put her fingers to the keys and sang the song in her head as she played.

❧

Ethan leaned against the side of the clapboard church. The song he'd written for Laurel drifted out through the open window. She played it beautifully, better than he. She'd almost caught him, but he'd seen her coming and slipped out in time.

After he'd spoken with her yesterday, he'd gone home, and the Lord had given him the new line. And soon He would give him the last. He listened to her play it through three times; then he headed back home with the copy of the music. He'd return for the service in an hour. He needed to add the new line to the second sheet so it would be ready when he finally knew the last.

Later, as he sat in his regular pew, he kept his gaze on Laurel. She didn't once turn his way or anyone else's way. She looked only at the piano and hymnal. After service, she left quickly, and he followed. "Miss Rivers."

She stopped and paused a moment before turning his way but kept her gaze down. "Good day, Mr. Burke."

He'd thought they were beyond the formalities. "I would prefer you call me Ethan."

"I really need to be getting back to Mrs. Howard. She's been feeling poorly as of late."

"I wanted to talk to you about the trip to California."

"I do truly appreciate all you have done for me, but I won't be leaving until after Mrs. Howard has her baby. She needs me."

I need you.

"At that time, I'll have my own means to get there. But thank you for your generous offer."

"But I want to help. I feel responsible."

There it was again—her shoulders shifting downward—but why?

"As I told you yesterday, I free you from any obligation you think you have where I am concerned."

But he wanted to be responsible for her.

"Pa did what he did, and you did what you had to do. I don't blame you. Honestly. He was not himself."

"But if I hadn't—if I had only wounded him."

"Then Pa would be in jail, he would still have debts, and my circumstances wouldn't be much different than they are now."

He gripped her shoulders. "But I did kill your pa, and I am responsible."

Tears rimmed her eyes. "I don't want you to feel you owe me a debt. The feeling I want from you is. . ."

"Is what, Laurel?" He searched the depths of her green eyes.

After a moment of silence, her words gushed out. "I want you to care about me, but not because of anything that has happened, not because you feel *responsible*."

"I do care about you."

"Because you feel responsible." She pulled from his grip. "I really do need to go check on Mrs. Howard. Good day, Mr.

Burke." She turned and walked away.

When would he ever hear her call him by his given name? Yesterday she said she'd forgiven him, so why did she seem to want to be far away from him? *Lord, what do I do now?*

Chapter 9

Laurel heard a crash. Mrs. Howard cried out. She glanced at Tommy stretched out on the floor asleep and raced upstairs. Mrs. Howard stood with one hand on the foot post of the bed, the other under her belly.

"Let me help you back into bed."

"Stay away from me." A small pool of water gathered at Mrs. Howard's feet.

She halted. The baby was coming. "Mrs. Howard, you must get back into bed."

"Leave. I want you to leave."

She backed up to the doorway. "I'll leave once you are back in bed." She watched Mrs. Howard struggle into the bed. "I'll go get help."

Mrs. Howard gripped her stomach and waved her away.

She was at the bottom of the stairs before she realized she had touched any of them.

Tommy stood there crying. "Mama hurt."

"Mama will be fine." She scooped up the child and headed out the door. "We have to go get the doctor."

Tommy struggled in her arms. "Want Mama."

"Shh. I know. We'll come right back." She hurried into town and turned the knob on the doctor's door, but it was locked. She pounded on it.

"Doc's not there." Mayor Vance stood a few feet away.

That was obvious. "Do you know where he is?"

"I think he's out at the Shepard place."

"How far is that?"

"Too far to help."

"Mrs. Howard is having her baby."

His eyes widened. "Martha Peabody just went over to the bank. She's a midwife."

She ran to the bank. Mrs. Peabody stood at Ethan's window. "Mrs. Peabody, Mrs. Howard needs you. She's having her baby."

"Calm down, child. Roberta's baby isn't due for at least four weeks yet."

"Ma'am, it's coming." She leaned close and whispered about the water on the floor.

Mrs. Peabody straightened. "Is her husband with her?"

"No. No one." She'd hated leaving Mrs. Howard alone in her time of need, but what choice did she have?

"I'll tend to her. You find Preacher." Mrs. Peabody hustled out the door.

Someone else in the bank piped up. "Heard tell he was heading over to the Myers' house."

Ethan appeared at her side. "I'll get the preacher."

◌◯

Laurel stood at the back of the Howards' bedroom, waiting to help in any way she could.

"I'm not having this baby while she is under my roof!" Mrs. Howard had become feverish and seemed delirious, thrashing her head from side to side.

"She can be of help," Minister Howard said.

"She'll steal the baby!" Then Mrs. Howard hollered in pain.

"If you won't do it, I will," Mrs. Peabody said. "She can't be this agitated."

Minister Howard nodded to her.

Laurel rushed to her room and put her few meager belongings in her carpetbag. As she walked back past the bedroom, she glanced in. Minister Howard gave her a small smile, then turned to his wife. "You can have our baby now."

She rushed down the stairs. Five ladies from the church stood in the kitchen; one held Tommy on her hip. Rosita and her ma were among them. Rosita's ma was also a midwife and rushed up the stairs with an armful of clean sheets. The three church ladies turned away. Could they really pretend she wasn't there? But Rosita's gaze didn't waver from her. Her big dark eyes filled with sadness as she watched her leave.

She had no place to go. *"When all around my soul gives way, He then is all my hope and stay."* Her only refuge now was God. She would go to His house. He alone was her source of help and hope.

She'd felt that the Lord wanted her to stay until the birth of the Howards' baby. That day was today. She'd thought she'd have a few more weeks, though. The little money she had must be enough to get her to the next place the Lord would have her go. Fear gripped her heart at the thought of traveling alone.

Rosita followed her out to the porch and started speaking to her in Spanish.

Laurel just shook her head. All she caught was Burke and Alonzo. "I don't know what you are trying to tell me."

Rosita pinched her face in frustration, then pointed to the church.

"Yes. I'm going to the church. Then I'm going to buy a stagecoach ticket that will take me as far as my small amount of money will let me go." Why was she explaining this to her? Rosita couldn't possibly understand.

But Rosita's eyes widened as though she did, then she stepped off the porch, heading into town, away from the church.

What was all that about? She heard Mrs. Howard scream and hurried on her way. She set down her carpetbags inside the door and knelt in front of the first pew.

"Please, blessed Lord Jesus, be with Mrs. Howard and her baby. Protect them both. It's too early for this baby, but I know that in Your hands the baby can live. Please don't take this little one from her. Please don't let anything I did harm either of them."

She thought she would pray for her own troubles, but the only words that came were for Mrs. Howard. She kept praying until she had nothing left. Then she just sat, exhausted, on the floor. She looked up at the cross hanging on the wall. "What now, Lord?" She supposed the only thing left to do was leave town.

Ethan looked up as the bell above the bank door jingled.

Rosita bustled in and walked right up to his window. She rattled off paragraphs in Spanish.

"Slow down. I need English."

Rosita took a deep breath. "*Señora* Howard—go—Señorita Rivers."

He nodded. "Yes, Mrs. Howard is going to have her baby, and Miss Rivers got help. Everything is going to be fine."

Rosita shook her head and started off in Spanish again.

He shrugged and held up his hands.

Rosita huffed out a breath. "*¿Dónde esta Alonzo?* Where Alonzo?"

"He was getting his hair cut at the barbershop." He started to make scissors with his fingers and bring them up to his hair, but Rosita had turned and was out the door. She understood far more than she could speak. Hopefully, Alonzo could make sense of what was upsetting her.

A few minutes later, Alonzo strode in with Rosita. "Can you come away?"

Ethan looked over at Mr. Yearwood. "Go. It's slow today. I don't expect much business with people distracted over the Howards' impending arrival."

"Thank you." He grabbed his jacket and followed Alonzo and Rosita outside. "What's this all about? Rosita came in upset, looking for you."

"No. She look for you."

Rosita started in rapid Spanish again.

"*¡Silencio!*" Alonzo ordered. "*El gringo no comprendo.*"

He understood that; *the American doesn't understand.* Rosita quieted. "She mentioned Mrs. Howard. I tried to tell her that we already got help."

"Rosita, she was there. She knows. Her *madre* help. Señora Howard has. . ."

Alonzo was searching for an unfamiliar word or phrase, so Ethan thought he'd offer help. "Had her baby?"

Alonzo shook his head in frustration. *"Echar a patadas."*

"Rápido, Alonzo." Rosita turned to Ethan. "Go, go."

"Señora Howard told Señorita Rivers to go. Leave," Alonzo finally said.

Ethan furrowed his brow. "She kicked her out?"

"That is not all. Señorita Rivers leaves town. She buys stagecoach ticket."

Ethan's insides twisted. He thought he would have more time to woo her. "I have to find her." He started off for the stagecoach ticket office.

"Rosita, she says Señorita Rivers go to church first."

He spun around and headed for the church.

Chapter 10

Laurel stood by the piano and picked up the sheet of music. She ran her fingers over it. She would never see the piece completed, but she would always carry it in her heart. It was time to continue her journey west. She would miss the song most of all, but she couldn't stay. Pa had ultimately let Ma's dream destroy him. California hadn't been good for either Ma or Pa, but maybe it would be good for her. She pulled out the thank-you note she'd written.

The door at the back creaked, and she heard footsteps. She kept her gaze on the piano. Whoever it was would leave once they saw her.

"Laurel."

She turned. Ethan! Her heart pitter-pattered at the sight of him. She wanted to run into his arms, let him take the undue responsibility he thought he had. But she didn't. She stayed rooted in place. "Mr. Burke." For the first time since Pa shot him, she didn't still see the sling. Forgiveness was a sweet thing.

He walked to the front where she stood. "What am I going to have to do to get you to call me by my given name?"

She lowered her gaze to the floor. "I don't know." She saw his foot take the last step between them and looked up.

His cobalt blue eyes met hers. They were trying to tell her something, but she couldn't figure out what.

"Rosita said that Mrs. Howard put you out. Is it true?" He held his hat in his hand.

"Yes." And there was relief in being put out. Though she didn't know just what she was going to do, she was glad to be out from under the Howards' roof.

"What will you do?"

"I have a little money now. I'll buy a coach ticket to another town where they don't know about Pa and get a job."

"Don't go."

"I must. The people of Hollow Springs don't want me here. It is best for everyone if I go."

"Not for me."

Her heart skipped a beat. Did he truly care? Or did he only feel responsible?

He stepped closer. "From the moment I saw you, the Lord put you in my heart. I don't want you to leave without me. Marry me. I can give you a place to live, provide for you, and I'll take you to California. Unless there is someone else. Someone in California?"

Ethan wanted to marry her? Her heart sang. The paper in her hand called out to her, and she looked down at the sheet of music.

He looked, too. "What do you have there?"

"It's a hymn. I don't know who wrote it, but I've been wondering about this person."

"Would you choose the unknown author over me?"

She stared up at him. Would she? If the composer walked in right now and professed his love for her, which she knew he wouldn't, would she choose him? The composer had only been the Lord's instrument to comfort her. To her, God was the true author of the music.

"It's okay if you would. More than anything, I want the truth."

Ethan was here and real. She'd loved him before she ever discovered the music, but the song had helped heal her. She set the sheet on the bench. "You. I would choose you."

His smile stretched his mouth. "You have made me the happiest man in the world." He picked up the music. "Would you play it for me?"

Glad to finally share it with someone, she sat and put her fingers to the keys. "I don't sing well, so I'll just play it."

"How about if I sing the words?"

She would like that. She hadn't heard both parts together yet. She began, and so did Ethan.

"I am here for you through everything." His voice was smooth and deep. "In the wind and rain, I am here." Deeper than his speaking voice. "Through good and bad, call on me; My love for you is true and faithful." The song fit his voice, seemed to be written for him. "Believe in me, I believe in you."

As she came to the last line, she knew he'd have to stop, but she would play to the end. But he didn't stop. He sang the last line, sure and strong. She stopped in the middle of the line, but he continued.

"No other man will love you more than I do."

She stared at the sheet of music as he finished. Ethan was the author. It wasn't a song about God's love, but a song about a man's love for a woman. She turned slowly on the bench. "You?"

He nodded.

"For me?"

"I wanted to give you something for what I took from you. I couldn't bring your father back, but I could give you my love. I didn't think you would let me in person, so I wrote it down, in a language I hoped you wouldn't reject."

Tears filled her eyes. "Thank you."

Ethan took her hand and pulled her to her feet. "I've loved you since the day you came into town."

"I love you, too."

He wrapped her in his arms and kissed her.

The clearing of a throat caused her to push away from him. The minister stood at the back of the church.

"Minister Howard, I'm sorry."

Ethan hooked his arm around her waist. "I'm not. I love her, and she loves me."

Minister Howard smiled back. "You two make a fine couple."

"Minister, has Mrs. Howard had the baby yet?"

He nodded. "Peter Sean Howard."

"Is he healthy?"

Minister Howard nodded. "He's tiny but a fighter like his mother."

"How is Mrs. Howard?"

"Right as rain. She's resting." He smiled at them. "Let me know when you two want to tie the knot."

Ethan stood taller. "Now."

She jerked her gaze up to him. "Now?"

"You need a place to live. I could pay for a room at the hotel, but that would start tongues to wagging. Marry me now? I don't want to wait one day and risk losing you."

She wanted to be Mrs. Ethan Burke right now, today. "I have Ma's wedding dress in my carpetbag. Can I change first?"

Ethan smiled, and the minister said, "I'll go round up a witness or two and meet the two of you back here."

"Alonzo and Rosita are probably not far away," Ethan said. "I'll bring them back with me."

The minister directed his gaze at her. "You can go over to the house to change. Mrs. Howard is asleep and won't even know you are there." He closed the door behind him.

"This is for you." She handed the thank-you letter to Ethan.

He tucked his eyebrows. "What is it?"

"I wrote a letter to the song's composer. That's you."

He unfolded it and read it. "I never knew if you were actually playing it until yesterday morning when you almost caught me here. I'm glad it helped you. I was praying it would."

"Some days, other than the Lord, it was the only good thing I had to look forward to. Do you have a title for it?"

" 'A Song for Laurel.' "

A smile stretched her lips. "I like that."

He took her hands. "So you're really going to marry me today?"

"Yes, Ethan. I'm going to marry you."

He shook his head. "So it took asking you to marry me to get you to call me Ethan. I should have asked you a long time ago, then." He drew her into his arms and kissed her before they went their separate ways to prepare.

⚬

Laurel put her carpetbag on the bed she used in Tommy's room and took out everything to get to the bottom, then she pulled out the bed sheet–wrapped dress. It was a simple white dress with a touch of lace at the cuffs and neck and wrinkles galore. Was there even time to iron it? She shook her head. Even if there was time, she would rather wear wrinkles than spend time in the kitchen with the clucking hens.

A light knock sounded at the door. She opened it, and Rosita walked into the room. "I help you." She gingerly touched the dress lying on the bed. *"Muy bonita."* She held the dress up to Laurel. "Bonita, señorita. You. . .make. . .beautiful bride."

"Thank you." Tears gathered in her eyes. Was it just because someone gave her a kind word? Or was it because she was getting married? Or was it because Ma and Pa weren't here with her?

Rosita scooped up the dress over both arms. "I go iron."

"You don't have to do that."

Rosita rattled off several sentences in Spanish, then swept out the door with the dress.

The tears that had gathered spilled over her cheeks at Rosita's kindness. She pulled out Pa's pocket watch and opened it. Ma and Pa on their wedding day looked up at her. "I wish you both were here." She paced the room until Rosita returned with her pressed dress.

Rosita laid it on the bed.

"Thank you so very much." Laurel gave her darling, black-haired angel a hug.

Rosita hugged her back, then helped her dress. "You wait." And Rosita left her again.

She wanted to call her back. Rosita had been so kind to her, she just wanted her to stay. She wasn't sure how long she would need to wait and suddenly grew nervous. She was going to get married today. She was going to be someone's wife. Her life would forever change. *Lord, am I doing the right thing?*

She knelt down beside the bed, careful not to undo Rosita's hard work, and poured out her hopes and fears to the Lord. When the knock came on the door, she was at peace with what her future held.

Minister Howard stood in the hall. "Are you ready?"

"Yes."

"Are you sure this is what you want? I can speak to Mrs. Howard. I can make her understand. Or I can make arrangements for you to stay with another family."

She didn't have to get married out of necessity. She had a choice. Did she want to marry Ethan for no other reason than that she could? *Yes!* her heart cried. From the day she'd first seen him, she'd known. She took a deep breath. "Very sure. I want to be Mrs. Ethan Burke."

"Ethan Burke is a good man." Minister Howard smiled and handed her a bouquet of wildflowers. "These are from Miss Menendez."

That was thoughtful of her. They were tied with a blue ribbon. Her dress was old, the flowers new, the ribbon blue. Rosita probably wasn't even aware of the tradition. The only thing missing was something borrowed. She would borrow Ma's favorite prayer: *Lord, from sun up to sun down, may my actions shine glory to You.*

Minister Howard walked her to the entrance door of the church. "Wait here until you hear the music start." The minister slipped inside.

Music? Who had he found to play the piano—and on such short notice? The music started, and she stepped inside, then stopped and stared. The pews were half full of the townspeople: Mr. Gonzales and his wife, Mr. and Mrs. Jones, the ladies from the Howards' kitchen, as well as a few others. They'd certainly not come for her. They must be here at the minister's request and for Ethan, but their presence gave her a sense of acceptance anyway. The Lord was working extra for her today.

She turned her focus to the front of the church and headed down the aisle. Ethan sat at the piano. Of course it would be him. As she walked down the aisle, she could see Rosita giving Alonzo a look that said she wanted to be getting married next. Alonzo just smiled back at her and winked. When she reached the front, Ethan played the final notes and then joined her.

She was very sure and couldn't wait to become Mrs. Ethan Burke.

After the vows, Minister Howard smiled as he said, "I now pronounce you husband and wife." Then he looked directly at Ethan. "You may kiss your bride."

Ethan cupped Laurel's face in both of his hands and gave her a gentle, lingering kiss.

Very, very sure.

Epilogue

One month later

Laurel stood on the sandy shore and stared out at the Pacific Ocean with the salt breeze caressing her face. "We made it, Ma." She pulled out Pa's pocket watch from her handbag and opened it, Ma and Pa gazing up at her. "We all made it."

She pulled the small photograph free. A cinnamon-colored curl lay beneath along with Pa's ashen one. She took them out. "I love you, Ma and Pa." She separated the hairs between her fingers and let the salt breeze take them away. How apropos to bring Ma to the Pacific Ocean on the anniversary of her death. Now Ma and Pa would forever be a part of California, and she could move on with her life.

She turned to her new husband, took his hand, and folded the watch into it. "My wedding gift to you."

Ethan opened his hand and stared at it. "I can't take this."

"Ma gave it to Pa on their wedding day. I know it's not our wedding day, but I want you to have it."

"Thank you."

She slipped her arms around his waist. "Thank you for bringing us here."

Ethan looped his arms around her. "My pleasure." He kissed the top of her head. "Now that we're here, where do you want to live?"

"Anywhere you are." She turned in his embrace to look up at him. "I love you, Mr. Burke." He didn't seem to mind her calling him Mr. Burke anymore.

He gave her a squeeze. "I love you, too, Mrs. Burke." He kissed her. "I think the Lord has good things planned for us here in California."

She was sure of it.

MARY DAVIS

Mary Davis is an award-winning author of eight novels with both historical and contemporary themes and one short story. She hopes to write stories with her husband one day. She is a member of American Christian Fiction Writers and leads two critique groups.

She enjoys walking, spending time with her family, and playing board and card games; she also enjoys rain and cats. She would enjoy gardening if she didn't have a black thumb. Her hobbies include sewing, quilting, crafting, porcelain doll making, crocheting, and knitting. She enjoys going into schools to talk to kids about writing. She loves creativity in various forms.

Mary lives near Colorado's Rocky Mountains with her husband of over twenty years, three teens, and six pets (only three are cats). She asked Jesus into her heart at age twelve and strives to have her writing point to and glorify God. If she had one wish to make, she would wish everyone Jesus, because when you have Jesus, you have the most important thing.

Please visit her Web site at http://marydavisbooks.com.

Cookie Schemes

by Kathleen E. Kovach

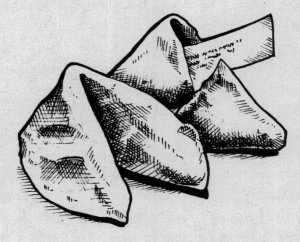

Dedication

To Jim, who wooed me not with cookies,
but used sweet words just the same.

For do I now persuade men, or God?
or do I seek to please men?
for if I yet pleased men,
I should not be the servant of Christ.
GALATIANS 1:10

Chapter 1

Prudie Burke hopped off the streetcar and felt the butterflies for the first time. Prescott Tower stood in proud importance at the top of the hill. She'd never interviewed for a job before, but after breezing through college, she felt confident. She reached into her handbag and pulled out the green and gold tassel—University of San Francisco, class of 1955. She smoothed it tenderly, as if she were petting a cat's tail. The tiny symbol represented a lifetime of dreams.

Her parents had needed convincing when she announced her plan to go to business college. But Prudie knew what she wanted, and it wasn't to stay home and be a baby-maker like her three sisters.

As the streetcar pulled away, she tugged the bottom of her cinch-waist jacket and smoothed the wrinkles from her blue pencil skirt, feeling quite fashionable in the just-below-the-knees style. She pulled on her white gloves, adjusted the tiny gray felt hat that hugged her red-brown waves, and tucked her handbag under her arm. No one could call her a tomboy now!

Her mother called her *special*. Any girl who could shinny up a tree since turning six must have unique talents.

As she approached the imposing building, her bravado faded. It looked much smaller from the street. She envisioned the revolving glass door welcoming people in but just as easily tossing them out. Would her dream of a career be whipped out onto the street?

Take a deep breath.

She entered the building and found the elevator. "Third floor, please."

The middle-aged operator in an impressive gray uniform touched the brim of his cap and pulled the controller handle. Prudie's spirits soared as the tiny car lifted her, symbolically, to success.

Her nervousness babbled out of her as the operator listened patiently. When she disembarked, his face lit, showing a toothy smile. "God's blessings on your interview, miss."

God's blessings?

She hoped God wouldn't have anything to do with this job. Where had He been when her brother died in Korea?

Prudie swallowed her anger as always. One couldn't function with such thoughts on the surface. *I must concentrate on this interview.*

The receptionist, a woman in her thirties with short, dark brown hair permed in pretty waves, greeted her and announced her arrival over an intercom. The woman led her into an office where a balding man in a gray flannel suit waited behind a desk. He rose and motioned to a chair. "Please take a seat, Miss Burke."

"Thank you." Placing her handbag on her lap, she fought

the urge to clasp her hands together in a death grip.

"I'm Harold Sweeney. Welcome to the Prescott Brokerage Firm." He sat down, slipped on a pair of black reading glasses, and opened a folder with her name written on it. "So you attended the University of San Francisco."

She sat up straight, pride filling her chest. "Yes, sir, I did."

"Majored in business, I see. And you're applying for the position of Mr. Prescott's secretary?" His brows knit together, and Prudie's butterflies turned into bats—large African bats. "Have you had any experience in secretarial work?"

Her mouth went dry. "No, sir, but as you can see, I graduated top of my class."

Mr. Sweeney tapped the edge of the folder with his index finger, then closed it. He took off his glasses and looked pointedly at Prudie, who suddenly felt small.

"Miss Burke, the ad was very clear as to what was expected in the way of credentials."

"I know, but I thought—"

"I'm sorry." His eyes took on a kind quality. "I must fill the position with someone more experienced. However. . ." He replaced the glasses and opened her folder again. "You type eighty words per minute?"

"Yes, sir." Prudie scooted to the edge of her seat.

"And excellent shorthand, too, I see." He removed the spectacles and placed them in his breast pocket. "Well, I'm impressed with your academics, but I'd like to see how you fare in the real world." When Mr. Sweeney stood, he tossed her folder into a box labeled TO BE FILED. "Follow me."

He led her to the elevator. The operator looked pleased to

see the two together, and he gave her a fatherly wink.

Mr. Sweeney joined her in the elevator. "Basement, please."

No, not the basement. She couldn't rise to success while plummeting the wrong way. When the doors opened, her heart sank.

The steno pool.

ॐ

Alex Prescott squeezed the receiver. His mother's perky voice invaded his ear, but he'd stopped listening after she said, "Come to the party tonight. There's someone your father and I want you to meet."

He rubbed his temple with his free hand. A quick glance at the calendar reminded him he only had three months to find a wife.

Sounds of clanging pots and pans beyond the office wall reminded him further. His staff continued to prepare the day's meals, oblivious to the fact that Alex could lose the restaurant for which his grandfather had worked so hard.

"Her name is Christine. . . ." Mother's voice droned on.

He twirled his chair to look at the portrait of the two men behind him. One would think that someone who'd built a business from the ground up would look more austere. But the artist had captured the compassion in Granddad's eyes.

Ho Woo stood next to him, the Chinese cook who'd shown Granddad that same compassion when he was down on his luck. He'd heard the story countless times. Ho, shedding centuries of Buddhist tradition, had recently converted to Christianity. He'd caught a young homeless and starved Edwin Prescott sneaking out of his restaurant without paying. Instead of calling the authorities, Ho took him in and taught him to cook, and together they formed a bond stronger than that of brothers.

". . .comes from a good family. . ."

After Ho and Edwin opened a Chinese/American restaurant and developed their own fortune cookie recipe, Ho heard of a man in Los Angeles who slipped words of encouragement into little cakes. They decided to put scripture verses in the cookies. Thus, they came up with the name Woo with Sweet, a play on Ho's name and a reminder that God woos with sweet words.

". . .and don't be late, because. . ."

Ho Woo died four years after Alex was born, so he barely knew the man. Edwin later wrote up a will. The oldest male would inherit the business as his predecessor retired. Edwin was Alex's maternal grandfather, making Alex the next in line to inherit. When he turned twenty, he began working closely with his grandfather, loving every minute. To ensure that the restaurant would remain in the family throughout the generations, Granddad had added the stipulation that the oldest male must be married by age thirty with the intent to have children—or forfeit his place in line to the next male.

That would be Cousin Corky. *Corky!* Five years younger by age, but about fifteen by maturity. He hadn't yet expressed a desire to take over the business, and Alex hoped he never would. He'd rather his family sell it than let Corky run it into the ground—or gamble it away in some drag race. Granddad couldn't have predicted there would be a Corky in the family.

"Alex? Are you listening to me?"

"Yes, Mother. I'll be there." But if he didn't sense something from God, he wouldn't pick this woman, either. *Pick*—what an ugly word.

After hanging up, he headed for the kitchen, glaring at the calendar on his way out.

His efficient staff was pulling together the lunch menu when he walked in. Although he often helped prepare the main dishes and entrées, the cookie baking fell exclusively to him. Since his grandfather's death five years prior, Alex was the only one who knew the secret recipe. And that, according to the food columnist in the *San Francisco Chronicle*, was what made Woo with Sweet unique.

Alex picked up two plates and asked where they needed to go. With both hands full, he backed through the swinging door and entered the dining room.

"Here you go, Mr. and Mrs. Leigh. Just the way you like it." He opened Mrs. Leigh's napkin and, with a flourish, laid it in her lap. She giggled like a teenager, though she must have been pushing fifty.

"Thank you, Mr. Prescott," Mr. Leigh said, digging his chopsticks into the chow mein.

"Young man," another customer called to him.

Alex approached the elderly Chinese gentleman who'd been eating alone. "How can I help you, sir?"

"I'd like to speak to the manager, please."

Alex adjusted his tie and said, "I'm the manager. Is anything wrong?"

A grin broke out on the octogenarian's face, displaying a set of yellowed teeth. "Not at all." With arthritic fingers, he picked up the slip of paper from his fortune cookie. "I just like to thank you for this message: 'For by me thy days shall be multiplied, and the years of thy life shall be increased' (Proverbs 9:11). Means much to me."

"Thank the Lord, sir. I simply write out verses and place them in a jar. He must have a special message for you."

As Alex walked away, he prayed silently for the man. This was his ministry. He believed God brought people into his restaurant so he could intercede in prayer on their behalf.

And while he was communicating with the Lord, he decided to toss up a prayer for himself. *Please, Lord. Bring a woman into my life whom I will fall head over heels for. And please let her have more than an ounce of sense, unlike the women my parents have been parading in front of me.*

At that moment, he turned and bumped into a customer, causing her to lose her balance. Before he knew it, they'd both landed on the floor, but he managed to break her fall with his own body. He felt her elbow pressing into his chest. As she tried to stand, her knees cocked at odd angles from a narrow blue skirt.

"I've lost my heel!" Her gaze darted around the floor.

"Wait a minute—*oof*—here it is." He pulled the spiked heel out from under his backside. When he stood, he held it out and asked, "Are you okay?"

She snatched the heel, adjusted her felt hat, and straightened her jacket. Then she glared at him with the most gorgeous cobalt blue eyes he'd ever seen.

"Do watch where you're going, sir." Her cheeks flushed a deep red.

"I'm s—s—sorry." Why was he stammering?

This is the one.

Excuse me, Lord?

He knew he'd heard the voice clearly. What was it he'd just prayed? To fall head over heels? It had to be his imagination. And yet. . .

"Come on, Prudie." One of her friends pulled her away. "We like to sit over here."

She wobbled to the booth, looking like a peg-leg sailor with a short peg. Her brunette friend scooted across the bench, allowing the one called Prudie to sit next to her.

Alex followed them in an effort to fix the mess. "If you give me your shoe, I'll glue the heel back on."

"While I sit here in stocking feet? No thank you." Icicles hung from her words.

Had he misunderstood the Lord? Wouldn't she have heard the same thing? "Then at least let me pay for a new pair." He reached for his wallet, but she held up her hand.

"The best thing you can do for me is walk away."

Alex felt his own anger rise. "I insist."

"Do you work here?" Her blue gaze bore into him, causing him to take a step back.

"Y—yes." He cleared his throat and tried again without stuttering. "I do."

She pressed her fists into the table. "Then I'd like to see the manager."

He pushed his shoulders back and looked down at Miss High-and-Mighty. "I am the manager."

She didn't seem at all intimidated. "There's no one else to report this incident to?"

"No, there is not." His gaze held hers in a standoff. "Is there anything else I can do for you at this time?"

"No."

Fine. "In any case, I'm very sorry. Please let me know if you change your mind." He spun abruptly, nearly spilling someone else to the floor.

He decided to remove himself from the dining room before he hurt somebody.

Before he could do so, a hot rod pulled up in front of his restaurant, its idle rumbling. Then it rattled the windows with a backfiring boom. He cringed as much at the noise it belched as at the scoundrel it spilled onto the street.

Corky.

Chapter 2

"Why are you here, Corky?" Alex stepped behind his desk and sat under the portrait of the two founders to assume an air of authority.

"Just thought I'd hang out with my favorite cousin." Corky pulled off his leather jacket and unrolled his sleeve, where he'd tucked a pack of cigarettes. "Mind if I smoke?"

"Yes." Alex sat ramrod straight. His cousin's slovenly appearance made him want to look the opposite.

Corky shrugged and rolled the pack back into his sleeve. He plopped into a chair and tossed his booted feet onto the desk. In the same move, he smoothed one side of his greased light brown hair. Alex wondered how he could be related to this man. Corky favored both of their mothers in looks. Otherwise, Alex would have sworn he was adopted.

Alex wished he could wipe the smirk off his cousin's unshaven face.

"So three months to the big day, eh?"

"What big day?" The hair on the back of his neck rose.

Corky reached into his pants pocket and drew out a small

knife. He picked at his nails. "Your birthday. There's talk you might have to retire from the restaurant biz early. No one interested in becoming Mrs. Alex Prescott?"

"A lot interested. None that interest me." How could he tell Corky, who had no standards, the wisdom of following God's will?

"Have no fear, Cuz. I've decided to step up to the plate."

Alex's heart plunged into his belly, his worst fears realized. He squeezed his eyes shut, hoping when he opened them again, Corky would be gone.

Nope.

"You see. . ." Corky slid his boots to the floor with a thud. "I think this joint has potential. Once I take over, it'll be a different ball game around here."

"How different?"

"Oh, I'm not going to spill the beans. But I have plans. Big plans." He stood and slipped his jacket back on. "Do you think they'll legalize gambling in California anytime soon?" With a cackle, he sauntered out the door.

Please, Lord. Please, was all Alex could pray.

❦

Prudie, more embarrassed than angry, could barely read the menu. And in front of her new friends! She glared toward the kitchen where she'd seen the offender disappear with an undesirable character.

"So," Loretta continued after she'd ordered, "you've just met the boss's son. What do you think?"

The tiny cup of green tea Prudie was sipping nearly slipped

through her fingers. "We work for *his* father? Swell."

She liked Loretta. Mr. Sweeney had asked her to help Prudie get oriented. She'd introduced her to the rest of the girls and then showed her the simple job she'd be doing. This willowy blond with the upswept chignon seemed much too sophisticated to work in a steno pool.

Gail, Loretta's friend, appeared more quiet and reserved. Her dark bobbed hair floated toward her face and encroached upon her black horn-rimmed glasses.

"The girls in the pool call him"—Loretta leaned in and lowered her voice—"Playboy Prescott."

"Him?" Prudie looked again at the kitchen door. Although tall, dark, and possessing incredible coffee-colored eyes, he certainly didn't seem as polished as a Casanova. In fact, now that her anger had cooled a bit, she thought he'd been quite vulnerable. That little stutter was kind of cute.

"If you read the social pages," Gail added, "you'll find mention of him with a different girl almost every week. Sure wish one week it'd be my turn." She leaned her chin on her hand and sighed heavily.

"Loretta," Prudie said after the food arrived, "Mr. Sweeney told me if I start in the steno pool, I might be able to work my way up into management."

Loretta and Gail looked at each other, then laughed. "Hon," Loretta said, "the only way upstairs is by the elevator."

"That's not quite true, Prudie," Gail said. "A few of our girls have made it into receptionist jobs."

Prudie wrinkled her nose. "I want to be more than a receptionist."

"I want to be a model." Loretta struck a pose straight out of *McCall's* magazine. "But I'm working because I like to eat." She demonstrated with a big bite of moo goo gai pan.

Prudie turned to Gail. "What about you? Are you content to take shorthand and type? Or would you rather be the one *giving* dictation?"

"Oh no. I'm only working until I find that special someone." A blush tinted Gail's cheeks.

Prudie shook her head. A model and a housewife. Couldn't she have made friends with more ambition?

Dessert arrived, a wafer-thin cookie folded and bent for each of them.

"Mmm. Aren't they to die for?" Loretta mumbled around the sizable piece she'd shoved into her mouth. "This is why we like it here."

"Well, this and to look at the boss's son." Gail's tawny eyes gazed longingly at the door where her object of desire had disappeared.

The cookies were, as the girls had said, *to die for*.

They each shared their slips of paper. Prudie's said, " 'Whatsoever thy hand findeth to do, do it with thy might; for there is no work, nor device, nor knowledge, nor wisdom, in the grave, whither thou goest' (Ecclesiastes 9:10)."

Scripture?

She started to wad it up, but something stopped her. She read it again. At least it didn't mention God. In fact, she found it comforting in a macabre sort of way. Compared to the grave, her job didn't sound so bad. She folded the paper and slipped it into her pocketbook.

"Listen," Loretta said after their plates were cleared, "Gail and I are looking into apartments. We could use a third roommate to help cut costs."

An apartment. Prudie licked her lips. Another step toward independence.

"Count me in!"

෬෧

"I still don't see why you have to do this," Prudie's sister said the next morning while brushing breakfast crumbs from her kitchen table.

"I'm helping the girls by moving in with them. And it's closer to work." Prudie accepted the cup of coffee Katie offered her.

No need for Mom to be around when Katie, ten years older than Prudie, served as a substitute. She barely knew her two older brothers. After the First World War, Teddy was born, twelve years older than Prudie; he'd inherited Mom's and Dad's love of music. Teddy was the special man in her life besides Dad. That was why his death hit especially hard. Then came the girls: Katie, Tessie, Abbie, and finally Prudie five years later.

When World War II ended, Prudie watched her sisters give up their jobs and marry. Each one, on their wedding day, looked at her all moony-eyed and tweaked her braids. "Someday it will be *your* turn, little one."

No, sirree! They couldn't understand why making a comfortable home for her husband would not be enough for Prudie.

"You know I supported you when you wanted a job." Katie lowered her eight-month pregnant body next to baby Livie's high chair. After spooning liquefied cereal into the baby's mouth and coaxing six-year-old Meg to eat faster, her attention finally turned back to Prudie. "But I don't see why you feel the need to move out. Haven't we made you a cozy home the last two years?"

"I appreciate you taking me in so I could go to college. Mom and Dad wouldn't have allowed me to attend otherwise. If you hadn't married Lon and moved to San Francisco, I might have had to"—she clutched her throat and gasped—"stay in the dorm."

"There aren't many women in college. They didn't feel it was safe for you to stay where the men outnumbered the women."

"I know; I heard all the arguments." Prudie leaned her cheek into her hand and swirled cream into her coffee. "I never did live up to their dreams for me." Mocking her mother's voice, she continued, " 'Prudie, did you bloody that little boy's nose? Prudie, don't bounce around too much in that dress, or you'll show your skinned knees. Prudie, you must learn how to cook so you can take care of your husband. Prudie! Prudie! Prudie!' " The spoon clinked against the cup in her agitation. "Excuse me while I don't dream of feathery nests, picket fences, perfect children, and the family dog. I want more than that."

The back door flew open, and Prudie's seven-year-old nephew Skip barreled inside with a rubber-band gun and his coonskin cap perched jauntily atop his head. His intended target was his sister. Meg squealed and ran from the table to the living room. The baby kicked her pudgy legs and screamed to get down.

"Okay, Livie, give Mama a minute." Katie wiped Livie's face and hands, causing the toddler to scream louder.

Prudie stifled a giggle as she watched her niece's feet running before her mother could lower her to the floor.

The baby toddled after her older siblings. Katie called into the living room for Skip to watch Livie, then added as an afterthought, "And don't shoot anything at her." She turned back to Prudie, patted her bulbous tummy, and shrugged. "What more is there than this?"

Prudie drained her coffee. "Look, I wore the folks down to let me go to college. And now you all expect me to set that aside to marry—who? Dennis next door?"

"He *has* asked you."

"And I said no."

Katie sighed as she reached for Prudie's hand, but Prudie pulled it away.

"I thought you, of all people, would understand." Prudie set her jaw. "You worked while Lon fought in Germany."

"I had to; you know that. I was helping with the war effort. But there's no way I could continue. It's a man's world, Prudie. I was replaced as soon as the men came home."

"I bragged to my friends about my sister who painted the American insignia onto battleship parts."

Prudie watched her sister intently. There it was. That flicker of regret. She'd loved that job, but she'd never admit it.

"Oh." Katie waved her hand as if batting at a fly. "You make it sound so glamorous! I'll bet you never told them I also stenciled thousands of letters and numbers, many more times than I was called on to draw freehand."

"Still, when the war was over, you should've continued your art in some capacity."

Lon walked into the kitchen twirling his car keys around

his finger. Katie smiled up at him and received his kiss.

"I love Lon more." She reached for a piece of toast and buttered it.

"Oops! Girl talk." Lon pulled open the back door. "Don't forget my suit at the cleaner's; I'll need it tomorrow."

Prudie narrowed her eyes at his retreating figure. She loved her brother-in-law, but he could be so dense sometimes. Couldn't he see the weary look in his wife's eyes?

Prudie didn't want that for herself.

"Please give me your blessing on this." Prudie leaned toward her sister.

"Which part? The job or the apartment?"

"Both."

Katie crunched into her toast and mumbled around the morsel. "Well, maybe you'll find a man there." Her eyes danced merrily.

Prudie hopped up and hugged her sister. "Where, at the job or the apartment?"

Katie pretended to choke. "It had better be the job, or Mom will have both our heads."

Laughing with her sister lifted Prudie's spirits. She knew her family thought of her as the rebel, the odd duck—*special*. Although Katie argued, she always let her maintain her individuality.

"I'm going to look at the apartment with the girls after work." Prudie reached over Katie to retrieve her coffee cup and kissed her on the cheek. "In honor of your support, I'll pick up the suit while I'm out."

Katie rewarded her with a grin.

Chapter 3

O kay, I'm done with your fingernails; now give me your foot." Loretta patted the footstool in their apartment. Prudie held her hands up like a surgeon and wiggled her foot as Loretta packed cotton between her toes. "Hey, that tickles!"

She wondered why she bothered to make herself pretty, not wishing to snare a man like the other girls in the steno pool. Perhaps for her own self-esteem. *A confident woman will get the job every time,* she told herself.

After living together for a week, the three friends had become quite comfortable with each other.

"Sunset Mauve is definitely your color." Loretta snapped her peppermint gum as she brushed on the first layer. "I think you should wear your blue sweater set with the plaid skirt. Your nails will pick up that subtle pink in the plaid."

"Whatever you say, Loretta." Prudie found Loretta to be an asset. Who else had a beautician and a fashion consultant living in their home? "I'm only allowing you to do this to me because I want to look professional."

With wide-eyed innocence, Loretta nodded her head. "Oh, that's why I'm doing this. Our career gal must look her best. By the way, do you own open-toed shoes?"

"No! Do you?" She'd never thought about displaying her new toenail color.

"Of course I do. And I'd let you borrow them, but your feet are at least three sizes smaller than mine." Loretta's gaze shifted around the room. "And if you tell anyone I admitted that, I'll deny every word."

Loretta glanced toward the easy chair where Gail was curled up with a book. "What about you, Gail? Looks like you and Prudie wear close to the same size."

"Hm?" Gail looked up and pushed her glasses up her nose.

"Shoes." Loretta waved the nailbrush toward her. "You got any open-toed shoes?"

"Heavens, no." Gail screwed up her face as though she'd eaten a pickle. "My feet are way too ugly for that."

"Well then, Prudie needs to go shopping today." Loretta winked conspiratorially at Prudie. "It would do you good to get out, Gail. That stuffy old book isn't going to find you a man."

Gail put a foot on the floor and waved the book in the air. "This, I'll have you know, is *The Fellowship of the Ring*. It's just been published."

Loretta looked at Prudie and shrugged. Prudie shook her head. "Never heard of it."

"And you, a college girl?" Gail huffed and pulled her feet underneath herself again. "Besides, I've found a man."

Prudie caught Loretta's incredulous gaze. She whipped her

head back to Gail. "Who?"

"When?" Loretta asked at the same time.

Gail sighed and shoved a bookmark between the pages. "Yesterday, when we walked home from work. I stopped at the bookstore while you two continued to window-shop."

"I thought you were in there a long time. Why didn't you tell us?" Prudie asked.

Gail shrugged. "I don't know. We both reached for the same book of poetry and something clicked. He's taking me to a poetry meeting tonight."

"Poetry meeting?"

"Yes, he calls it a beat club, where people share their favorite poems or those they've written. You drink coffee by candlelight. It sounds fun."

Loretta's worried glance reflected Prudie's thoughts. "Please be careful, Gail. I've heard. . .things. . .go on at those clubs."

Gail waved away Prudie's protest. "I'm sure that's all rumors. Barry seems perfectly normal, in a scruffy puppy dog sort of way."

"Is Barry a poet?" Loretta dipped the brush back into the nail polish bottle.

"Oh, he's more than a poet. He's a. . ." She drew her shoulders toward her ears. "A philosopher."

"Oh, brother!" Loretta rolled her eyes.

Gail tossed a throw pillow at Loretta's head.

"Watch the nails!" Prudie tried to defend herself from the ricochet, only to smudge her pinkie nail.

Gail, obviously satisfied after hitting them both with one throw, began reading again.

"Looks like it's you and me, kid," Loretta said as she finished Prudie's toes. "Let's go shoe shopping, then stop at our favorite restaurant." She switched to a singsong voice. "I'll bet someone would be pretty happy to see you."

"Don't be ridiculous."

"Well, the man did fall all over himself to meet you."

"The man fell all over me! Why would you think he'd be interested in this small-time college gal?"

"Instinct. I saw how he looked at you when he thought you were hurt. And then that smacked-on-the-nose-with-a-newspaper look when you told him off." Her smug grin unnerved Prudie.

But she had noticed all that, too. And she knew she must put up her barriers.

⟪❧⟫

Why did I agree to dinner? When his mother pressed, Alex insisted on hosting Christine and her mother at Woo with Sweet for the home-turf advantage. They sat toward the back of the restaurant at a nearly secluded table. His dad and Christine's father had conveniently begged off, leaving Alex with a numbers disadvantage. Three to one. He imagined they were sharing their little joke on the back nine.

"And then," Christine blathered, "we traveled to Nice, where Father met his dreary business partners while Mother and I shopped. And, of course, you can't be that close to Monaco without zipping over. We visited the Monte Carlo Opera and saw an absolutely wonderful rendition of Verdi's *La Traviata*. Do you remember, Mother, how we cried when Violetta died in Alfredo's arms?" She spoke with animation while her mother beamed proudly.

Alex pasted a smile on his face but, in fact, was bored. Dead bored. He tried to like Christine; he really did. She was a tall, blond beauty with a straight back and polished airs. She came from a good family, which mattered not a whit to him. She attended church, but he'd yet to hear anything from her that suggested she shared his beliefs. In truth, Christine was no different from the half dozen other socialites he'd already met in his parents' quest to find him a wife. After listening to her talk about her favorite subject—herself—he knew Christine was not his idea of a wife. He didn't care how much stock her father owned.

"What do you think, Alex?" Christine's voice pulled him back to the current topic.

Noticing the warning look from his mother, he decided he'd better start paying attention. "I believe the Grimaldis have reigned there for centuries."

"Oh, Alex!" Christine's twittering grated on his spine. "The Grimaldis aren't in Austria!"

Wait. What had they been talking about? Apparently, there had been a turn in the conversation.

Mother hid her embarrassment unsuccessfully behind her napkin, but Alex caught the raised eyebrow.

Finally, after all the opera and shopping talk he could take, Alex decided to throw meat into the conversation. "May I ask you something, Miss Fletcher?"

"Certainly." She touched the corners of her cherry-colored mouth with her napkin.

"What do you think of the homeless mission down the street?"

"Well. . ." She looked at her mother as if she had no thought apart from her.

"We support all kinds of charity, Mr. Prescott," Mrs. Fletcher chimed in.

"I was asking your daughter." He bit the inside of his cheek, immediately regretting his bark. "Forgive me, but I need to know her thoughts on the matter."

Christine shifted slightly in her seat.

While waiting for an individual thought to form in that pretty head, he glanced toward the door. The auburn beauty and her blond friend had just walked in. His heart did a little jig. He tried to settle it down, but it danced right out of his chest and over to the booth where they were led.

Maybe she'd heard the music, too. Their gazes locked, then hers shifted to the floor. Was she still angry over her little spill?

"As Mother said, Mr. Prescott," Christine said, regaining his attention, "Father gives to all kinds of charities. However, the mission is not one of them. You want my opinion, so I'll give it. I think it should be flattened and an office building put in its place. Those people are just lazy. They should be forced to get jobs and stop living on someone else's dime."

Mrs. Fletcher had the grace to place her gloved hand over her mouth, now agape.

"I see." He felt his lips press together, a futile attempt to hold his tongue. "Have you heard my grandfather's story, Miss Fletcher?" She suddenly looked like a rabbit caught in a trap.

"He was homeless as a youth. When he got back on his feet, he made it his mission to encourage the homeless and the hurting. I've invited a few people down on their luck into my home, even hired a couple." Christine's gaze shifted about the room as if searching for the homeless employee who might brush against her at any moment. Alex, in his growing anger, couldn't bite back his next words. "I don't suppose you would do the same?"

"Well, I never. . ." Christine started to rise, but her mother pulled her back into her seat.

"We're in a public place, dear."

Through clenched teeth and a fake smile, Christine sealed their non-future together. "I would not disrespect my home in that way."

He closed his eyes. Never—never would he make a rash decision that he felt was against God's will. And marrying Christine was not in God's will.

Mother and daughter rose to leave, acting as if the meal were truly over. Christine leaned in to kiss his cheek. In his ear she whispered, "Don't bother calling me—ever."

His mother rocked in her seat after they left, acting as if he'd just shot someone in cold blood. "What have you done?"

He felt remorse for his actions, but not for his beliefs. He pulled a chair close to his mother and stroked her hand. "It couldn't have worked, Mother. We have nothing in common."

Her eyes flashed with anger. "You don't understand. If you had married Christine, not only would you have inherited, but with Mr. Fletcher's connections, you could have opened another restaurant in a more lucrative spot, charged more, and grown. This tiny operation will not fare well as the bigger companies start moving in. And now, with the economy picking up after the war, we have to make some big changes."

"Why hasn't Dad discussed this with me?"

Through clenched teeth, she hissed, "I've done the research. I've chosen the women you should meet. Your father doesn't care about the restaurant. He only keeps a hand in it for me."

The light finally dawned. *Mother should be the one running the business end of the restaurant.* But her role in society prevented that.

"Mother," he said and took her trembling hand, "does Father know you've been choosing women with backgrounds that can further the business?"

"No."

All throughout the Bible, Alex had read stories of scheming women who'd tried to help their husbands. Mother's plan was just as flawed as theirs, and he hoped by now she knew that.

He glanced over at the booth by the window. Would he be helping God if he were to pursue this woman, knowing she was the one? He'd received the go-ahead—hadn't he? Maybe they'd just gotten off on the wrong foot. Well, right now, he needed to get to know her better, so he resolved to turn on the charm.

⁊❦

"Come on, Prudie. You must have seen it," Loretta pressed.

Prudie tried to pretend she hadn't seen the beautiful woman kiss Alex Prescott. It wasn't her affair. But she did wonder why the two older women were there. It looked like a cozy engagement party to her.

"New shoes, I see." The male voice startled her. She hoped

he hadn't overheard Loretta.

"Not because of you." Must he remind her of that embarrassing moment?

"They're lovely."

She wiggled her toes and then scolded herself for trying to draw attention to her Mauve Sunset.

"I'll be happy to take your order tonight. May I recommend the lo mein?"

"Actually. . ." Loretta batted her eyelashes.

What was she up to?

"We're celebrating. We just moved into an apartment up the street, and—ow!"

Loretta scowled at Prudie for the swift kick under the table.

Alex's face lit up. "Oh, we're neighbors." He held out his hand and shook Loretta's first. "My name is Alex."

This was more embarrassing than getting knocked off her feet. Only because she suspected Loretta had an ulterior motive.

"I'm Loretta, and this is Prudie. We work in the steno pool at Prescott Tower. Our other roommate is Gail, but she had plans tonight."

"Well, if we're celebrating being neighbors, please let me choose the menu, on the house."

"That won't be nec—ow!" Prudie rubbed her shin under the table.

"Thank you, Alex. We insist you join us." Loretta's eyes twinkled. That scamp was playing matchmaker.

"Thank you for the offer, but I've just had dinner with my

mother and. . .her friends."

Her friends? The young one sure acted like *his* friend.

"I will take a rain check, however. Now that you live close, I'm sure we'll see more of each other. In fact. . ." He dug into his breast pocket, pulled out a business card, and wrote something on the back. Then he handed it to Prudie. "Ten percent off anytime you come in. That goes for your friend who made other plans, too." Then he winked.

The nerve! What a flirt! Maybe he'd actually earned the name Playboy Prescott. Prudie thought about tearing the card in two, but Loretta snatched it out of her hand.

"That's very generous of you, Alex."

When he left, Prudie leaned across the table and hissed, "I can't believe you accepted that."

"Well, technically, he gave it to you. But I'm part of the package deal." Her chuckle bubbled out of her like water out of a fountain.

Their meal arrived, and amid Loretta's chatter, Prudie couldn't stop thinking of the owner of Woo with Sweet. Why was he eating with those three women? Why did the pretty one kiss him? Why would she care? She glanced at her painted nails. Would they attract a man like Alex? Is that what he saw in the pretty one?

Stop it! You have no use for a man!

She frowned, and Loretta said, "What? Is something wrong with your duck? Mine is absolutely delicious! We never could have afforded duck if Alex hadn't taken a liking to you."

"Oh, prattle!" She couldn't think of anything else to say. She knew Loretta was right. But she also knew she had to stay angry with Alex Prescott, or his charm—and those coffee-colored eyes—would be the end of her independence.

At the end of the meal, their cookies arrived. She'd been salivating for them even before the duck.

Her slip said, " 'Hatred stirreth up strifes: but love covereth all sins' (Proverbs 10:12)."

Hatred? She didn't hate Alex. Did she? A quick search of her heart confirmed that wasn't the case. Fear, maybe? That was more like it. She feared what a man would do to her newfound freedom. But she wasn't about to show fear in front of him.

After fingering the slip one more time and shoving the last bite of cookie into her mouth, she realized it was just a silly phrase and probably didn't apply to her at all. Even so, she folded it up and tucked it into her purse.

Chapter 4

A lex entered the house in which he grew up, the house that never seemed like a home. He remembered his grandfather's house—much more modest compared to the Victorian monstrosity located in Pacific Heights. He longed for the smell of vanilla, the scent that represented love and lingered on Granddad long after he'd made a day's batch of fortune cookies. He couldn't associate a scent with this house, unless it would be the liquor that flowed freely at his mother's numerous parties.

He rarely saw his father, and with his mother on the hunt for the perfect wife, he tended to avoid her. But they had asked him to join them on Saturday. He suspected it had to do with his future, as did most of their conversations lately.

"Mr. and Mrs. Prescott are waiting for you in the garden," the new maid informed him. He missed Margaret, who had retired five years ago. She and Granddad kept him sane in his childhood years. "Shall I announce your arrival?"

"No need. They're expecting me." He dismissed the young woman with a wink.

Jamming his hands into his pockets, he strode through the parlor and out the open French doors to the garden. His parents were rarely together on a weekend afternoon. Dad's penchant for golf usually kept him away until dinnertime. He imagined Mother had manipulated this meeting. Yet she acted innocent, sipping iced tea at the glass-topped table while Dad lounged in the padded wicker chair reading the day's paper.

Alex kissed his mother on the cheek and waited for his father to look up from his paper.

"Hello, Dad."

"Alex." The man retreated back to the business section without a further word.

"Have a seat, dear." His mother craned her neck toward the parlor door. "Where's the maid? Didn't she walk you out?"

"I told her there was no need. She disappeared somewhere in the back of the house." Doubtless afraid of her employers, like every other maid since Margaret.

Mother picked up a bell and hammered it back and forth until he feared the clapper would fall out. Finally, the maid popped out of the door, her cheeks flushed, probably from running through the house.

"Phyllis, did you happen to offer my son something to drink?"

"No, ma'am."

"Mother—"

She held up her hand to silence him. "Didn't you think he'd be thirsty since we're experiencing warm weather today?"

"Yes, ma'am."

"Mother, I'm not—"

"Phyllis? Do you have something to say?"

Alex guessed the woman to be in her early twenties. Was this her first job? If so, he felt sympathy for her.

But she rallied nicely as she pulled herself up straight. "Mr. Prescott, would you like something to drink?"

He couldn't submit her to any more scrutiny. "No, thank you. I'm fine."

"Nonsense! Phyllis, bring my son an iced tea, with two sugars."

"Yes, ma'am." She curtsied and walked away with her dignity intact.

"I'm not thirsty, Mother."

She fanned herself lightly with her napkin. "You will be if we sit out here all day." She turned to the man behind the newspaper. "Terrence, please come out of that hole you've burrowed yourself in and talk to your child."

His father lowered the paper, and for the first time, Alex could see stress lines in his trim face. Was Mother's badgering affecting them both? "Your mother is concerned about you."

Here it comes.

"It seems," his father continued, "you're not taking the restaurant seriously."

Alex leapt to his feet. "I work hard; you know that."

Dad folded his paper and waited patiently for Alex to sit again. "Yes, you're a very hard worker, but I'm afraid your grandfather failed in preparing you to take over the business. There's more to running a restaurant than merely keeping the doors open and serving superb food. Have you thought of opening another one on the other side of town?"

So Mother had run straight to Dad after their conversation the other day at the restaurant. "Shouldn't I follow Granddad's vision and keep it small and intimate?" He thought of the homey feel, his regular customers whom he knew by name, and the cookie scriptures he sometimes chose for special people. He couldn't do that if he had several restaurants. This was more than a business to him. It was a ministry.

"Since Korea, things have changed in this country, son. We're experiencing an affluence never before realized in our lifetime. Here's what I read this morning." He opened the *Chronicle* and began quoting. " 'The whole of San Francisco is going to change. . . .' This fellow, Ben Swig, says we're going to become another New York. He not only owns the Fairmont Hotel; he's also a successful real estate developer. He knows what he's talking about."

Alex swallowed hard. Glancing out past the garden area of the backyard, he noted the other Victorians on the sloping hill, built in San Francisco's heyday. The bay shimmered off in the distance on this unusually fogless day, and to his right, the forbidding Alcatraz Federal Penitentiary—the Rock—stood in the cold San Francisco Bay, impervious to the waves crashing against its stone. The last few years, he had equated himself to the men imprisoned behind those walls—his father telling him how to run a business, his mother telling him whom to marry. Now he prayed he could be as solid as that island. The waves of change were crashing at his shores, and he could either give way to their erosion or build barriers. Downtown San Francisco drew his gaze to the right. The skyline would change drastically if Mr. Swig had his way. *And they call that progress?*

His father continued. "My business is booming, and I'm thinking of going nationwide with it. Now if you'd rather give up the restaurant, since it doesn't look like you'll meet your grandfather's conditions anyway, you're welcome to join me at Prescott Brokerage."

"No!" Alex thrust himself from his chair again and began pacing. "That restaurant is all I have left of Granddad's legacy. It was his dream. And now it's my dream. But I'll run it the way I choose."

Phyllis tried to slip out to the garden unseen with a glass of iced tea on a tray.

"Not now, Phyllis!" his mother bellowed, startling the poor girl.

"Thank you, Phyllis." Alex reached for the tottering glass. "I'm suddenly very parched."

She gave him a grateful smile, curtsied, and disappeared into the house.

"Well," Mother said, dabbing at her upper lip, obviously agitated, "none of that matters if you don't find a wife. It will all go to your cousin Corky. Would that make you happy?"

Alex caught the distasteful look on his father's face at the mention of the black sheep. Nobody liked Corky, but he was family and clearly second in line to inherit the restaurant. Alex dropped into his chair, accepting defeat. If he didn't marry in time, he'd lose his grandfather's legacy. If he did marry but didn't begin thinking like a businessman, he could lose the restaurant anyway. He clasped his hands behind his neck and plunked his elbows on the table.

Lord, please tell me what to do.

Mother's voice broke the silence. "I hope you plan on coming to my July Fourth party on Monday evening. I've invited several prominent families." At his glare, she clarified. "Some with daughters, some without. I'll let you choose this time."

"Thanks." It was still the same old game, but now the young women would be clamoring to meet him. Maybe it hadn't been so bad one socialite at a time.

His excuses were on his tongue when his father spoke up. "And the day before, I've invited my employees for a picnic in Lafayette Park. Kind of a mid-year bonus. I thought an early Fourth of July celebration would be a grand time to meet their families and create a feeling of well-being in the company. You see, Alex, this is thinking like a businessman." He tapped his temple and winked wisely. "Why don't you come, and we can discuss more business options."

A warm ember sparked in Alex's chest and spread to a comfortable flame. "The employees will be there? All of them? Even the steno pool?"

⌘

Loretta's voice called to Prudie from the kitchen. "I'm sure glad you moved in with us. If Gail is going to skip out on the housework every weekend, I'm grateful I don't have to clean this place alone."

After dusting the living room, Prudie joined Loretta in the kitchen. "If I weren't here, there would be less to clean."

"Oh, sure. You're such a slob." Loretta wrinkled her nose. "Gail, on the other hand. . ."

"Didn't you know Gail was like this? I thought you were best friends."

"We became friends after she joined the steno pool about a year ago, but I had no indication she was so. . .untidy." She emphasized her statement by picking up a scrap of paper Gail must have tried to throw into the trash can that morning. "Is it so hard to pick up after oneself?"

They had been in their apartment for two weeks, and Prudie was beginning to learn her roommates' quirks. Loretta moved like a sanitizing tornado from room to room. Gail was more like the aftermath of a storm, with clothes strewn everywhere. She had no problem leaving the work for them, as long as they left her tottering stack of books alone.

Discarding the dust rag and tackling the breakfast dishes that had been Gail's responsibility, Prudie asked, "Where did Gail go this time? Out with her new beau?"

"Probably. I don't like it. This new boyfriend is claiming all her free time."

"That's what she wants, though. She thinks she'll find fulfillment in marriage."

"I know, but I worry about the man she's apparently chosen." Loretta adjusted the bandanna around her blond ponytail. Prudie found her more attractive with no makeup and her hair in a soft flip.

Loretta wielded the broom in her war on dirt and used each sweep to emphasize her rant against Barry. "He's unkempt, a poor dresser, and has no ambition apart from his poetry." With a heavy sigh, she swept the dirt into the dustpan and poured it into the trash can. "I just wish she'd stay away from those clubs."

Prudie rinsed the last dish while Loretta swished her hands in the remaining dishwater before its final *glug* through the drain.

Prudie also wished Gail would stay away from the beat clubs. She'd heard that dangerous substances were often served along with the coffee. But she couldn't prove it to Gail, who had promised to be extra careful. In her eyes, Barry was the perfect man and would never let any harm come to her.

While Loretta dried the dishes, they heard a knock on the door. "Lunch!" she called out while sprinting to the living room.

Not feeling like leaving the apartment—and seeing Alex again—Prudie had ordered two meals from Woo with Sweet, complete with dessert.

They both tackled their chow mein and then tore into their cookies. Before eating hers, Loretta read her slip.

" 'Let not mercy and truth forsake thee: bind them about thy neck; write them upon the table of thine heart' (Proverbs 3:3)." She lowered it, closed her eyes, and smiled. "What a beautiful thought. Write them upon the table of my heart."

Prudie swallowed her first bite of the sweet dessert. "Be careful, or you'll get as starry-eyed as Gail with her poetry."

"Aren't you going to read yours?"

"Eventually, I suppose."

Loretta reached across the table to snatch it from Prudie but wasn't fast enough.

"Fine." Prudie held the slip out of Loretta's reach. "I'll read it. 'Reprove not a scorner, lest he hate thee: rebuke a wise man, and he will love thee' (Proverbs 9:8). Happy now?"

Again, Loretta closed her eyes. "Rebuke a wise man, and he will love thee." When she opened her eyes, a mischievous twinkle danced in them. "Alex is a wise man, and you sure rebuked him."

"Oh, prattle!" She needed to escape. "I'm going downstairs to get the mail."

Prudie finished her cookie while descending the three flights of stairs to the lobby. Several items were in their box. Prudie thumbed through the stack.

She scanned the various flyers put out by local businesses to entice new renters. Leaning against the wall, she read aloud. "Nunzio's Italian Eatery. Mmm, a spaghetti special, and it's only a block away. Hunan Dragon. One of Alex's competitors. Oh, here's a place to get a great steak." What a perfect neighborhood. North Beach, or Little Italy, was close to Chinatown, where Woo with Sweet was located. Now if she could find a place that served her mother's pot roast, she'd be a very happy woman.

Three square envelopes caught her eye. Each with their names addressed individually. She drew in a sharp breath as she read the return address.

She scurried back up the stairs. "Loretta, look what was in our mail." Prudie, breathless, handed Loretta's envelope to her, keeping the other two.

"Looks like an invitation or announcement of some kind." Loretta's gaze traveled the same route Prudie's had. The handwriting, then the return address.

"Did you open yours?"

"No, I was waiting to do it with you."

They both tore into their envelopes and read the words together.

" 'In honor of your excellent service to the company, Terrence Prescott invites you and yours to Lafayette Park for a company picnic, Sunday, July 3.' "

Loretta waved the invitation like a victory flag. "Do you know what this means?"

Prudie shook her head.

"This means you might get to talk to Alex without a dinner menu standing between you." She beamed like the proud matchmaker she was.

"Don't you remember that woman we saw him with last week?" Prudie asked, shaking her head to dislodge the memory. "The one dripping in wealth? If he isn't engaged to her yet, I'm sure it won't be long. He wouldn't be interested in a bargain-basement catch like me." She tossed the invitation onto the table, making it skitter toward Loretta. "Besides, I'm not looking for a man. I have a career, and a man will only slow me down."

Loretta grabbed her hand and hauled her to her feet. "Come on. We've got to find you something to wear."

Chapter 5

When Prudie arrived at the picnic, she found herself grateful the coastal weather had cooperated and warmed comfortably. Loretta had talked Prudie into wearing lavender shorts and a sleeveless blouse with a Peter Pan collar. She noticed her friend had managed to cover herself with pink pedal pushers and a matching print shirt with three-quarter-length sleeves. Gail and Barry were dressed in black, the color of choice for the Beats, people who hung out at the poetry clubs in North Beach. They all now milled about.

Prudie scanned the grounds for a certain bachelor, even though she knew there was no reason for him to be there. He didn't work for Prescott Brokerage.

Yet as she tried to remove him from her mind and focus on the crowd, a sporty white car drew her attention as it pulled up and parked along the street. As Alex got out, her heart argued with her brain. She tried to convince herself not to become attracted to the man. But she found it impossible to look away from his dark tan against the white tennis shorts and light blue polo shirt. He waved and smiled, and her heart fought to win the debate.

"It seems Playboy Prescott came to the party alone," Loretta whispered in her ear. "I wonder what that could mean."

"Nothing. It means absolutely nothing," Prudie hissed as Alex approached.

"Well, hello to my favorite neighbors. Are you enjoying the picnic?" Alex took off his sunglasses and ran his hand through his hair, causing the slight breeze to play with it. Prudie commanded her imagination to kindly not think of her fingers in those soft, dark locks.

"We just arrived ourselves. We've been introducing Gail's friend around. Barry, this is Alex Prescott, our employer's son and owner of Woo with Sweet Restaurant."

Alex held out his hand. "Pleased to meet you."

"Man, you the Clyde with the cool cookies? Me and my subterraneans were cranked when we discovered your pad. And that's the word from the bird. Dig it?"

Prudie and Loretta stood with their mouths open. Barry hadn't uttered that many words altogether since they'd met him, but whatever he'd said sounded like a compliment.

"Thank you." Alex reached into his wallet, pulled out a business card, and wrote on the back. "You and your. . .er. . . subterraneans are welcome anytime."

"Cool." Barry flipped the card over and grinned. Prudie knew he'd received a sizable discount.

Witnessing Alex and his gentle ways, Prudie yielded to her heart's debate. Try as she might, she could find nothing to dislike about this man.

Gail pulled Barry away to meet someone else. As they left, Prudie could hear her telling Barry, "See, not everyone in the establishment is a drag. Alex is a cat who really digs us."

Oh, Gail. Are you becoming one of them? While Barry seemed nice enough, Prudie still worried about her friend.

"I'm starving. Would you girls join me for a hot dog?" Alex held out both elbows. Loretta latched on as if he were a carousel pony at Playland down by Ocean Beach. Prudie hesitated, but with both Loretta and Alex cocking their eyebrows at her, she realized the two weren't going anywhere until she placed her hand through his arm.

After picking up their food, they found a shady spot under a tree. Alex excused himself for a moment to get them all something to drink.

"What are we doing?" Prudie whispered to Loretta through clenched teeth.

"I believe we're having lunch with an attractive man. What did you think we were doing?" Loretta daintily played with her potato salad. "I thought about leaving you two alone, but I decided to come along to make sure you didn't bolt."

"Why would I bolt? He's just being nice to us."

"To you. Again, I'm only part of the package deal." Her gaze darted upward. "Here he comes."

Alex sat down with three bottles of pop in one hand and three fortune cookies wrapped in a napkin in the other. "My restaurant just delivered these." He handed one to each of them.

"Alex," Loretta said, "how did you come to be in this business?"

He told them an interesting story of his grandfather as a

young homeless man, trying to survive. A Chinese cook caught him stealing and took him in. The two formed a partnership and created Woo with Sweet back in 1921.

He paused, frowned, and picked at a dandelion. "May I ask you both a question?"

"Of course." Whatever could have changed his mood?

"What do you think of the homeless?"

Prudie, though taken aback by the question, understood its importance after hearing about his grandfather. "I think they need love and someone to champion them as they get back on their feet."

Loretta wholeheartedly agreed.

By his broad grin, she knew he must feel the same way.

After more small talk, Prudie's head for business began calculating. "So. . .you've followed in your grandfather's foot-steps. Why not go into insurance with your father? That seems more lucrative."

"Because this is my grandfather's legacy. If I don't fulfill my obligation, I'll lose it to. . ." He stopped and frowned. "Never mind. This must be boring you. Please, let's have our dessert."

Prudie picked up her cookie but kept an eye on Alex, whose emotions were riding a roller coaster. He'd seemed so animated when talking about his grandfather, a man he clearly loved. But the word "obligation" caught her attention. She sensed more to this story than a loving relationship and the desire to fulfill a legacy.

෯

Alex dabbed at sweat on his upper lip as Prudie opened her

cookie. He'd arranged for the restaurant to bring the cookies after he got there so he could claim the one he'd made especially for Prudie. Would she understand the scripture he'd picked? Would her reaction prompt him to reveal his feelings for her?

She broke the cookie in two and pulled the slip of paper out but began munching without reading. Meanwhile, Loretta tore into her dessert and seemed eager to read her scripture.

" 'Ointment and perfume rejoice the heart: so doth the sweetness of a man's friend by hearty counsel' (Proverbs 27:9)." She closed her eyes as if savoring every word.

Alex smiled inwardly; he hadn't chosen that verse for her. It amazed him how the Lord always knew what to say.

Prudie peered at her friend. "I suppose you're going to tell me my heart should rejoice from your hearty council."

"It had occurred to me." Loretta grinned at Prudie, which only seemed to put her in more of a huff. "Read yours."

Alex's heart thumped hard against his chest.

Prudie cast a glance toward Alex, and he wondered if she was embarrassed to read her slip in front of him. To make her feel more at ease, he read his next. He never knew what he'd get in his cookies.

" 'He only is my rock and my salvation: he is my defence; I shall not be moved' (Psalm 62:6)." He wanted to close his eyes as Loretta had done—to savor God's soothing confirmation that he was to continue in the work his grandfather had started.

Prudie, prompted by a shove from her friend, opened her slip and proceeded to read. " 'As the lily among thorns, so is my love among the daughters' (Solomon 2:2)." She blushed a pretty pink, folded the slip, and set it aside. What disconcerted him, however, was the frown puckering her eyebrows.

"Well, I like that!" Loretta placed her hands on her hips. "God just called me a thorn." She laughed, hopped up, and gathered their trash. "Dare I say, if I sit next to this 'lily' any longer, I'll grow spikes. See you later, Alex. It was great having lunch with you. I see someone across the park I want to catch."

Alex noticed the wink Loretta intended for Prudie. He also saw the scowl on Prudie's face. She rose to leave also, but he captured her wrist and asked her to stay a moment longer.

"You seem troubled by your verse."

He could tell she was warring inside herself. Emotions played on her face like a featurette at the local movie theater. Her next words stumped him.

"Why scripture?"

"Excuse me?"

"Why do you put scriptures in the cookies?"

Alex caught his breath. Was that animosity he heard in her voice?

He told her about his grandfather learning about someone else in California who used little cakes to encourage the homeless. Thus began their ministry through the fortune cookies. "I've continued that ministry and seen lives changed as a result."

"I see."

But did she? Her frown spoke volumes.

"Why does it bother you?" Alex didn't truly want to know the answer. He'd already assumed she was a Christian since God had chosen her.

Prudie's face clouded over, like an angry thundercloud anxious to rain on his parade. "God stopped caring about my family three years ago when He allowed a grenade to take my brother's life in Korea. None of our prayers for his safety worked. Now Teddy's body, or what's left of it, lies in a grave."

"I'm so sorry, Prudie." Alex's heart broke for her. He prayed for words of comfort. "I'm not sure what to tell you, except God didn't kill your brother. This sinful world did. All God has ever promised us is that He will be with us in the good times and the bad. But He's given us a better promise, one that transcends all of our problems."

Prudie swiped at a tear trailing down her cheek and sniffled. "Yeah? And what would that be?"

"Eternal life with Him. Our bodies aren't made to last forever. And some are taken much too soon. But our souls will go to live with Him if we only accept the gift of His Son who died in our place. Jesus died a physical, painful death so our souls could live eternally."

"Teddy believed that."

Alex felt relief upon hearing those words. "Then I believe Teddy is with the Lord right now."

Prudie grinned, changing the track of another tear as it floated into her dimple and pooled there. "Teddy used to say, 'Know what, sis? God is even bigger than that old oak tree out at Uncle George's farm.' I couldn't believe it. That tree was big enough to put two tree houses in."

"And now he's living with the Creator of that tree."

Prudie looked up at the spreading limbs above. "Before he died, I'd climb the tree and hug it, pretending I was hugging God. But after we buried Teddy, I couldn't bring myself to climb it again. How could God have taken someone who loved

Him? Teddy was good and decent; he didn't deserve to die."

"If you can stand one more scripture, try this one: 'For God sent not his Son into the world to condemn the world; but that the world through him might be saved.' That's from John 3:17. Death is not condemnation for the one who loves God. It's merely a stepping from this life into the next."

He let that sink in a moment. She hugged her knees while her expressive face told the whole story. She'd been angry with God for so long—was she trying to reject what she'd just heard? Tears pooled in her blue eyes, and she blinked them away. Was the Lord dealing with her heart?

Alex lay down on the grass next to Prudie. He put his hands behind his head and gazed up at the dancing green leaves overhead. He also felt closer to God when beholding His nature.

"Alex." She'd been so quiet her tiny voice startled him. "Thank you for taking the time to explain it to me. I've heard those words all my life, and for a time I believed them. But when faced with a tragedy, I guess I bailed out on God." She twirled a blade of grass between her fingers. "Don't get me wrong. I'm still upset with Him, but I'll try to be more open to Him."

"That's all He wants, Prudie."

Alex noticed the picnic was breaking up, but he didn't want his time with Prudie to end. "Say, would you be up to another party tomorrow? It's fancier than this picnic, and it will be horribly boring, and you'll have to tolerate my parents' friends."

Her light laugh tickled his ear. "With an invitation like that, how could I possibly refuse?"

Chapter 6

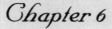

Alex pulled up to the Prescott home. Prudie stared up at the large Victorian structure, feeling insignificant. She waited for Alex to open her car door. What was she doing here? Was this a date? Or did she simply want to discover more about this man whose faith put it all into perspective for her?

The car door opened, and the breeze ruffled the netting of her royal blue dress, threatening to float up and smother her. He held his hand out to her. Of their own volition, her fingers slipped inside his palm. A perfect fit.

"I apologize once again for what you are about to endure." His crooked grin made her laugh.

"Oh, please, stop hard-selling me. Are you a restaurant owner or a salesman?"

They stepped onto a large curved porch supported by impressive white columns. Prudie, awed by the grandeur, discreetly pinched her lips closed to keep them from whistling.

A young maid opened the door and welcomed them into the foyer. Prudie's heels clicked on the polished marble floor.

Alex, with hands in his front pockets, leaned down and spoke to the maid in a conspiratorial tone. "What's the mood in there, Phyllis?"

"It's as if they're waiting for James Dean at his first movie premiere."

Alex winced, then pulled Prudie's arm over his elbow—she imagined more for moral support than to be gentlemanly. "Our public awaits."

They walked through a set of double doors where the assembled crowd consisted of mostly young women and their mothers. Prudie wondered where the men were. Then she caught a glimpse of the patio and realized they'd all gone out there to smoke cigars.

"Alex! I'm so glad you are finally here." A matronly woman glided toward them. Prudie recognized her from the dinner she had witnessed a couple of weeks earlier. A brief scan for the polished blond she'd seen kissing him on the cheek that day proved fruitless. However—she stifled a gasp—the room was full of polished blonds, brunettes, and redheads. Glancing down at her secondhand dress, she suddenly felt like a battered penny lying on some forgotten street in the Mission District.

"And who is this?" The woman raised her eyebrows and regarded Prudie with what she felt was false courtesy. The voice was friendly, but the eyes were not.

"May I present Prudie Burke? Prudie, this is my mother, Florence Prescott."

The woman held out her hand, knuckles first, and Prudie thought for a moment she was expected to kiss her ring. But she managed a handshake and said, "Pleased to meet you."

"Yes. . ." And with that, Prudie was dismissed. "Alex, you're such a naughty boy. I know I told you to be here at six o'clock. And here it's almost seven." She wrapped her arms around his elbow and began to steer him in the direction of the twittering troop. Alex stopped, looked over his shoulder at Prudie, and held out his hand. Warmth spread through her chest like wildfire. She knew he wasn't about to let her be devoured, by his mother or anybody else.

❧

Throughout the evening, Alex introduced Prudie to everyone, despite the women who tried to ignore her. He hated watching ten jealous women and their mothers dissect her, slashing her with their words and their looks. But Prudie was a trouper. She seemed to know her own mind and didn't appear intimidated at all.

He felt a stab of guilt for bringing her to the party. Did he want to show her his world, to introduce her slowly into his life? Or was she merely a buffer to the attention he knew he'd have to bear? Admittedly, he'd thought of that yesterday when he invited her. But he also wanted to get to know her better. If God had chosen her for him, he needed to develop this relationship.

Even if God hadn't chosen her, her beauty would have attracted him. That dress made her eyes a deeper blue, like the night sky under which he wanted to draw her.

Despite his best efforts to slay the dragon tongues, she needed a break. He led her through the house toward the small patio. They passed the grand piano, and she brushed her fingers over the keys, a gentle smile on her lips.

"Do you play?" He suspected his question had pulled her from a beautiful memory.

"A little. Not as much as I used to. My dad taught me 'Claire de Lune.'" She sat on the bench and played the beginning notes of that haunting strain. "My father courted my mother with a song, and she didn't even know it was him."

He sat next to her. "Really? How did that happen?"

"My mother found a piece of sheet music on the piano at church—a work in progress. Every time she'd look at it, a new line would be added. She eventually fell in love with the songwriter, and they married."

"That sounds very romantic." Would Prudie fall in love with him through the scripture he chose for her?

After dinner, while the guests mingled, Alex's father seemed especially interested in Prudie, probably because she was the only woman in the room who understood his language.

"Business school, you say? Sounds like you've got a good head on your shoulders, young lady."

"Thank you. I'm hoping someday to apply for a job higher up in your company."

"Higher up?" He raised a brow, clearly perplexed.

Alex realized his father hadn't recognized Prudie. And he wanted to get closer to his employees? "Prudie works for your company, Dad."

"Really? What department are you in?"

Her gaze dropped. "The steno pool."

"Well, come to my office tomorrow morning. I'll see if there's a better fit for someone of your abilities."

"Thank you, sir." Her glow stole Alex's breath. He wished his conversation had caused as much pleasure on her face.

He suddenly became aware of the whispering.

"*Steno pool?*"

"*What's he doing with a girl like that?*"

He ignored them. They didn't deserve any explanations. All that rabble wanted was a lucrative business merger, for which they were willing to sell off their daughters. It sickened him.

"Take Alex here." His father suddenly thrust him into the conversation. "Doesn't have a lick of business sense."

Alex felt his face flame. How dare his father berate him in front of Prudie.

But she defended him. "Well, his restaurant always packs them in. And the food is marvelous, especially those cookies."

"Cookies!" He raised his gaze to the ceiling. "Now *that's* something to put stock in."

The dining room broke into laughter. Alex glanced toward his mother, who was not laughing. Father had slapped them both with that remark.

"Insurance!" He continued to emote. "That's where the money is."

He launched into his postwar society speech, but Alex interrupted him, not willing to hear it again. "Dad, no one is interested in such things."

"Excuse me!" Prudie's eyes shot blue flames. "I find your father's thoughts quite enlightening. Are you saying that I, as a woman, am not interested? Honestly, Alex, you shouldn't pigeonhole women like that. We're not all like. . ." She scanned the room and then seemed to realize her mistake. A mob of perfectly penciled eyes glared at her, daring her to finish that sentence.

She clamped her lips shut and took a deep breath. "Mrs. Prescott, this was a lovely party. Thank you."

As she fled from the room, Alex pursued her. "Wait, what are you doing?"

"I'm calling a cab." She stopped in the middle of the foyer and balled her fists. "Where's the phone?"

Alex spoke to her back. "I'm sorry. You're right. I shouldn't have said that in there. I'm not used to strong women, especially women who can carry a conversation with my dad."

When she turned to face him, he saw her crimson cheeks and the tears that threatened to spill. "It's not that. I just humiliated myself in there. You know what I was about to call those women?"

Alex now understood her dilemma, and he attempted to ease her mind. "Empty-headed ninnies?" She smiled, and he went on. "Mindless mice? Down-filled decorative pillows? Believe me, I've thought of them all." He traced her chin with his thumb, catching a tear before it reached her dimple. "Come on, no harm done. You made a graceful exit, and they all think you're angry with me. How about we ditch this party? My mother has accomplished her purpose."

"And what was that?"

"Frankly, I'm too ashamed to tell you. Suffice it to say, it's the last time. She no longer has a purpose to accomplish."

As he led her to his car, Fourth of July fireworks erupted all over the city. Alex thought it apropos. He had a real firecracker right next to him. Would there be sparks if he kissed her?

☙

The next day, while clattering along in the streetcar, Loretta grilled Prudie all the way to work. Gail feigned disinterest, her nose in a book.

"Come on, Prudie! There has to be more to it. Did he take you out into the moonlight? Did he kiss you under the fireworks? Please tell me you had some kind of a Cary Grant moment with him!"

Prudie simply smiled. No, Alex hadn't kissed her, under the fireworks or anywhere else. He'd been the perfect gentleman and walked her to her door. True, she didn't give him much time, slipping into the apartment after politely thanking him for the invitation.

And now she had a date with destiny.

Loretta had been so engrossed with her interrogation, she failed to realize that Prudie was dressed for an interview. Apparently, romance overruled fashion.

When they reached the elevator, Prudie said, "Go on down, girls. I have an appointment upstairs."

As the door closed, they both looked as if they'd already lost her. But Prudie steeled herself.

The elevator arrived back at the main floor, and the operator looked at her with surprise when she asked for the top floor. "You going to see Mr. Prescott himself, Miss Burke?"

"Yes, I am. At his request."

As she stepped off the elevator, she heard him mumble, "Will miracles never cease?"

Miracles. Was that what had happened? If she hadn't met

Alex, if he hadn't shown up at the picnic, if he hadn't invited her to the party, she wouldn't be going to the top floor of Prescott Tower. She thought of her conversation with Alex at the park and her change of opinion about God. Was that a miracle, too?

No time to ponder. She now stood face-to-face with Mr. Prescott's personal secretary.

Chapter 7

Prudie couldn't believe her good fortune. Mr. Prescott promoted her! And not to just any position, but one higher in rank than receptionist. She was going to be a personal secretary. Not for him, obviously, but the next best thing.

For his son.

The morning of her first day working for Alex, Loretta sat on Prudie's bed. "I don't know if I should kick you or congratulate you. How can you leave our cozy office? It won't be the same without you."

Prudie had laid two skirts on the bed: a black pinstripe pencil skirt and a more flattering ruffled pale green one. She held both up for Loretta's opinion. Her friend pointed to the ruffled skirt, so Prudie chose the black one instead. She assumed Loretta would choose the one more appealing to Alex, and Prudie wanted to look professional. The matching austere jacket, although stylish, resembled a Salvation Army coat. Alex couldn't get the wrong idea when she walked in wearing this outfit.

"Loretta, we still live together. It's not as if we'll never see each other again. Besides, I thought you'd be happy I'm working for Alex."

Her friend lay back on the bed and winced when her curlers poked her head. "I'm happy for you, really. But office relationships don't often work out. You don't seem the type to marry the boss."

"Well," Prudie said as she tied the silk bow attached to her blouse around her neck, "I'm not in any way interested in a relationship with Alex. So there is nothing to jeopardize, is there?" After one last glimpse in the mirror, she grabbed her handbag and headed for the door. "Aren't you going to work today?"

Loretta, still lying prone on Prudie's bed, tossed her arm over her eyes. "No, I think I'll call in lonely."

"Come on." Prudie hauled Loretta to her feet. "Get ready for work. I'll walk as far as the streetcar stop with you."

❧

Alex drummed his fingers on his desk loudly enough to compete with the banging pots and chatter from the kitchen. If he didn't feel small enough in his father's eyes, add the fact that Prudie was now involved. He'd gotten the call yesterday after Prudie's interview. Dad never asked but rather told him that Prudie would be his new secretary. What did he need a secretary for? And why did it have to be Prudie?

After the tiny rap on his closed door, he wanted to shout, "Go away!" but checked his infantile thought.

"Come in."

She entered with an air of confidence that impressed even him. He rose and held the back of the chair for her. She delicately removed her white gloves and laid them in her lap.

He tried small talk to drown the angry voices in his head. "How are you today?"

"I'm well, and you?"

He rubbed the back of his neck. How was he? Livid. Confused. He wanted to send her back to his father, and he wanted to gather her in his arms. How was he supposed to work in these conditions?

He leaned back in his chair and tapped a pencil on his desk. Prudie's large eyes regarded him with part curiosity and part impatience. Apparently, she was waiting for him to make the first move.

"I'm going to be honest with you, Prudie."

"Miss Burke."

"Excuse me?"

"If we're to be professional with each other, we shouldn't be so informal."

All Alex could think of was two nights ago when he contemplated kissing her. He believed she was now wearing the same lipstick she had worn that night. "I don't think that's necess—"

"Please, Mr. Prescott. Other than the steno pool, this is the first professional job I've ever had. I'd like to do it right."

He tamped down his anger. If she wanted professional, he'd give her professional. "Very well, *Miss Burke*. I'm going to be honest with you. My father hired you without my consent, and technically, I could refuse your employment and send you back to the steno pool."

Her eyes narrowed. "Then why don't you?"

"Because," he said as he sat forward and leaned his elbows on his desk, "I respect my father, even when I don't agree with him. I'm not sure how he thinks you can contribute to my restaurant, but in business matters he's rarely wrong."

"I see." She glanced toward her lap.

He wondered if she'd get up and walk out, but he soon realized what a locomotive Prudie Burke was.

"Now *I'll* be honest. Your father asked me to look at your books. He'd like me to help you cut the fat and bring in more profit."

"That doesn't sound like secretarial work to me."

"No, it isn't. And I'll be happy to file, take shorthand, and type. But I have a talent, Al—Mr. Prescott. I received top honors in accounting. I haven't had a chance to apply that talent, however. If you'd allow me to work with you, not only would it be helpful to you, but I'd consider it a personal favor."

Her unwavering gaze disconcerted him. He tossed up a quick prayer, something he'd failed to do in his anger. *Lord, should I go along with this?* A tentative peace settled in his chest, one he felt might abandon him at any moment. He knew he was still fighting the arrangement despite God's affirmative answer.

"Okay, I'll show you the setup here, then we'll open the books. I'm not sure what you can do with them. I'm pretty tightfisted when it comes to spending money on the business."

"We'll see."

After a brief tour of the restaurant, Prudie sat down at Alex's desk with the accounting books spread out before her. For the most part, her new boss seemed to have everything in order. His debits and credits matched, and he'd logged everything neatly. But when she wrote out her own profit-and-loss statement over the last three years, she noticed no significant rise in profit. It seemed all Alex cared about was keeping the doors open.

"Lunch!" Alex called from the hallway.

Prudie rubbed her stomach, which had been growling for the last hour. The smells coming from the kitchen were marvelous. It wouldn't surprise her if she gained weight while working there.

She sat at a table toward the back of the dining room. At first she thought Alex might join her, but he busied himself waiting tables and chatting with customers. This moment to observe him proved eye-opening for her.

In the half hour during which she ate, Alex had accepted three of his own business cards—discounts for meals promised— given away two more business cards, and refused payment from a scruffy vagrant who looked as if he hadn't had a solid meal in ages.

While this endeared him to her, from a business standpoint, she could see why the restaurant hung by a thread. She knew she'd have to crack down on those discounts. But the look of pure joy on his face was priceless.

As she finished her meal, he brought her a cookie, then sped off to greet more customers. Prudie smiled. He really enjoyed himself.

This time when she opened her cookie, she read the slip first. " 'We are confident, I say, and willing rather to be absent from the body, and to be present with the Lord' (Second Corinthians 5:8)." She closed her eyes as Loretta had done, savoring what that must mean. At first it didn't make sense, and she wondered how she could apply it to herself. Then it hit her. Teddy. Did this mean that since he was absent from his body, he was indeed present with the Lord, as Alex had said?

She found herself praying. *Dear God, help me to have the same love for You that Teddy had—that Alex has.*

She opened her eyes to see Alex holding the frail hand of an elderly woman eating by herself. Was he praying with her?

Oh, Alex. How can I do my job if it means killing your spirit?

Chapter 8

Prudie chose not to tell Alex he mustn't give away free food anymore. Instead, she showed him where he could cut back in other areas. Using discount cleaning supplies, installing dimmer lighting, changing to a less expensive vendor—all of this helped, but not if the customers decided to go elsewhere. She had received three flyers in her mailbox for new Chinese restaurants that week alone, all offering deeper discounts. It seemed the cookies were the only draw to Woo with Sweet.

Meanwhile, Katie had given birth, so Prudie moved back home temporarily to help with the other three children. One rainy night, Alex offered to drive her so she wouldn't have to take the bus.

He pulled up to the house, and she turned to him. "Come on in and meet the family."

He surprised her with how quickly he agreed. Before long, he was romping on the floor with Skip and tickling Meg and Livie. All three children needed baths before going to bed after playing hard with the man they called *Uncle* Alex.

As Alex was about to leave, Lon challenged him to a game of chess. Prudie, perplexed by her own emotions, felt her heart quickening as her boss eased himself into her family. He seemed more comfortable in her sister's modest home than in his own.

Prudie and her sister chose to watch television while the men played their game. Soon baby Cindy started crying from her nursery upstairs. Katie, now curled up on the sofa, snored softly. Prudie rose from the other end of the couch, but Alex waved her to stay seated.

"Please, allow me to get her for you. Your brother-in-law's strategy is brutal, and I need to retreat."

He noiselessly padded up the stairs, and soon the baby's whimpering stopped.

After several minutes and no Alex, Prudie went to investigate. Her heart leaped when she entered the nursery to find Alex in the rocking chair with the infant, cooing at her and letting her wrap her tiny fingers around his. They both gazed at each other, oblivious of Prudie's presence.

She made a move to leave but stepped on a creaky board. Alex looked up with a sheepish grin and said, "I gave her the bottle sitting on the dresser. Hope that was okay."

Prudie nodded, dumbfounded. "Katie made it earlier, but Cindy wasn't ready to eat." She knelt before the two of them, rubbing the baby's downy head but looking at Alex. "Excuse me. You fed her? Lon doesn't even do that."

"Then Lon doesn't know what he's missing."

Soft nursery light, music playing from a windup toy, and the scent of baby powder created an ambience. Alex touched Prudie's face with his right hand while cradling the baby with the other. She never knew who made the first move, both drawn to each other magnetically. Their lips touched in a feather-soft kiss that promised so much more.

When he left that evening, she walked him to the door. With both arms free, he pulled her into an embrace.

"What are you doing to me, Alex?" she whispered against his cheek.

"Loving you." Then his lips found hers.

When he left, she held on to the doorjamb to regain her equilibrium. Then something happened to Prudie that she'd always feared. She fell in love.

❦

The next day, Loretta came to the restaurant for lunch and Prudie sat with her during a lull. She wondered if she should share her feelings for Alex. Would Loretta gloat over her matchmaking skills or warn her again of work-centered romances?

Her friend assessed her appearance. "A hairnet?"

Prudie's hands flew to her head. "Sometimes I help in the kitchen." Indeed, and sometimes she waited tables. She loved the interaction with the regular customers whom she knew by name now. She loved working side by side with Alex, and she loved when he included her in small prayer sessions.

She loved the cookies, too—and not only for their decadent sweetness. She looked forward to the scripture inside. Every slip seemed lavished with love, and she found herself equating God's love with that of Alex. It was as if God was wooing her through the scriptures, yet Alex easily could have penned them.

She shared one with Loretta.

" 'Behold, thou art fair, my love; behold, thou art fair; thou hast doves' eyes within thy locks: thy hair is as a flock of goats, that appear from mount Gilead' (Solomon 4:1)."

Loretta guffawed. "Maybe God is trying to tell you something. Comb that mop—it looks like goats!"

Prudie didn't want her two new loves, God and Alex, mocked, so she changed the subject. She asked about Gail, whom she rarely saw anymore.

"I don't know," Loretta said while picking at her thumbnail. "She's hardly ever at the apartment except to sleep. She never wears makeup, and her hair looks worse than yours. And her clothes! Always clad in black from head to toe."

"Other than the clothes, that sounds normal for Gail."

Loretta's gaze softened, and she reached out to cover Prudie's hand. "What about you? Are you happy here? It's not quite the executive position you'd hoped for."

Prudie leaned her cheek in her hand. "No, but it's fun. I have free rein of the accounting and all business-related duties, but Alex has drawn me into his ministry, and I like it."

"I think you like Alex."

She wanted to tell Loretta how working with Alex had made her feel special to God. But she still guarded that information in her heart. Loretta was fun but not too deep, and Prudie didn't think she could share these things with her.

Just as she felt close to God in the old oak tree on Uncle George's farm, she felt Him near within the four walls of Woo with Sweet. Her career would take her elsewhere someday, but for right now, this was home.

Alex sat in his office cutting slips of scripture and dropping them in the jar on his desk. A second jar, Prudie's, sat there, too. He delighted in handpicking her verses and then hearing how they had made her day. Of course, she didn't know he'd been doing this, and he had to be extra careful she didn't catch him.

The door swung open, and Alex jumped, thinking it might be Prudie, but then again, she always knocked. Corky, on the other hand, wasn't so polite. He sauntered in and plopped himself into the chair.

Alex crossed his arms. "Why are you wearing a suit?"

Corky looked down at his jacket and smoothed his silk tie. "Just getting into character. It won't be long before I take over the business." He ran his hand down the side of his head, ending at the ducktail. Once a greaser, always a greaser.

"What do you want, Corky?"

"Thought I'd follow the master around. See how you run things." He grabbed the two jars. "What are these?"

Alex cringed as Corky clunked them together. "Scripture. It's what I put in the cookies."

"Why do you do that?"

Alex sighed. If he didn't answer his cousin's questions, he might not go away. "Granddad Edwin started that tradition, and I'm making sure it's continued."

"I never could understand that dotty old man. Why not put stuff in there like a fortune-teller? 'You will be rich shortly.' I've heard of some places doing that."

As Alex was about to educate Corky on the evils of fortune-telling, his cousin's grip slipped and one of the jars crashed to the floor.

Alex jumped from his seat. "Watch what you're doing." It was bad enough to lose the jar, but now his cousin stepped on the slips, soiling them with his grimy shoes.

"Sorry. Hey, what's this?" Corky carefully picked up what was left of the jar's thick bottom. "There's a name written under this one." Corky raised his head slowly to look Alex in the eye, looking like a cobra about to strike. Leering, he said, "*Prudie.* That waitress out there? You pick special verses for the help?"

Alex's anger burned in his belly. "What's wrong with that?"

"Does your mother know you've fallen for a servant?"

Alex bristled. His cousin sure knew how to push all his buttons. "She's not a servant; she's my bookkeeper. Prudie is gracious enough to help wherever she's needed. And what makes you think I've fallen for her?"

"The look on your face when I mentioned her, cuz." He made a tsking sound. "In fact, you've got it bad."

Alex had no idea Corky could be so astute.

"Anyway. . ." Corky's snake eyes continued to try to hypnotize Alex. "I was wondering where you keep the cookie recipe. I should probably start learning how to make them so they're perfect when I take over."

Oh no, you don't. Alex knew if Corky ever got his hands on the recipe, he'd sell it to the highest bidder. "I'm not telling you the recipe, and you can't find it on the premises. It's locked safely away."

His cousin cocked his head, as though he knew that would

be the answer. "Well, I'll learn it eventually. It can't be that hard. I'll probably have someone else make it anyway."

"No! That recipe has to stay a secret."

"Relax, cuz." He patted the air, palms down. "If you don't get married in the next two months, you won't have any say in the matter, now, will you?" He rose to leave, grabbing a slip from Prudie's jar. He waved it as he headed for the door. "For research."

❧

That same objectionable man Prudie had seen her first day at the restaurant now appeared from the back office and plunked himself down into a booth.

He waved her over. "Hi there, sweetheart. How about some lo mein?"

Prudie was rankled over this man's attitude, but she took his order quietly. When she delivered his meal, he asked her to sit.

"I'm working, sir."

"Aw, come on. I'm the boss's cousin. We're practically family." He held out his hand, and she fought the desire to recoil. "Name's Corky."

Alex's cousin? He hadn't mentioned him, but then, apart from his grandfather, Alex rarely talked about his family. She ignored his hand and slid into the seat across from him, cautious yet curious about this part of Alex's life.

He tossed a slip of paper toward her.

Prudie picked it up. "Alex puts these in the cookies. It's scripture." What did this have to do with anything?

"Seems your boss chooses special verses just for you." He wound the noodles around his fork as if they were spaghetti and shoved a large bite into his mouth. Around chews, he said, "I got one word of caution."

Her stomach churned. "What's that?"

"If Alex marries you in time, it still won't make any difference. If he marries anyone beneath his station, he'll be disinherited anyway. Cut off from the family. So he'll have the restaurant, but that's it. Nothing from the insurance biz." He glanced around and half whispered, "You and I both know he'll need that money just to keep this joint afloat."

Prudie's mind whirred. "Wait a minute—back up. What do you mean, if Alex marries in time?"

He looked up, clearly surprised. "You don't know? I had you pegged for one of them gold diggers trying to get their pickaxes into the mother lode." He leaned forward and lowered his voice. "If Alex doesn't get married by his thirtieth birthday, he forfeits the restaurant. He thinks anyone will do." He sucked on a toothpick and pointed to Prudie.

His insolence caused her ears to burn from an adrenaline rush.

He continued to leer. "But he doesn't know his dad will cut him off. If you really like him, you'll back off and let him meet someone else. Then he can inherit what he's due."

Prudie's lungs stopped taking in air. She would have discounted this man for spreading lies, but his words actually shed light on many half conversations she'd had with Alex. Her anger began to boil. Who was the real villain? Had Alex been using scripture to soften her up? Had he been manipulating her into marriage so he could inherit the restaurant? According to this man, he didn't know about the clause that would cut him off from his father's money. When he found out, would he discard her like a used dishrag?

"It's a man's world, Prudie."

Her sister's words reached forward in time and slapped her. Women were ignored in the world of business.

Well, not this woman. Prudie stood, ripped off her apron, and glared at it. Alex had managed to domesticate her after all. Their first kiss had been in a baby nursery! Had he orchestrated that? She marched to the back office and hurled open the door.

Chapter 9

Y ou pig!"

Alex looked up, stunned, as Prudie burst into his office and threw an apron at him.

"What did I do?" Alex disentangled himself from the apron strings.

She grabbed at her hairnet and ripped it from her head. Bobby pins went flying in all directions. "The question is, what didn't you do?" Her eyes blazed fire, and she began counting on her fingers. "You didn't tell me you were preparing me to be a wife so you could inherit this restaurant. You didn't tell me you were manipulating me with scripture. I thought God was truly speaking to me. And you didn't tell me you never really loved me but I was just a pawn in some silly man-game!"

She spun and disappeared out the door, "I quit!" lingering in the air.

"Wait, Prudie!"

She stormed through the restaurant with him in pursuit. He caught up with her on the sidewalk and grabbed her arm, spinning her around. Tears streamed down her cheeks, no dimple in sight to catch them.

"Let me explain."

"Explain? So it's true." She tore her arm away from his grasp and stormed down the street.

"Hey, cuz!"

Alex turned to see Corky leaning on his hot rod and sucking on a toothpick. By his smug expression, Alex knew his cousin had something to do with this disaster. He was tempted to walk over and punch the black sheep in the nose. While making that decision, the window closed on chasing Prudie. She'd hopped onto a streetcar and disappeared.

He walked back to the restaurant, kicking himself. Everything Prudie said was true—except the part about him not loving her.

"She seems pretty angry there, cuz. What did you do? Forget to tell her a few things? Doesn't your Bible say something about honesty being the best policy?" With a cackle, he slid into his car. "Back to the old drawing board, eh, cuz?" The rumbling muffler and screeching tires drowned out any spontaneous thoughts of revenge.

❦

Prudie lay curled up on her bed at the apartment when she heard the front door open.

Loretta's voice called from the living room. "Prudie? Where are you?"

Prudie slogged into the living room, knowing she looked like a soggy mess. "How did you know I was here?"

"I stopped by the restaurant. Alex wasn't there, either, but the staff filled me in on what happened." She pulled Prudie to the sofa and smoothed the hair from her face. "You want to talk about it?"

"Oh, Loretta." Prudie began sobbing anew. She told her about Corky and about Alex's having to marry someone, fast. "I felt used, manipulated. How could he not tell me he needed to get married? I might have understood. Instead, he tricked me with those beautiful verses. He softened me up so I'd fall into his arms." She blew her nose into her hanky. "And I did. I'm such a fool."

"Now, now," Loretta crooned, "men have been devious from day one. Didn't Adam blame the woman for making him eat the forbidden fruit? Couldn't he have said no?"

Prudie looked up at her friend. "I didn't know you read the Bible."

"Well, truthfully, I didn't until I started reading the scripture cookies. They opened my eyes to what I was missing. I'm glad, too, because now I can pray for you and Gail."

Prudie sat up straight and wiped the last tear from her chin. "Where is Gail? Was she at work today?"

"No. She didn't even call in sick. She's going to get fired if she doesn't straighten up soon. What about you? Are you coming back to the steno pool?"

Prudie hadn't thought that far. She needed money if she wanted to stay independent. "I suppose I'll go back to Mr. Prescott and ask for my old job back. Technically, I work for him anyway."

She hated the thought of working in the basement again, but she hadn't proven herself in the executive world, so where else did she belong? She'd broken all the rules, being too soft on Alex when making suggestions over the books, then falling in love with him. She wasn't "dog-eat-dog" like her instructors at college said she would need to be. She was just Prudie. *Special* to her mother, loved by her sisters, deceived by the last man she ever thought would break her heart.

⚭

Alex sat in his apartment feeling utterly alone. He couldn't talk to his parents about what had happened with Prudie, and God suddenly seemed silent on the matter. What had he done wrong? Maybe he should have been more up front with Prudie, but he knew if he'd mentioned marriage, she would have run.

Should he have trusted God to work out the details?

After a long, restless night, he concluded he didn't want the restaurant if he couldn't share it with Prudie. He smashed his face into his pillow.

Let Corky have it.

He jerked his head up. Certainly that thought wasn't from God. He leapt from the bed and knelt on the rug. He didn't know what to pray. It seemed that if he'd truly heard God the day he met Prudie, then God would smooth things over. But was there enough time? How could he start at square one? And if Prudie was his destiny, was God telling him to let go of the legacy?

He was so confused. He'd been so concerned about his grandfather's legacy—but what was that really? The restaurant, or the ministry? In his mind, they intermingled. Without the restaurant, he wouldn't be able to put God's Word into the cookies. Wait a minute. A thought struck him. The cookies! Now wide awake, he hopped out of bed. He needed to look at that will again.

⟨∽⟩

Prudie was grateful Mr. Prescott allowed her to go back to the steno pool. When he apologized about Alex's refusing any more help, she realized that although she was the one who left, he'd let his dad think he couldn't handle a secretary.

So maybe he wasn't a creep—but he was a worm. She would have to be starving to death before she'd set foot in his restaurant again.

Thank goodness for takeout.

A couple of weeks after she quit, she was eating lunch with Loretta at the apartment.

"So what does your cookie say?" Loretta, happy now that Prudie was back after helping her sister, was still relentless when it came to the scripture cookies.

"I don't know. I don't read them anymore."

"Not true. I noticed every one of them on your dresser the other day."

It was true; she had read and kept the scriptures from all the cookies she'd eaten. At first she was incensed that Alex would be so bold as to continue wooing her in that manner. But as she read each one, her heart started to thaw. She found herself growing more in love with Alex for choosing them and more in love with God as each verse spoke directly to her heart.

She wondered why he hadn't called. Was he giving her time

to cool off? It vexed her that she'd have to be the first to make amends.

Since her hasty departure, she missed the work she'd done at the restaurant, the people, and Alex's ministry. Alex would lose all of that in a few weeks. Every day she pored over the newspaper, afraid the real reason he hadn't called was because he'd found someone willing to marry him before his deadline. But Playboy Prescott seemed to have dropped off the society pages.

The telephone rang, interrupting the girls' Saturday afternoon. Loretta answered.

She mouthed, "It's Alex."

Prudie's first instinct was to sprint to the phone, but she decided she'd make him squirm first. She waved away her friend's offer to take the receiver.

Loretta listened for a moment, then in alarm said, "What?" Another moment passed. "No, I assumed she was visiting her mother over the weekend. . . . She's where?"

Prudie pressed her ear next to Loretta's in time to hear "found her at the rescue mission. I'm with her at the hospital now."

Prudie grabbed the phone. "Who, Alex?"

"Gail. I was at the mission this morning, and I saw her on a cot. At first I thought she was ill, but. . .I think she'd taken some kind of drug. She was lethargic and wouldn't respond."

"We'll be right there." Prudie and Loretta grabbed their purses and dashed out the door.

Chapter 10

Gail's dark hair lay in a tangled mess around her pale face. The crisp white sheet contrasted with her filthy hands, and Prudie understood why the mission thought she was homeless. The doctor confirmed Alex's initial thought. Gail had a dangerous amount of morphine in her system.

"It's all Barry's fault," Loretta lamented as she worked a comb through Gail's hair. "He must have slipped it into her drink at one of those awful clubs."

Prudie found a wet washcloth and wiped Gail's face and hands. She glanced across the room at Alex. He looked good. Too good. She'd expected him to be thin and gaunt over worry of losing her. She shook the crazy thought away. Gail was her main concern right now.

"Thank you for calling us," she said.

"I was so surprised to see her there. If I had decided not to deliver cookies today. . ." He let the thought fade as he rubbed the back of his neck. "Or I could have still been in China."

"China?"

"Yes, I was there on business." He paused and glanced at Gail. "I'll explain later."

Gail's mother arrived at that moment, and Prudie, Loretta, and Alex left the room. Prudie didn't press for Alex's explanation. The man had a good excuse not to call if he were truly halfway around the world.

Loretta opted to stay in the waiting area in case Gail needed her, but she told Prudie and Alex to go home. "No reason for all of us to stay. I'll call if I need you."

Alex held out his hand to Prudie. "Come back to the restaurant with me?"

⊗≬

Alex thanked God for this second chance. They worked side by side during the dinner rush, and when the last customer left, Alex flipped the CLOSED sign and pulled Prudie to a booth by the window. He reached across the table and laid his hand over hers. "I'm so sorry I deceived you."

She flipped her palm up and squeezed his fingers gently. "I know you don't have a conniving bone in your body, Alex. I'm sure you prayed it through before withholding anything from me."

He fidgeted. "Well, to be honest, no. If I had, I'm sure our courtship would have run more smoothly. But I have been on my knees lately. I prayed God would speak to both of us."

She winced but offered a small smile. "Yes, He's been dealing with my heart. I'm not nearly as mad at you as I was when I walked out."

"But you're still a little angry?"

"I don't know. I guess I can understand why you didn't confide in me." She laughed softly. "I made it pretty clear what my agenda was, didn't I?"

"You had me scared, Prudie."

With a jaunty cock of her head, she said, "Well, Mr. Prescott, am I hired back on, or will some other floundering company benefit from my expertise?"

Recognizing her teasing tone, he played along. "Actually, Miss Burke, I was thinking of putting you back on the payroll, but only under one condition."

She crossed her arms on the table and cocked an eyebrow. With a confidence that came only from God, he knelt next to her. "I love you, this crazy deadline notwithstanding."

☙

Prudie's heart pinged against her lungs, and she gasped as Alex pulled a black velvet box from his breast pocket.

"Marry me, Prudie."

She couldn't make herself reach for the box. Tears stung her eyes. "But what about your family?"

He looked confused. "What about my family?"

"Corky told me your father would disinherit you if you married beneath your station."

He stood and drew her to stand in front of him. Prudie felt the burden on her heart lifting.

"First of all, never listen to Corky. Second, my father loves you. And third. . ." He opened the box for her. "This was my grandmother's ring. I remember Granddad Edwin telling me God had chosen her for him. He said God smiled when they worked together." He slipped the band on her finger, not even surprised it was a perfect fit. "I fell head over heels for you, Prudie Burke, and that was an answer to prayer. I believe God chose you to be my helpmate in the ministry my grandfather founded."

Prudie's emotions rose into her throat, making it difficult to say what she knew she must. "Before I tell you my answer, it's my turn to apologize. I don't know why I got so angry when I found out you had picked the scriptures for my cookies. They were lovely and prompted me to renew my commitment to God."

His smile made her apology all worthwhile.

"And," she went on, thoroughly humbled by this dynamic man of God, "all the scriptures since I quit were beautiful, too. Thank you; they were absolutely perfect."

He tilted his head. "I was out of the country, remember?" They both smiled as the revelation dawned. "Prudie, God has been wooing you with His own sweet words."

"Then I accept—both of you."

⚬⚭⚬

Alex was surprised that his mother supported their choice to hold the reception in the restaurant. Between the odious socialite matchmaking and the push to make him more enterprising, he'd somehow missed the woman who had devoted herself to the business her father had started. He knew Granddad Edwin must be smiling down upon them as they celebrated together in the place he had created to bring joy into the lives of others.

As they walked through the door, Alex couldn't wait for Prudie's reaction to the fortune cookie cake, which had been a late inspiration. His staff had pulled it off to perfection attaching each cookie to the three-tiered cake with fluffy icing. He had instructed for the table to be positioned at the same spot where he met her—where he fell head over heels.

"Oh, Alex! It's beautiful." She approached the table, her train wrapped over her arm to keep it from dragging.

After the cake-cutting ceremony, Prudie's sister Katie, her matron of honor, helped cut the rest of the cake while her husband held baby Cindy and corralled Skip, Meg, and toddler Livie. The older two had been perfect as ring bearer and flower girl, but now they were ready to play. Alex suspected his new brother-in-law had received a strict dressing down from Prudie on his behavior concerning equal care of his children. His new bride's mother and father stood talking to his own parents. After learning his new in-laws were Christians, he prayed they would somehow be able to break through the barriers his mother and father had built.

Barry had loaned them his spinet piano and even offered to play. It seemed someone had drugged both him and Gail that night, unbeknownst to either. The day Gail came home from the hospital, Barry told Alex he'd lost track of her while in his own stupor. The incident opened their eyes, and neither had been to a beat club since.

In a touching moment that caused Alex's eyes to mist, Prudie's father, Ethan, sang a song to his baby daughter that he'd written. Her mother, Laurel, played on the borrowed piano, miraculously turning it into a grand with her professionalism.

The rumbling of an engine outside disrupted the festive gathering. Corky, who hadn't attended the wedding, blustered in, ready to swing at the first thing that moved. It took both

Alex and his father to contain him as they ushered him to the back office.

Prudie joined them there.

"You can't do this to me." Corky's anger toward Alex seethed through his teeth.

Alex's father frowned at his nephew. "What's going on?"

"Ask him." Corky tossed a poisonous glare toward Alex.

"I nearly lost my bride-to-be over Granddad's will. Yet I couldn't lose the legacy to this spoiled brat." Alex pointed to Corky. "God prompted me to find a loophole. It seems the restaurant can be passed down, but it doesn't say a thing about the recipe."

His dad rolled his eyes. Alex sighed. Why couldn't he grasp the importance of the recipe and, thus, the ministry?

Nevertheless, Alex continued. "While researching the loophole, I made another discovery. Not only can Granddad Edwin's family inherit, but Ho Woo's, as well. Remember my trip to China?"

"Yes. Your mother asked if I could fund it. She said you were going to collect authentic recipes for the restaurant."

"I did, but I was actually looking for Ho's family and discovered his great-grandson. It seems his granddaughter left San Francisco to live in China with her new husband shortly before Ho's death. Cheng was born a year before Corky, so according to the will, he would inherit the restaurant as next in line after me." Which was a relief when he thought Corky would get it all.

Corky kicked at a file cabinet. Grabbing the scruff of his neck, Alex's father bellowed, "Sit down!" and shoved him into a hard metal chair near the desk.

Prudie motioned to the black sheep of the family, compassion showing in her eyes. "Corky is upset because after I agreed to marry Alex, we both decided to approach Cheng and offer him a partnership. He's successful in his own business, but he's agreed to be a silent partner and investor in Woo with Sweet."

Alex's father nodded his head, an approving smile on his lips. "Very smart. See, I knew she'd help you turn things around."

Alex gazed at Prudie. "You were right, Dad. She's just what I needed."

"So," Alex's father said, addressing Corky, "what are you upset about? You wouldn't have inherited the restaurant anyway."

"They could have made me that offer; I have money. This guy is halfway around the world. Why don't I get part ownership?"

"Because. . ." Alex scowled at his cousin. "You can't be trusted. Grow up and we'll talk."

Corky crossed his arms and legs, harrumphed, and swiveled on the chair so he couldn't look at them directly. "You can have your stupid restaurant. All I ever wanted was the recipe anyway. Stupid old man. He could have shared that recipe with me. I was his grandson, too."

At that moment, Alex saw Corky in a new light. Had he been rebellious all this time to gain attention?

Corky stood abruptly and bolted for the door. "You'll hear from my lawyer."

Alex shook his head as Corky left with Alex's dad escorting him out.

Prudie's concerned blue gaze watched Corky leave. "He needs love, Alex."

He felt the muscles in his jaw relax. "You're right again." He pulled her into his arms. "Tell you what. If Corky ever changes, I'll consider cutting him in."

Prudie wrapped her arms around his waist. "You're an unusual man, Alex."

"You're an unusual woman, Prudie." He held her close and kissed an auburn ringlet that peeked out from the lace she wore on her head.

She gazed up at him, a mischievous glint in her eye. "Would you call me special?"

He didn't need to consider the question. "Yes, I would. You are incredibly special to both of us."

"Both of you?"

"God and me." He kissed her and rejoiced in his heart when she returned the kiss with equal abandon.

Before rejoining the party, they shared another kiss that sealed more than their future; it secured a legacy of their own.

KATHLEEN E. KOVACH

Kathleen E. Kovach was born the year Prudie and Alex met, 1955, and grew up in Denver, Colorado, where she married Jim. He joined the Air Force, and together they spent over twenty years living a nomadic lifestyle, which took them overseas to Germany twice. After retiring from the military, they returned to Colorado, where they hope to plant deep roots. They have two sons and three grandchildren.

Kathleen loves to camp and fish in her spectacular Rocky Mountains. She sings on the praise team at her church, writes the weekly bulletin, and helps in the library. Kathleen has written fiction all her life, but the Lord finally released her to write full-time at the 2002 Colorado Christian Writers Conference when she won first place with her article about writing with God's voice. Her first novel was published with Heartsong Presents in 2006.

Now Kathleen eagerly shares her writing journey with others through speaking, leading a local writers' group, and serving as the Colorado coordinator for American Christian Fiction Writers. She hopes her readers will giggle through her books while learning the spiritual truths God has placed there. Get to know Kathleen at www.kathleenekovach.com.

Posted Dreams

by Sally Laity

Delight yourself also in the LORD,
and He shall give you the desires of your heart.
PSALM 37:4

Chapter 1

Spring 1980

Oh, the comfort, the inexpressible comfort of feeling safe with a person, having neither to weigh thoughts nor measure words, but pouring them all right out, just as they are, chaff and grain together; certain that a faithful hand will take and sift them, keep what is worth keeping, and with a breath of kindness blow the rest away.

—Dinah Marie Mulock Craik

Checking the whimsical handwritten thought over one last time for misspellings, Bethany Prescott attached the yellow sticky note to the library bulletin board, then gathered her belongings and headed for her Chevy Caprice. She hoped the books she'd checked out would clear her mind of the trying day she'd experienced as new kid on the block at Granger Realty.

A ten-minute drive took her from the Beale Memorial Library downtown to her home in southwest Bakersfield. She pulled into the driveway of the ivory stucco house she shared with her mother, Prudie. Looping the strap of her summer purse over her shoulder, she started up the curved front walk.

"How was your day, dear?"

Bethany stepped onto the shallow landing of the porch, smiling as she set down her belongings and took a seat beside her mom on the padded glider. "You know first days. My head's filled with a jumble of numbers, names, and faces. There's *so* much to remember."

"Ah, but I know you." Nudging the glider into motion with her sandaled foot, Prudie gave Bethany's hand a comforting pat. "It won't take long before you feel comfortable there. Everything will become routine. What sort of people will you be working with?"

"Mainly the owner of the real estate office and his son, plus some other sales agents. According to the girl who's training me, the son was widowed a few years ago and has a young daughter."

"What a pity. How unfortunate there's so much sadness in this world. We must remember to keep the man in our prayers, him and his little girl. Imagine growing up without a mother."

Bethany didn't respond but tilted her head, studying her mom in the pleasant quietness of late afternoon. The sun's slanted rays lent fire to the older woman's wavy auburn hair, its rich hue now fading gently as silver threads began to make an appearance. She'd lost some weight in the weeks since contracting Valley Fever, and her paisley blouse and trim navy slacks seemed loose on her slight frame. Bethany was thankful that the sometimes deadly fungus infection, caused by windborne spores, hadn't erupted into meningitis—or worse, been fatal. The flu-like symptoms had lasted over a month, however, and tiredness still manifested itself during the slow recovery. "Well, it's great to see you outside again. I hope this means you're starting to feel a little more like yourself now."

"I am. The sunshine streaming through the miniblinds seemed so glorious, and the birds were singing so beautifully, I decided to come out for some fresh air."

"Good. It'll do you wonders to get out of the house for a while. Just don't overdo. How about if this weekend we drive somewhere for a picnic? Lake Isabella, maybe. Would you like that?"

She nodded, clasping her hands together atop the scrapbook in her lap.

Bethany suppressed a wry grin. "Looking at pictures again?"

Her mother's cobalt blue eyes sparkled as they met hers. "There are always so many hours to fill when you're not here. It's comforting to reminisce about a time when I wasn't much older than you and head over heels in love with the handsomest man who ever crossed my path." She paused momentarily, and when she spoke again, her voice held a wistful quality. "I still miss him. I wish there wasn't any such thing as a brain tumor. Your father was so vibrant and funny, such a thoughtful and godly man. I wanted the two of us to grow old together and have the joy of watching our grandchildren come into the world." She blinked a sudden mistiness away.

Fighting her own emotions at the tender memory, Bethany struggled to keep the moment light. "Grandchildren! I'm not even dating anyone! Anyway, there's too much I want to do with my life before I settle down with a husband. You of all people should understand that, seeing as how you had a career going when you met Dad."

Her mom laughed softly. "Funny. I believed I'd find fulfillment in doing something *important* with my life. Didn't take me long to discover the Lord's plans for me differed greatly from my own lofty intentions. He programmed each of us with different needs—personal ones. My true fulfillment came when your father encouraged me to stay home and raise you. When the time is right, He'll bring the right man across your path, too, if you seek His will. You'll see. A girl like you: sensitive, sweet, pretty. . ."

Bethany swallowed a chuckle. She hadn't felt pretty since she'd turned twelve and compared herself to the thin, popular, wealthy girls she knew during her high school years, who considered her too *religious* to include her in their parties and girlish confidences. Nor did she possess her mother's slight build. It had been her lot in life to take after the sturdier Prescott side of the family. Now that she'd begun following a daily aerobics program, though, she'd noticed her body's contours were becoming more defined—a change she rather liked.

April's sweet breath wafted the heady fragrance of roses around them, and Bethany averted her attention to the profusion of yellow blooms gracing the lattice on the opposite end of the porch, which provided a measure of privacy from the similar red-tile-roofed house next door and other dwellings along the street. Lovely as roses were, they seemed pale in comparison to the breathtaking display of spring wildflowers that still carpeted much of Southern California's undeveloped land in a fragrant rainbow of soft pastels and vibrant hues.

"I seriously doubt anyone as nice as Daddy will come along in my lifetime," she finally admitted.

"You never know. You just seem so listless since Jillian married and moved away. You should have more going on in your life besides going to church or burying your nose in books. I was sharing an apartment with my friends Loretta and Gail when I was around your age."

"So you expect me to desert you now and leave you here by yourself?" Bethany teased.

"Not at all. You know what I mean."

She leaned closer to give her mom a hug. "Right. But I *like* to read. Ever since I was Miss Hollis's star reader in third grade."

"And books are fine. But you used to like to go places, too. Shopping, concerts, restaurants. . ."

"I can still do that with you, when you're better. Anyway, they're no fun without Jill. Her marriage spoiled everything." She snickered at her jest. "It would've been bad enough if she'd stayed within driving distance, so we could at least visit sometimes. Boston's on the other side of the world." She waved at a neighbor driving past in a white Honda. "I don't suppose there was a letter from her in the mail today."

Her mother shook her head.

"Well," Bethany said on a sigh as she stood to her feet, "stay here and relax. I'll go rustle us up some supper before *burying my nose* in the new library books I picked up on the way home." With a saucy wink, she kissed her mother's cheek and went inside.

She couldn't help smiling at the thought of Mom forever

poring over photo albums and scrapbooks. There was no lack of pictures of her father and other relatives displayed around the house, yet her mother felt compelled to focus on old snapshots and the treasured collection of yellowed scraps of paper she'd lovingly saved over the years. Daddy had plied her with his famous fortune cookies, made from a secret recipe passed on from Grandfather Edwin and his adopted Grandpa Woo—who passed away only a few years after the birth of Bethany's father. Her dad had continued the tradition the older pair had started, tucking Bible verses into the sweet treats and eventually snagging her mother. But after he became sick, his restaurant, Woo with Sweet, closed its doors forever and was replaced by a more upscale establishment.

Brushing a wisp of hair away from her eyes as she pondered her parents' sweet love story, Bethany sprinkled seasoning on the chicken breasts she'd thawed this morning and slid them beneath the broiler. Then she popped a pair of potatoes into the microwave. She and her mom didn't exactly live like royalty, but Daddy's insurance policy and inheritance had provided sufficient funds to leave the San Francisco Bay area and relocate to this smaller city, where the cost of living wasn't so expensive. With the balance, the Lord had kept them afloat these seven years since her father had succumbed to the inoperable tumor. Bethany had been able to finish school and take some college classes in graphic design, where her chief interest lay. Perhaps one day she'd finish the required courses for her deg___ ___d put her talent to good use. Until then, the secretarial po___ ___t the real estate office would have to do.

Her thoughts again drifted to her late father. S___

she imagined she could hear his footsteps in the halls of her mind and smell his tangy aftershave. Often, at the end of a long day, he would brush his sandpapery five o'clock shadow against her cheek, a sensation that would never completely vanish from her mind. His hearty laugh had tickled her insides, and its memory brought a twinge of sadness.

How she wished she could still find a fortune cookie under her pillow, as she often had during her childhood years, with a message he'd penned just for her. They'd instilled within her a deep appreciation for written sentiments, and she loved collecting lovely thoughts from books and passing them on via anonymous notes.

❦

"I feel awful about having to skip out on you the day after tomorrow already," Gwen Michaels said the following morning. "I wish I had another whole week before I had to throw you to the wolves. Three days seems such a short time."

Bethany shrugged at the slender, green-eyed brunette idly tapping a pencil tip against the desk they shared in the reception area of Granger Realty. "Don't worry about it. I'm just glad you're here now. I've taken tons of notes on everything, including the proper order of all the bazillion forms that make up each real estate file. How hard can it be?" But even as she asked the question, she feared the answer. Day two, and she had yet to meet the members of the sales staff who'd been occupied with appointments the previous day.

"Well," Gwen commiserated, "since Mr. Granger hired you on the spot after your interview, he must feel you'll fit in okay.

I know you'll like working for him. He's a real teddy bear, always a big help if you have any questions. And his son, John, whom you've also met—he's a touch moody since his wife died. But he's a decent guy, and you'll adore his darling little girl. He's just not one to crack a lot of jokes, like some of the other guys do." She stuck the pencil behind her ear, carving a narrow path in her short locks.

Bethany thought about the owner's tall, brooding son with the glossy mink-brown hair that waved softly over his ears and light brown eyes that seemed clouded with painful memories. He was easily every inch as handsome as any male cover model for *GQ* magazine. As she recalled the way he had greeted her with a reserved smile and polite handshake, her heart went out to him. It was too soon to tell whether she'd made a good first impression on *him* yesterday, but she hoped the high standards she set for her work would speak for themselves. She'd already added him and his daughter to her daily prayer time.

Gwen's ongoing monologue cut across her musings. "The other guys, Craig Franklin and Rick Peters, are a hoot. They should be here any minute, unless they have to sit open houses again today. Craig's married and has a couple of kids, but Rick thinks he's God's gift to women. That leaves only Cynthia Hargrove—who just happens to be right outside." She lowered her voice to a whisper. "Miss Priss has her cap set for the boss's son, so don't get in her way."

A willowy young woman in a fashionably cut pantsuit stepped inside and closed the door behind herself, leather brief-case in hand. Cool, brown-black eyes widened, then narrowed slightly as they focused on Bethany. An exquisite gold-link bracelet glistened as she brushed a dark lock of her feathered haircut back into place with the manicured fingers of her free hand.

"Morning, Cynthia," Gwen said brightly. "I'd like you to meet Bethany Prescott. She'll be taking my place here."

Cynthia's expression remained composed and unsmiling, though perfectly shaped brows rose a notch on her forehead. "How do you do." Before Bethany could respond, the woman's gaze slid to Gwen. "So you're leaving us?"

" 'Fraid so. My sister in Spokane is confined to bed with a difficult pregnancy. She needs someone to come and look after her twins until the baby comes. They're a little too much for our mom to cope with indefinitely."

"Oh, really. What fun," she said on a droll note, barely pausing for air before getting right to business. "I need you to call this owner and schedule an appointment for me to show her home this afternoon." Depositing a slip of paper on the desk with a tap of a long fingernail, she tipped her head and sashayed off to one of the three cubicles occupying the other end of the large, carpeted main room.

"Friendly, isn't she? No wonder her husband dumped her," Gwen quipped under her breath, then grew serious. "Actually, she's quite professional—can be sweet as syrup around John and his dad. Don't let her get to you."

Bethany nodded. "We'd better make that call, before I get on her wrong side."

For the remainder of the day, Gwen sat back and allowed Bethany to take charge, offering assistance when needed. With the staff coming and going much of the time, Bethany found most of her duties typically secretarial and assumed they'd quickly become routine. Her confidence went up a few degrees.

But the next day, when Gwen bid her a final good-bye at noon, Bethany felt a new sense of aloneness. Now everything was up to her. She surveyed the attractive surroundings that made up her new world, tastefully coordinated in muted hues of gray and mauve, with ficus trees and containers of artificial greenery placed in strategic spots for a pleasing effect. The upholstered chairs for customers looked comfortable and inviting, flanking a marble-top table with a silk flower arrangement and a pewter lamp. She drew a deep breath, and in the silence of the deserted office, she breathed a prayer for strength and wisdom not to mess up.

John Granger was the first person to return after lunch. Attired in a navy pinstripe suit and burgundy silk tie, he offered a thin smile as he stopped at Bethany's desk. "On your own already, I see."

"Looks like. I enjoyed working with Gwen—she was super nice."

He gave a nod. "That she was." A slight pause. "By the way, any messages? I'm expecting a call from Steve Cochran."

"No calls so far, Mr. Granger."

He tucked his chin. "That title belongs to my dad. John will do for me."

"Right, sir."

"The *sir* can go, too."

"Right." Bethany thought she detected a humorous glint in his eyes, and for no reason she could grasp, she fought a blush.

With the barest hint of a smile, John rapped on the edge of her desk with the knuckles of one hand and strode away to his private office.

Bethany let out a suppressed breath. *Strange. . .he doesn't seem as moody as Gwen led me to believe. Even if he doesn't smile a lot.*

⌘

John relaxed against the plush leather of his office chair and leafed grimly through the stack of papers on his desk. Always so many details to slog through before a deal closed. Offers to purchase, counteroffers, appraisals, termite inspections, roof inspections, half a dozen separate disclosure statements required by California bureaucrats, escrow instructions to be signed and carried out, anxious sellers, irate buyers, lenders and title companies dragging their feet, final walk-throughs. And despite all of his best efforts, at any moment a deal that appeared flawless could fall out. He detested the aggravation. If it weren't that his dad appreciated his taking part in the family business, it would be tempting to ditch it all and link up with his buddy Steve, designing and building tract homes.

John would never desert his father, though. Granger Realty's small but aggressive staff of salespeople managed to hold their own against the bigger conglomerates like Century 21. Even now, with the market in the recession's downward cycle, many newer, younger agents in the big offices were leaving real estate for greener pastures. But the Granger staff seemed determined to hang in until things improved.

The city of Bakersfield retained a small-town atmosphere,

despite its constant state of growth. It boasted a decent down-town business district, good shopping centers and hospitals, and a fine assortment of churches, theaters, and restaurants. Along with its own community college, the city also housed a branch of California State University and an airport. The convention center drew top names in the entertainment industry, and the fairgrounds hosted all kinds of exhibits and rodeos. Located on one of the state's major north-south arteries, there was never a lack of traffic coming through town.

With California's population steadily increasing, a number of bedroom communities were already springing up along Interstate 5 to house LA commuters willing to put up with the hassles of freeway driving. Anyone with vision could foresee that soon enough, investors from the larger metropolitan areas like Los Angeles and San Francisco would set their sights on Bakersfield's affordable housing market, likely driving prices to a scale beyond what the local oil and agricultural industries could support.

Still, with things certain to improve in time, getting in on the ground floor of a housing boom with Steve would be exhilarating. . . .

Yeah, leaving Granger Realty had been pretty easy for Gwen Michaels. A family crisis, and she was history. She'd probably never give the lot of them a second thought.

But what about the new auburn-haired gal—Bethany? How long would *she* last? With gentle hazel eyes and a beguil-ing smile, she exuded a serene peacefulness that seemed pro-foundly spiritual, yet she looked as though she'd just graduated high school! *Sure hope Dad knew what he was doing when he hired that slip of a girl. Time will tell.*

Chapter 2

John slid his hands into the pockets of his jeans and idly meandered around the carpeted lobby of the Beale Memorial Library. From the juvenile section, a few yards away, a childish chorus of *oohs* and *aahs* interspersed with an occasional "yes" or "no–o" drifted from the circle of youngsters enthralled with this week's Story Hour with Miss Stacey. His daughter, Jessica, nearing her fourth birthday, counted the days until Saturday each week, eager to visit the library and hear a popular children's book read aloud by the college-age blond with the expressive voice. John knew that any dad worth his salt would do his best to make sure his only daughter didn't miss her favorite outing any more often than necessary.

Waiting for her, he'd already browsed the national newspapers regarding the failed military expedition to rescue the fifty-two American hostages held by Iran. He'd also checked out the shelves of surplus books and the magazine discards on the sale rack. Now, on his way back from the drinking fountain, he noticed a colorful display of announcements and posters on the bulletin board and moved closer. He scanned the list of library fees and a sheet regarding a writing workshop. A well-known author of children's books was scheduled to make a personal appearance in two weeks, possibly something Jess would like. The biannual used-book sale hosted by the Friends of Kern County Library would take place next month—another item of interest. He'd picked up several good finds at those events.

Then his gaze fell upon a smaller handwritten message on a yellow sticky note. He leaned closer, admiring the small, obviously feminine script as he read the message:

Oh, the comfort, the inexpressible comfort of feeling safe with a person, having neither to weigh thoughts nor measure words. . .

The statement struck him as sad, though he couldn't fathom why. Perhaps some lonely soul needed a friend. On the other hand, maybe the individual just liked to write pretty things for others to contemplate. Not that it was of any importance to him.

"Daddy! Daddy!" A tug on his pant leg brought him back to the moment. He looked down into his redheaded daughter's sea green eyes—so reminiscent of Lisa's it made his heart ache. He wondered if the pain of that loss would ever pass.

"Can I get"—she counted on her fingers—"four books this time? Please? Pleeeease?" She held up the coveted treasures, the corners of her rosebud lips curving upward with a hopeful smile.

As if a man could refuse that sweet face with tiny freckles sprinkled across the bridge of her nose like specks of glitter. "Sure, princess. We can handle four." He took them from her and feigned enthusiasm as he read the titles.

"Oh, Daddy, I love you this much!" She spread her arms wide.

"I love you, too, sweetheart. Let's go get these checked out. Then you and I can head over to McDonald's for a Happy Meal and a Big Mac. Would you like that?"

"Yippee!" She clapped and nodded, two long, softly curled ponytails dancing with her movements. They'd taken him awhile to master but tamed her curls nicely. Placing her hand inside his, she skipped along beside him to the checkout desk.

∞

A mild breeze ruffled Bethany's hair as she sat in a chaise lounge copying sayings from a book of quotations onto index cards. She paused and looked skyward.

Only a cluster of cloud puffs off to the west marred the otherwise clear blue reflecting against the rippled surface of Lake Isabella, and the temperature was a perfect eighty degrees. The spring rains had been generous, so the lush green on the hills had yet to parch to their normal golden brown, and some spring flowers were still in bloom at this elevation. Bethany drew her gaze from the man-made mountain lake and checked to see that her mother rested comfortably in the other lawn chaise they'd stowed in the car trunk.

"It couldn't be a prettier day," Mom remarked, as if sensing Bethany's scrutiny. "I'm getting a little hungry already, even if it isn't even noon. Must be this clean mountain air."

"Must be. My stomach is about to growl, too. I'll get out the cooler, and we'll dig into the deli sandwiches and potato salad we bought at Albertson's." Swinging her legs over the side of her chair, she stood and walked to the car. After removing the ice chest from the trunk, along with a checked cover for the nearby picnic table, she brought them back to the tree-shaded spot they'd chosen on a hillside overlooking the expanse of water. Then she spread out their small feast.

"Mmm. Looks delicious, honey," her mom said as she approached the table and took a seat opposite Bethany, who was setting out paper plates and plastic silverware.

"The sandwiches are both alike: ham, provolone, the works. Help yourself to the potato salad and pickles." Brushing away a pesky fly, Bethany withdrew two cans of root beer from the cooler and popped the tabs as she took her own seat. She reached across for her mother's hand and bowed her head. "Thank You, Lord, for this beautiful day and for the beautiful spot to enjoy Your handiwork. Please bless our food and make us ever conscious of Your presence in our lives. In Jesus' name, amen."

Both too hungry for small talk, they watched the activity below them on the lake while they ate. A handful of small boats sported individuals with fishing poles, and near the water's edge, kids flew a pair of brightly colored kites. Here and there along the shoreline, other families were gathering at tables, tossing Frisbees, or lying about on blankets working on their California tans. Some romped with dogs or waded in the cold shallows. The wind carried bursts of laughter and the occasional few bars of music from portable boom boxes, but coming from the distance, the sounds were hardly intrusive.

"Ready for some cherry pie?" Bethany asked.

Her mother patted her stomach. "I'm not sure I've got room, but I'll never turn down my favorite pie."

"Just as I figured." Smiling, Bethany cut a slice for each of them and slid the remainder back into the box.

"This has been the nicest day. I'm so glad you thought of coming here. It's been ages since our last visit, hasn't it?"

"Last summer, at least."

"I'm glad you suggested it. It's been a real treat."

"I know what you mean, Mom. It's been great for me, too, getting out of town for a few hours."

Another short rest after lunch, and Bethany packed things up for the long homeward drive. Instrumental praise music from the car's tape player lulled her mom to sleep before they'd covered the first five miles of the winding Kern Canyon road that descended into the San Joaquin Valley. Noting the roses beginning to reappear in her mother's cheeks, Bethany smiled and breathed a prayer that God would continue to give her strength with each new day. Hopefully she'd be back to normal soon.

⚬⚬

Hearing the office door open bright and early on Monday morning, Bethany looked up from the forms she was attaching to the file folder bracket. A thirty-something man in a camel blazer and brown slacks entered.

"Well, well," he said, spying her at the desk. "Who might we have here? I'm Craig Franklin, one of the regular staff."

"Yes, I've heard your name mentioned, Mr. Franklin. In fact, I have a few phone messages for you." She picked up a small stack of pink message sheets and handed them over. "I'm Bethany Prescott."

"What happened to Gwen?" Puzzlement creased his olive

forehead, making his heavy dark brown sideburns even more prominent against eyes of clear blue.

"A family emergency. I'm taking her place."

"I see." He gave an understanding nod.

"What do you see?" another male voice piped up from behind him.

He turned. "Seems we have a new secretary, Rick. Come and meet Bethany. . .Prescott, was it?"

"Right." She smiled to greet a wiry young man with sandy-blond hair, a touch on the bushy side.

"Rick Peters," he said, coming forward and gripping her hand, his deep-set gray eyes assessing her from head to foot. "Glad to meet you, Beth."

Gwen's warning had prepared her for the once-over, so Bethany ignored it. She was glad she'd chosen to wear a simple cotton blouse and plaid skirt rather than something in clingy jersey knit. His familiarity was less than endearing, however. "I prefer *Bethany*, if you don't mind."

"Oh. Sorry." He had the grace to look abashed.

Gathering a second stack of papers, she held them out. "Your phone messages, Mr. Peters."

He snickered. "We don't stand on ceremony here, Bethany. We're all friends. Just call me Rick." He leafed through the messages, tucking one into the breast pocket of his gray suit jacket.

"And Craig for me," his sidekick added. "We'll try not to make life too hard for you."

"Thanks. I'd appreciate that." With a pleasant nod, Bethany returned her attention to the file as the pair crossed to the other two cubicles. Within minutes she heard them both on their phones and let out a nervous breath.

At that moment, gray-haired Mr. Granger exited his office and approached her desk. She looked up and met his gaze, noting how similar his eyes were to his son's; they were not only the same size and shape, but also the identical light brown shade. They lacked the sad factor, though, and instead had a tranquil quality. Laugh lines bracketing his mouth deepened as he smiled and gave her a handwritten sheet from a yellow legal tablet.

"I need this letter typed to go out in the morning mail, if possible."

"Of course."

"Oh, and when Mr. Seward comes in, please show him to my office. He should be here a little before ten."

"No problem."

He hesitated a moment. "I really appreciate your willingness to step in for Gwen so quickly, Bethany. If you have any questions, please don't be afraid to ask. We want you to feel at home here."

She found his words encouraging. "I appreciate that. I'll do my best, sir."

"I'm sure you will." With another polite smile, he turned and walked back to his office.

Watching after him, Bethany saw other similarities between father and son, in height and bearing. *Well, what else would one expect?* she berated herself. *They* are *related.*

Glancing over the letter he'd written, she removed the vinyl cover from her electric typewriter and turned it on, inserting a sheet of company letterhead from the drawer. Cynthia, who had already come and gone out on an appointment, had left her with numerous other tasks to take care of. This was shaping up to be a busy day.

❦

As Bethany finished washing the supper dishes and wiped down the marbled Formica counter, her mom finished drying the last piece, placing the iced tea pitcher back into its place in the oak cupboard. "Oh, I nearly forgot, dear. You got a letter today in the mail. It's on the buffet."

"From Jill?"

She nodded. "Sorry it slipped my mind."

"No problem, Mom. I wouldn't have had time to read it anyway until supper was over. I'll be glad to have her new address so I can finally write to her. I sure miss that girl. I can't wait to hear what's happening in her life." Giving her mother a quick hug and a peck on the cheek, Bethany flew to the stack of mail, retrieved the letter, and dashed off to the privacy of her room.

Unlike the rest of their traditionally furnished house, her haven was filled with antiques passed down from her grandmother. She took a seat at the mahogany drop-leaf desk and slid the opener along the edge of the envelope as the faint notes from the *Jeopardy* theme song drifted from the television set in the living room. She smiled and unfolded the single sheet of blue stationery, drinking in her friend's familiar script:

Dearest Bethy,

How weird it feels to be writing instead of talking to you! I do miss seeing your face, your smile. Seems like forever since Troy and I packed up all our worldly possessions and

196

left sunny Bakersfield for Boston. We get tons of rain here, but so far the wetter climate hasn't caused much inconvenience. We found a cute little furnished apartment on the second floor of an older Colonial-style home with a huge backyard for us to enjoy whenever we desire. There's a lot to see in this area—neat historical buildings and famous sites. It's like living inside a history book! I think I'm going to enjoy living here.

Have you been successful in your job hunting? If so, be sure to write me all the details. Troy says we'll be having a phone installed soon, so I'll be able to call you when I'm desperately lonely for my best bud.

How is your sweet mother? Fully recovered from Valley Fever, I hope. Do give her my love.

I know this is just a short note, but we seem to be on the go a lot of the time, and as usual, Troy has plans for tonight. Mostly I wanted you to have my address. I'll write a longer letter next time, I promise.

Do take care, my sweetest, dearest friend. I keep you in my prayers, but nothing is like being with you. I suppose I'll get used to this eventually.

Love,
Jillian

Bethany couldn't help wondering if *she* would get used to being without *Jill* anytime soon. Taking a seat at her desk, she took out some writing paper and flicked on the desk lamp. There was so much to tell her friend. Where to start was the problem.

Chapter 3

On Friday of the following week, John pulled into the driveway of his parents' spacious, Spanish-style home and headed for the double front door. Tired after a long day of mental aggravation, he looked forward to picking up Jessica and going home.

He'd barely stepped inside before his daughter flew into his arms.

"Daddy! Come on. See what me and Nana made." Eyes shining, she took him by the hand and drew him toward the kitchen, where a luscious-looking chocolate layer cake occupied a portion of the granite counter. "It's special."

"It sure is, princess. Is Nana expecting company?"

"Uh-uh." Her twin ponytails shook along with her head. "It's special for *us*, 'cause we're family."

"That's right, sweetie," her grandmother said, removing gardening gloves as she came in the back door. "Hi, John. Want to stay for supper? We're doing steaks on the grill."

The thought of his father's juicy filet mignons invigorated John, easing some of his weariness. He grinned at his mom, who managed to look regal even in her casual summer slacks and top, her silver hair drawn into a French roll. "Sounds great."

"Good. Sit down and relax while I wash up and set the table. Or you can visit with your dad. We'll be eating out on the patio."

"Push me on the swing, Daddy?" Jessica asked. "I can go high now."

"Sure, we can do that. Just let me get rid of my tie."

While she skipped happily off, John shrugged out of his suit jacket and removed his tie, draping them both over a chair back in his mom's elegant delphinium blue and white dining room. Then he exited the back door. Obviously the gardeners had been around today, as the smell of freshly mown grass mingled with the tantalizing scent of sizzling beef. He greeted his dad with a nod and a wave and strode around the pool's edge to the elaborate wooden play set constructed especially for their granddaughter. She sat already poised on one of its two swings, pushing herself into motion with her foot as he stepped behind her. "Hold on tight."

"I will. I'm big now. I go high." She scooted more securely onto the seat.

"Is that right?" he teased. "Then I guess we'll see *how* high, won't we?" He gave a few shallow pushes, gently increasing the force as she gained momentum until he had her shrieking with glee. He lost himself in her girlish giggles until a melancholy thought surfaced of how much Lisa was missing. Was there anything in heaven that could equal the pure joy in a child's laughter? Blinking to ease a burning sensation in his eyes, he stepped back to allow the swing to slow naturally while his gaze roamed the manicured shrubbery and profusion of flowers his mother lovingly attended.

John knew that Jessica, too, was as lovingly attended by his mom. He would forever be grateful she had taken on the responsibility of looking after his daughter. Rather than see Jess farmed off in some day-care center, she'd put aside her own commitments and activities and stepped in for Lisa. And even though his daughter was surrounded by luxury, she was not spoiled or coddled but was growing up instead with a sense of appreciation for God's blessings. Some days John still had to remind himself about those—

"Soup's on," his mom called from the patio.

"Come on, princess. We're being summoned." Taking hold of the ropes, John brought the swing to a stop while Jessica dismounted, and they walked hand in hand to the glass-topped umbrella table, festive with floral place mats and coordinating napkins. Tall, frost-coated glasses of iced tea topped by slices of lemon sat at each place setting.

"Oh, Nana," Jessica remarked, eyeing it all. "It's pretty."

"And everything will taste as good as it looks," John's father said, carting over a platter of steaks fresh off the grill. He set them down between the bowls of coleslaw and garden salad and took his seat.

They joined hands for prayer.

"Dear Lord," he prayed, "we thank You for Your tender care and the bounty that surrounds us. Make us ever grateful for Your Son and His sacrifice for us, and keep us faithful day by day. Bless this food to our bodies, and us to Your service. In Jesus' name, amen."

"Amen," everyone echoed.

"Well, help yourself," Mom said cheerily, taking a warm roll from a napkin-lined basket and handing them on to John while his father started the steak platter on its rounds.

"Thanks. Everything smells great. I'm starved."

"Do I like this white stuff?" Jessica asked when John served her a spoonful of coleslaw.

"We don't really know that until you try it, do we? Anyway, when you're company at somebody's house, you eat what you're served. Quietly. It's good manners."

"Oh yeah. I forgot." She sampled a smidgeon. "I had this before. It's good."

"Nana makes *all* good food," he assured her. Slicing a chunk off his steak for her, he cut it into bite-sized pieces on her plate, then concentrated on his own meal.

"How's everything going at the office?" his mom asked after several quiet minutes. "I hear you two got a new secretary a couple of weeks ago. Is she working out okay?"

"Sure is," his father piped in. "Bethany's a great gal. Good worker, too. No complaints at all."

She nodded. "How about you, John? Do you like her?"

He swallowed the meat he was chewing. "Bethany? Sure. She's a quiet kid, but competent. Already settling in." He forked the last bit of his garden salad and ate it.

"So she's fairly young, then."

John met his mother's gaze. "Around twenty or so—right out of college. Cute, with auburn hair and hazel eyes. Any other details you'd like to know?" His wink softened what she might have taken as a rebuke.

"Not at all. I just like to keep up with what's going on with the people I love." She blotted her lips on her napkin and glanced at the near-empty serving containers before getting up and gathering them. "Well, I hope you've all saved room for cake. Jessica and I made a special one today."

"The icing is yummy," Jessica admitted, while the family tried not to chuckle. "Nana let me lick the bowl."

"I can't wait to try it," John said. "Nothing like a girl who knows her way around a kitchen."

After dessert and coffee, his mother took Jessica to the bathroom to wash her face and hands, while John retrieved his jacket and tie from the dining room.

"Here she is, all bright and shiny and ready to go home," his mother said, smiling on her return.

"So I see." He leaned closer and gave his mother a hug. "Thanks, as always. For the great meal—and for being you."

She blushed. "That's what moms are for. See you next time, honey," she told Jessica and gave her a hug and a kiss.

"Bye-bye, Nana. I love you."

"I love you, too. Don't forget Annie." She gave the child her worn rag doll.

"Tell Dad good-bye for us," John said as he ushered his daughter to the door.

Outside, he buckled Jess into her car seat and went around to his own side. "Thought we'd pick up some ice cream for the fridge on the way home. Sound good to you?"

"Mmm. I like ice cream."

"I know. Let's go to Albertson's and check out the flavors."

Moments later, a half gallon of chocolate and another of

butter pecan in hand, the two of them were on their way out the sliding doors to their BMW, when John happened to catch a glimpse of a yellow note on the public board. Out of curiosity he stopped to read it:

> *How sweet, how passing sweet, is solitude!*
> *But grant me still a friend in my retreat,*
> *When I may whisper,*
> *Solitude is sweet.*
>
> *—William Cowper*

"What's that, Daddy?"

"Hmm? Oh, nothing, princess. Just a note." But for some reason, it made him smile.

❧

Easy-listening music played on the radio as Bethany sat in the lunchtime quiet of the office. Except for the occasional phone call, interruptions were rare during the noon hour. This week, Rick was deep-sea fishing on his vacation, which also added to the slowness of the day. Finishing the last of her iced tea, Bethany took out a sheet of blank paper and began doodling. So engrossed was she in her task that she never heard the door open.

"What are you doing?" John asked, appearing out of nowhere as he gawked with interest over her shoulder.

Bethany started in surprise. A maddening flush rose upward from her neck. "I—nothing. Just fooling around." She folded her hands over her work, trying nonchalantly to cover it up.

"That's our logo, isn't it? Let me see."

"I was just—just passing time. It's nothing, really."

"Hey, I'm not grilling you, Bethany," he said gently. "What I saw looked pretty good. I just wanted to take a closer look. Honest."

Bethany raised her lashes and met his gaze. Seeing that he appeared sincere, she reluctantly uncovered the design she'd fashioned and pressed her lips together as he bent to examine the drawing.

"I have to say I'm impressed." John smiled. "I'd been thinking for a while that our logo was looking dated. It's time Granger Realty signs and stationery had a new, more modern look. If you have any spare time, see what you can come up with. I'll check out your sketches with Dad and see what he thinks about updating our stuff. Agreed?"

"Agreed." She smiled. "I like designing things."

"It shows. Well, have at it." A friendly grin, and he walked off to his office.

Relieved that he hadn't made light of her doodling, Bethany relaxed and took out another blank sheet for some serious graphics work.

෨෬

On his way back to the office after doing a final walk-through inspection with a customer, John realized he was about to pass his pal Steve Cochran's work site. He turned into the housing tract, parked, and climbed out of his car. The *rat-tat-tat* of automatic nail guns and the whine of saws filled the air. John stepped gingerly over some piled-up Sheetrock and debris outside a partially constructed house in a group of others in different stages of progress. Workmen at various sites moved around, busy as bees.

Steve had obviously spied him coming and strode toward him, wiping his hands on a rag and stuffing it into the back pocket of his work jeans before holding out a hand. "How's it going, buddy? Aren't you afraid you'll get those shiny shoes of yours all dusty?"

John took his friend's proffered hand and shook it. "Yeah, yeah, rub it in. You know I'd rather be up to my armpits in sawdust and nails than warming a desk chair every day."

Steve snickered. "So when are you gonna make the break?" A mischievous twinkle glinted in his gray eyes.

"Not until Dad doesn't need me around."

"Guess that means never. Well, come see what we're doing. This model is one you helped design when we were tossing those ideas around a couple weeks ago, remember? With the extra built-ins and handy features?"

"Oh yeah. So they were workable, some of those suggestions?"

"Pretty much. Had the architect make adjustments in the blueprints so the subtrades wouldn't have problems following the plans." Doffing the hard hat from his dark curly hair, Steve swiped a shirtsleeve across his forehead, then replaced the hat. "Man, it's hot already. Why can't Southern California have a real spring, like other places? All we get is winter or summer. That sun is a killer."

John had to chuckle.

"How 'bout a soda? I have some in the house."

"Sounds great." John followed his wiry friend inside the

framed dwelling, inhaling the pungent scent of new lumber, trying to ignore the way his hands itched to be working with it.

Stopping at a picnic cooler, Steve opened it and plucked out two cans, handing one to John, and they gulped the drinks as they walked around. "Over here will be the built-in bookshelves," he said, indicating a wall in what was to be a library or home office. "Thought we'd build a desk in this nook. There'll be phone jacks in every room in the house. Oh, and the laundry room over here," he continued, leading the way, "and here's where we'll put that fold-down ironing board. Chelsea likes that feature, that and the cedar-lined closet off the master bedroom."

"How is Chels?" John asked. "Your wedding's coming up this fall, right?"

"Yep. Can't be soon enough, but summer's our busiest time building houses, so there's no way I can take time off for a honeymoon now. She's going nuts with plans for the big day. I'm sure her dad's laying out a fortune to keep her happy."

"That's the way life is." Even as John spoke, he couldn't help recalling how happy his own wedding day had been, despite the headaches associated with the plans. He would have been celebrating his sixth anniversary in a month, if Lisa hadn't contracted uterine cancer. Her pregnancy had complicated things, stalling treatments that could have kept her alive. But neither of them would consider terminating the pregnancy. It gave her a sense of fulfillment to live long enough to give birth to a daughter and enjoy her for a year and a half before cancer claimed its grim victory. He exhaled a ragged breath.

"In a couple weeks," Steve rambled on, "the rock guys'll start on the built-in gas barbecue out back. That alone will probably sell this place once it's done. That and some of the upgraded fixtures we're putting in."

John nodded.

"Doing anything this Sunday?" Steve asked. "Besides church, I mean."

"Nothing special. Why?"

"Thought maybe I'd get some tickets for the Angels game. Chelsea's gonna be occupied at her best friend's bridal shower. Great chance for us guys to whip down to LA for the day."

"Sounds good. I haven't been to a game for a while."

"Tell me about it. I'll arrange for tickets, then."

"Great. Well, I'd better let you get back to work. It's lookin' good, buddy."

"Thanks. It'd be better if you were working on it, too, though."

"Maybe someday. See ya." With a jaunty wave, John returned to his BMW, more disenchanted with real estate than ever. This slow market might provide the opportune time to approach Dad regarding the benefits of partnering with Steve, with him helping in construction and his dad marketing the homes. After all, Granger Realty would have some fancy new signs for all of these front lawns. He wondered what designs Bethany had come up with.

Chapter 4

For some unexplained reason, John found himself counting the hours until Saturday morning came around
again. As soon as he and his daughter got to the library,
Jessica wasted no time in traipsing off to snag a chair for the
story hour. John's first stop would be the bulletin board. For
weeks he'd been fascinated by the quotes he'd come across here
and at the grocery store. He could still remember the one he'd
seen last time on the library's board:

> *When I am attacked by gloomy thoughts, nothing*
> *helps me so much as running to my books. They quickly*
> *absorb me and banish the clouds from my mind.*
> *—Michael de Montaigne*

The underlying thread in all of the notes he'd read seemed
to be loneliness—which he could easily relate to—so in his
daily devotions he'd begun praying that God would send the
writer of the quotes the friend she longed for. Approaching the
board, he couldn't help wondering how someone with such a

sensitive spirit could feel friendless.

As he expected, the writer had posted a new sentiment:

> *Give me a few friends who will love me for what I am, or am not, and keep ever burning before my wandering steps the kindly light of hope. And though age and infirmity overtake me, and I come not in sight of the castle of my dreams, teach me still to be thankful for life and time's old memories that are good and sweet. And may the evening twilight find me gentle still.*
>
> *—Author unknown*

John smiled as he admired the small, neat writing, contemplating the statement momentarily before filling his lungs and heading for the national newspapers.

The whole country was in shock over last week's violent eruption of Mount St. Helens. Reading about the extent of the damage and the ongoing search for survivors, John breathed a prayer for the unfortunate souls involved. Then he skimmed other items of interest while he waited for Jessica. But his thoughts kept wandering back to the bulletin board.

On a whim, he decided to post a reply—a short word of encouragement. What harm could it do? He tried to think of a verse of scripture to suit the occasion, but none came to mind. He checked his watch. Still a good half hour before Jess would be done. He sprinted up the steps, taking two at a time, and searched the card index for books of quotations, then went to the proper section. After flipping through one thick volume, he found what he was looking for, and another smile broke forth.

Bethany's feet were tired by the time she and her mother finished browsing through the Valley Plaza shopping mall and then stopped for groceries on their way home. After the food had been put away and Mom went to lie down for a nap, Bethany decided to return the library books she'd finished and choose new ones. Perhaps novels, for a change.

Arriving at the library, she parked her car and went inside, dropped off her books at the return bin, and took the elevator to the second floor. The card file pointed her in the direction of the inspirational romances. She chose several, then went down to the checkout desk.

"These'll be due in two weeks," the plump, middle-aged clerk told her, peering over her reading glasses.

"Yes. I know the drill," Bethany said with a smile. She picked up the new selections and went through the security gate toward the main entrance, stopping at the bulletin board to remove the quote she'd posted last time and put up a fresh one. But as she reached for the sticky note, her arm paused in midair. A comment had been added!

Choose thy friends like thy books, few but choice.
—English proverb

Her heart skipped a beat. She'd only been posting a thought for the day, never expecting to draw a reply. Bethany stared at the sentiment, musing for several seconds over the meaning behind it. The block letters made it impossible to conclude whether it had been written by a male or a female, but it didn't matter. She smiled inwardly. Maybe there was at least one other person in town who appreciated the quotes she'd been passing along. Her only intent was to brighten someone's day. Drawing a calming breath, she put last week's note into her purse and fastened a new message to the board:

A friend is a person with whom I may be sincere.
Before him I may think aloud. . .
A friend may be well reckoned the masterpiece of
Nature.

—*Ralph Waldo Emerson*

When she exited her car at home, soft notes from the piano met her ears. She recognized her mother's favorite piece, "Claire de Lune," and smiled. Another good sign of normalcy—Mom was playing the piano again, continuing the legacy of music she'd acquired from her parents. Bethany never ceased to marvel at the story of how her grandparents had fallen in love over a sheet of music while a touching song unfolded. Surely that had to be one of the great romances of all time. Her own mom and dad's romance had been the other. Sadly, Bethany couldn't help doubting she was destined to continue that tradition. No wonderful, strikingly handsome man had ever caught her attention—or, closer to the truth, noticed *her*. Shaking off the silly thought, she opened the door and went inside.

"I'm home," she called out. Setting her novels on the hall table, she continued on into the living room.

Her mom paused and turned, resting a hand on the piano

211

bench. "Oh, hi, dear. I was just trying to get rid of some rust. Seems eons since I've touched these keys."

"I know. It's wonderful to hear your music again. I've missed it."

"So have I. Well, now that I'm starting to feel more like myself, lots of things are going to change. No more sitting around day after day. Time I get back to living."

Bethany chuckled. "That's good news. Just don't overdo. No sense in having a relapse."

"Don't worry; I'm a big girl. I know when to quit."

"I'm sure you do." Leaning closer, she gave her mom a hug. "Getting hungry? I'll start supper."

"It's done. I whipped up some chicken salad for sandwiches while you were gone and tossed a garden salad to go with them."

Surprised, Bethany hiked her brows. "I can at least make some fresh iced tea."

"That's done, too. Since it isn't awfully hot, I thought we could eat outside."

"Boy, you really are feeling better. Just let me take my books to my room, and we'll have supper."

Moments later, Bethany opened the sliding glass door and stepped onto the covered patio, where her mother had already set out their food and drinks. Overhead fans helped dispel the late afternoon heat, and the light breeze stirred by the blades felt refreshing as they ate. Bethany touched her mom's hand and pointed to the edge of the patio, where a pair of humming-birds flitted around the hanging feeders.

"Don't you just love those tiny creatures?" her mother

remarked as they watched the little birds, not much larger than bees. "Yesterday when the sprinklers were on, I watched them playing in the spray. It was so cute. I wished you were here to see it."

Bethany smiled and bit into her sandwich as the sweet scent of jasmine drifted from the trellis at the back fence. Hummingbirds, jasmine, and Mom returning to her music and health—what more could she desire?

∽∾

"Read me a story?" Jessica asked, slipping into her summer nightie after her bath.

"Sure, princess." Reveling in her sweet soap-bubble smell, John turned her around so he could brush the tangles from her red-gold hair. "First we'll read a Bible story, and then you can pick one or two of your new library books. How's that?"

She nodded. "Nana reads me Bible stories, too. She says they're 'portant. Why are they 'portant, Daddy?"

He gently turned her to face him and put his hands on her shoulders. "Because they tell us how to live. And how much God loves us."

"Did He love Mommy, too? Is that why He took her to heaven when she was sick? So He could make her all better? That's what Nana says."

John had asked himself the same question a hundred times. Even though he had to fight bitterness over fate's cruelties, he didn't want to pass those feelings on to his daughter. He swallowed a lump in his throat and gathered his thoughts. "Most likely. I guess sometimes people can't get better down here."

"That's sad. I would have helped her get better. I wouldn't do bad things."

"I'm sure you wouldn't," he said, drawing her close to his heart. "I'm sure you wouldn't."

That seemed to satisfy her. Her misty green eyes were radiant when she smiled up at him. "I hafta brush my teeth."

He nodded. "Then it's off to bed with you, young lady." As she turned and stepped onto the footstool at the sink, he hung her towel and drained the tub.

Having Jessica to look after had kept him alive, given him a reason to go on living when it would've been easier to curl up and die. Somehow, answering her questions was a balm to his own spirit, and caring for her needs and praying for her were helping him to heal. It still hurt to recall how he'd stood helplessly by, watching his wife's beautiful form wither away as she suffered, remembering the unspeakable emptiness he'd felt as her body was laid to its final rest. But with the passage of time he was beginning to accept the comfort of knowing she was beyond pain and living in the magnificent presence of the Lord. One day they'd be reunited where pain and sadness were banished for all time. And what a joy it would be to present Lisa with the sweet little girl she'd left behind—possibly all grown up and a mommy herself. He just had to make sure he did a good job raising their daughter, as he was sure Lisa would have done herself.

"All done, Daddy. Can you read to me now?"

"Sure, princess." Taking her by the hand, he led the way to her white canopy bed, where he moved the assortment of stuffed animals so he could turn down her coverlet.

❧

Unable to sleep after her evening devotions, Bethany put a Carpenters album on her portable stereo and let the music fill the quietness while she got out some stationery. Even with Jillian on the other side of the country, it helped to confide in her through the mail.

Dear Jilli,

I hope this finds you well and happy. I pray for you every morning and night. Somehow knowing the Lord has me by one hand and you by the other makes it seem like we're not so very far apart. I know He will take good care of my best friend.

Mom is starting to return to health now. It's so good to see her starting to be more active. Next thing I know she'll be calling the ladies at church to announce she's ready to get back to weekly Bible studies and sewing those lap quilts her group makes for shut-ins. She was always on the go until she got sick. This has been a long siege. I won't be sorry to see it end.

Things are going okay for me at work. I've gotten used to all the people—even prissy Cynthia. She's not really as snooty as I first thought. I think she's insecure.

But enough about her. The most amazing thing happened today! You won't believe this, but somebody actually wrote a comment on one of my notes. I about fainted when I saw it, but then I realized it wasn't threatening or anything. I decided there must be another person in town who's lonely and needs a friend. Of course, I may never find another comment, but I'll still keep leaving notes around town anyway. It gives me pleasure to pass along some beautiful thought from someone's mind. There's nothing wrong with bringing joy and pleasure to others, right?

It's getting awfully warm here now. You know Bakersfield. But who can dislike all the gorgeous flowers that make it smell like Eden? I hope your weather is nice. Write when you can.

Love,
Beth

Folding the letter, she slipped it into an envelope and addressed it. Writing to Jill was almost as good as visiting with her. But not quite. Yawning, she crawled back between the cool bed sheets and plumped her pillow before lying down.

Her thoughts returned to the library bulletin board and her surprise at finding a response to the quote she'd posted. What sort of individual could have done it? Would she comment again? After all, it couldn't possibly be a man. That species was too busy to waste time going to libraries and taking notice of items on bulletin boards. It had to be a woman. Somebody lonely. Someone who needed a friend.

Whoever it is, Father, please be with her—or him—and make Your presence felt day by day. Ease the lonely times and show that person Your love. Help me to find sayings that will touch the heart and help him or her to focus on You. In Jesus' name, amen.

Chapter 5

Hazy June sunlight streamed through the textured windowpanes of Hope Community Church, turning lowly dust mites into specks of glittering splendor. At the piano, Rachel Maxwell, the pastor's attractive wife, played the offertory, a symphonic arrangement of "Great Is Thy Faithfulness." Her slim teenage daughters, Heather and Laura, accompanied their mother on the organ and flute, adding to the majesty of the piece.

The song had always been a favorite of Bethany's. Seated with her mother halfway down the rows of dark oak pews, she felt her heart swell as the lyrics scrolled through her mind, stirring her senses along with the music's incredible beauty.

The offering plates being passed along each row were hardly a distraction as she observed the young musicians. Similarly dressed in pastel florals, with softly curled shag haircuts shimmering in the overhead light, they made a pretty picture as they concentrated on their task.

Pondering God's faithfulness, Bethany's mind drifted to the response she'd received to the quote she'd posted on the library bulletin board two weeks ago, regarding friendship: *"Delight yourself also in the LORD, and He shall give you the desires of your heart" (Psalm 37:4).* The thoughtful sentiment had touched her deeply. Even now she squelched a smile and returned her focus to the front of the sanctuary.

The hymn's final crescendo lingered on a sustained chord and the song came to an end. A breathless hush hovered over the congregation as the women quietly took their seats.

Pastor Stu stepped up to the podium, attired in a dark gray suit and striped tie. "No one could ask for more lovely or talented gals," he said, beaming. "I believe I'll keep them." He nudged his bifocals a touch higher on his nose as a collective chuckle echoed from the audience. Then his smile dimmed as he opened his large black Bible. "Our text this morning will be from First Corinthians, chapter 13, the last verse: 'And now abide faith, hope, love, these three; but the greatest of these is love.'"

He looked out over the congregation. "As you know, we've been in a three-part series studying these aspects of our salvation experience. Last week we looked closely at faith and discovered from Hebrews that without faith it is impossible to please God. We learned that faith, as defined in the scriptures, is a firm conviction based on the Word of God, and that God is the object of that faith. In our everyday living, it's a decision to act with dependence on Him, focusing on His Son, Jesus Christ. In return, we're given the promise that one day our faith will become sight.

"This morning we'll turn our magnifying glass on the second item listed: hope. It's a word that relates chiefly to our future, yet it clearly affects the present, as well. Hope always refers to something good. For us as Christians, that hope embraces all of God's plans for His people. It's like a beautiful rose that unfolds from a tiny bud to the fullest flower, growing increasingly beautiful along the way."

Bethany smiled to herself at the image the pastor's words painted in her mind. Her father had been an eternal optimist, always making sure she and her mother kept their hopes alive. Never once had he focused on the negative. Even at his weakest point, as death grew imminent, he reminded them of the surety that one day they would all be reunited. She returned her attention to the minister.

"Turn with me, if you will, to Hebrews 6, verse 19." He paused for the rustle of pages to cease. "Look at this statement: 'This hope we have as an anchor of the soul, both sure and steadfast.' Here we see that hope affects our daily lives. Hope inspires and motivates us to live in obedience. Just as we have God's promise that one day our faith will become sight, we have His vow that one day in His perfect time, our hope will be fulfilled. . . ."

∞

Seated in a cushioned pew at the Life in Christ Center, the sprawling church he'd attended throughout his life, John stared over the sea of heads in front of him as portly Reverend Sheldon's authoritative voice droned on. If John hadn't been part of this congregation and grown up along with the membership roster, he'd have preferred being part of a smaller, homier place of worship. Over the years, he'd watched the place evolve from an average-size church into a worship center with a modern campus of high-tech buildings. Even the sound system was the best money could buy, and renowned recording artists often came here to display their talent to their adoring fans. In fact, before this morning's sermon, a group who'd given a concert the previous evening had performed one more extremely loud number for the offertory before boarding their bus to go on to their next gig.

But John took comfort in knowing that at least he was able to fade into the woodwork here, after dropping out of so many activities when Lisa became ill. Maybe that was one benefit of being in such a crowd. No one singled him out to fill in for a Sunday school teacher or an usher.

He felt Jessica go limp against his arm. He gazed down at his daughter as she dozed, met his mom's smile on the child's other side, then returned his concentration to the minister's sermon, entitled "God's Abundant Things." Even though most of the passages covered were familiar to him, it was always good to be reminded of the various blessings making up each sermon point—mercy for the lost, grace for the needy, and peace for the troubled. It made him yearn to dust off the Bible on his nightstand and get back to reading it regularly. Taking that as an encouraging sign of God's abundant *healing for the wounded*, he shifted slightly to make sure Jessica was comfortable. The short nap would do her good.

⚭

"That was a stirring message," Bethany's mom commented on the drive home. "And wasn't the music especially lovely? Even better than we heard last night at the concert held at the Life in Christ Center. Oh, it's good to be getting out to church regularly again. Maybe next week I'll start attending my Sunday school class. Seems ages since I've been with my lady friends."

"Mm-hmm," Bethany agreed, only half listening as she drove.

"The more I think about it, the better that sounds. I might even have Pearl Marshall pick me up for the ladies' Bible study Tuesday morning. You should start back in your class, too. No telling how many activities you've missed out on, being stuck at home with your sick old mother and dropping choir and everything else except the church services."

"You're far from old, Mom," Bethany assured her. "But I no longer want to be a part of that college and career class. I skipped out so long ago, the friends I knew have probably gotten married and moved on, just like Jillian. There's probably a whole bunch of new people now. If I decide to go to any class, it'll be the pastor's. It's general, for all ages, and I like being anonymous."

"There's still choir."

"But they don't need one more alto. Anyway, I'd feel awkward. There are too many new faces in that group. People I don't even know."

When her mother didn't respond right away, Bethany cut a glance in her direction and saw her face creased with worry.

"I'm afraid you're going to let life pass you by, Bethy. You've become a recluse. And I'm to blame."

"No, you're not." Bethany patted her mother's hand. "I'm fine. I'm happy. I'm normal, even. I meet people at work—"

"And the rest of the time your life centers around me and around books," Mom interrupted.

"So what's wrong with that? If I don't mind, you surely shouldn't."

"I'd just like to see you more involved in outside activities again. You never know if you might be missing out on something the Lord has for you."

Bethany rolled her eyes. "I'm sure if the Lord wanted me to fill my life with extracurricular activities, I'd sense His leading. Besides, I still have devotions every day. And I'm kind of enjoying this quiet lifestyle. Honest. There's nothing different I wish I could be doing."

"Maybe, but that doesn't mean I'll stop worrying about my favorite daughter. You deserve some happiness in this life."

"I told you, Mom, I *am* happy. But you're sweet for being concerned. Now where would you like to eat? Hungry for anything special?"

"We haven't gone Mexican for a while. How about Don Pepe's?"

"My sentiments exactly. Let's see if we can beat the members of First Assembly to the restaurant."

Her mother chuckled at the joke.

෨෨

Bethany had spent weeks working on the drawings for Granger Realty, pouring her whole heart and all of her skill into each one. Now, eyeing them critically one by one, she gathered them together to give to John when he had a free minute. Not only had she changed the basic design of the Granger logo; she had chosen a different color scheme, too, changing from forest green and white to a more patriotic red, white, and blue. She'd worked with several different style possibilities, utilizing varying kinds of lettering and embellishments to enhance each one. Wondering how they'd be taken, she decided that the worst he and Mr. Granger could do was hate them and toss them into the circular file. It shouldn't bother her if they were content with the status quo.

John came out of his office and went directly to the small break room. She could hear him pouring coffee and opening the fridge, where the half-and-half was kept. She also heard Cynthia in there.

"How's it going, John?" the saleswoman asked in honeyed tones.

"Not bad. Get everything with that Hawkins woman straightened out? I hear she was giving you grief."

Cynthia snorted. "Yes, finally. I see now why Craig was so willing for me to take that deal. That lady is a—well, you know."

"Yeah. I've dealt with a few of those myself. I don't seem to fare well with single gals. I've learned to keep my distance."

"I don't see why—a handsome man like you. Seems they'd be falling at your feet."

"Right. More like using me for a doormat. I've gotten a bit more selective in choosing clients these days."

"Whatever." She paused. "By the way, I'm having a few people over at my place this Sunday afternoon. Would you like to come? You could bring your little girl, too, of course. I have swim rings available for my nieces and nephews, and she'd be quite safe in the pool. We'd be nearby to keep an eye on her."

"Decent of you to ask, but I don't think so. I don't go in much for parties these days."

"Oh, too bad. You should get out more, you know. Do things. Meet people. Make. . .friends."

"Maybe. But it's still no."

"Well, if you change your mind, come anyway. You're always welcome. You know where I live."

The phone in Cynthia's cubicle interrupted the interchange, and Bethany feigned absorption in her work as the woman returned to her desk. If not for the carpet muffling the sound of her heels, Bethany sensed the clipped steps would have ricocheted off the walls. In mere seconds, the agent had her purse and briefcase and was out the door without a word.

"That went over well," John quipped, coming to Bethany's desk after Cynthia had taken her leave.

"Excuse me?" She looked up at him as if she hadn't heard a single word of their conversation.

"Never mind. By any chance, have you finished any of those designs you were working on? Not that there's any hurry. I was just wondering." He took a sip of coffee from the mug he held.

"Yes, I have." Suddenly doubting her abilities, Bethany fought reluctance at showing them to him. She knew she'd been quite bold in revamping the entire design.

"Well? May I see them?"

"Of course." Pursing her lips, she braced herself and handed them over.

He set down his cup and took his time leafing through

the pages. "Hmm. Not bad. Pretty radical, though. Don't you think?"

"Is that. . .bad?"

"Nope. More like you're making us part of this century. I'm impressed. It'd be a good change, updating the logo *and* the colors."

Bethany shrugged a shoulder. "Well, as the old saying goes, 'To change the name and not the letter is a change for the worse and not the better.'"

A look of puzzlement creased his forehead. "An interesting thought." He gave her a quizzical look, then nodded. "I'll show these to Dad when he comes in and see what he thinks. And thanks for the effort, Bethany. You do good work."

"Thank *you* for the opportunity to do something I truly enjoy. It was fun."

❧

John closed his Bible and switched off the light. His thoughts reflected back to Sunday. He'd been on his way out the door after the morning service when he glimpsed a note on the public board in the foyer, written on the familiar paper, in the handwriting he easily recognized. Since it was the first time he'd seen one there, he could only surmise it had been posted by a visitor who'd attended Saturday evening's concert.

Those who know the path to God can find it in the dark.
—*Ian Maclaren*

Somehow, that particular sentiment, on the board of his

own church, seemed to have been put there especially for him, and he'd been unable to get it out of his head. No one had to tell him he'd been in the dark far too long. Lately, little by little, he could feel himself crawling out of the pit and returning to life. Kneeling down beside his bed, he bowed his head.

I know it's been a long time since I've spent time in Your Word, Father. Please forgive me for being wrapped up in myself and my grief for so long that I've neglected feeding on the Living Bread. I'm aware that even my prayers have been mere surface requests; it's easier to pray for Jessica and for the person I don't even know—who leaves those strange, fascinating notes around town—than to face my own demons and ask for forgiveness for myself. But I've always felt Mom's and Dad's prayers, and I know You've still been there. Thank You, Lord, for bringing me through the rough time since You took Lisa home to be with You. I'm asking You to forgive me and revive my heart, and make me a faithful servant once again. This I pray in the name of Your Son. Amen.

Feeling as though a great weight had been lifted from his spirit, John climbed between the cool sheets and lay down on his back, his head cupped in his hands.

And he breathed a prayer of blessing for the note writer—whoever she was.

Chapter 6

While her mom sequestered herself in one of J. C. Penney's dressing rooms to try on an assortment of new outfits, Bethany browsed through the display of purses before meandering to the jewelry department. Always appreciative of the store's fine selection of seasonal accessories, she gave a carousel of clearance earrings a slow turn, eyeing the various styles. Then she moved on to the newer summer jewelry.

"So they let just anybody come here and shop," a male voice said from the base of the escalator nearby.

Bethany turned, hiking her brows in surprise at the sight of her employer stepping off the motorized stairs with a little girl. As striking as he looked in business suits, he was positively devastating in jeans and a polo shirt. She wished she had dressed in something nicer than the dull khaki slacks and peach blouse she'd grabbed out of her closet earlier that morning. "Seems strange to see you outside of the office," she blurted, embarrassed by the inane comment.

He nodded. "Saturday's our day on the town. We try to hit

all the high spots. The library, McDonald's, the works. This is my daughter, Jessica." He beamed down at the redhead with dual ponytails. "Jess, this is Bethany. She works at the office with Grandpa and me."

"Hi, Jessica," Bethany said, taking in the child's jean shorts, appliquéd T-shirt, and white sandals. She bent slightly to be on her level. "My, what a big girl you are. You must be. . .four years old?"

"Almost." She hugged a faded Raggedy Ann close.

"So you'll be having a birthday pretty soon. Well, it's so nice to meet you. What pretty hair you have. And I like your dolly. I used to have one like her."

She gave a shy smile. "I'm gonna get new shoes."

"Oh, I'm sure you'll find some nice ones. Maybe at Payless, down the mall. I always see lots of kids there."

"That's where we're heading," John supplied. "They had a pair here that she liked, but not in her size."

"Story of my life," Bethany added with a droll smile. "I dread trying to find new shoes."

"We're going to the food court," Jessica piped up.

"Yum. That's one of my favorite places." She glanced at John. "Your little girl is very articulate."

"Jess spends a lot of time with my mother," he said. "She used to teach kindergarten."

Bethany gave an understanding nod.

"I. . .don't suppose you'd care to join us for lunch. I'm buying."

The invitation about floored Bethany. This John seemed relaxed and jovial, far removed from the somber one she'd met her first day on the job. She raised her lashes to meet his eyes. "Thank you, that's really nice. Only I'm not alone. My mom is here—somewhere." She craned her neck to see if she could spot her.

"No problem," he said. "We'll be tied up at Payless for a little while. You and your mother can join us at the food court in, say, twenty minutes? If you're interested, of course."

Seeing no negative reaction in the child's expression, Bethany smiled at John. "Well, again. . .thanks. I'll check with Mom, and then maybe we'll see you guys there."

He gave a nod. "Well, come on, then, princess. Somewhere there's a pair of new shoes with your name on them. It's up to us to find 'em."

"Oh, Daddy," she giggled, slipping her tiny hand into his. "That's silly."

With a tip of his head at Bethany, John led his daughter toward the exit to the mall.

No one could miss the adoration in Jessica's green eyes as she gazed up at her hero, Bethany realized, watching after the pair. The depth of love between the two was almost tangible. Her heart ached for the darling little munchkin growing up without a mother, almost as much as it ached for the child's daddy.

Her mom's voice interrupted her musings. "*There* you are."

Bethany turned and smiled as she saw the bulging shopping bag in her mother's hand. "I see you found a few things, huh?"

"I sure did. They had some great buys. I'll show you everything when we get home."

"Sounds good." After a brief hesitation, she decided to go for broke. "Well, tell me, are you more worn out or more hungry?"

A thoughtful look brought a sparkle to her mom's blue eyes. "To tell you the truth, I think I worked up an appetite trying on all those clothes. I can rest any old time."

"Good, then let's head up to the food court. There's someone I'd like you to meet. I'll carry your bag."

On their way to the food court, Bethany and her mother stopped inside a few specialty shops. By the time they reached the open area dotted by tables and surrounded by various fast-food chains, John and Jessica were already seated at a table sipping drinks.

He stood and gave a slight bow as they approached. "Hello, ladies. I'm glad you've decided to join us."

"Hi," Bethany said. "John, I'd like you to meet my mother, Prudie Prescott. Mom, this is John Granger, one of my bosses."

"Mrs. Prescott." John smiled and shook her hand warmly. "Very nice to meet the mother of such a talented young lady. Thanks to your daughter, our entire office is being redesigned."

Bethany blushed at the exaggeration but took comfort from the twinkle in his eye.

"I'm pleased to meet you, too. Bethany speaks highly of you and your father."

"That's good to hear," he said, flashing a grin her way before returning his attention to her mother. "If you two will have a seat with my daughter, Jessica, I'd be happy to go order us up some food. Or you can tag along, Bethany, and choose what you and your mom would like. Either way."

"I'll tag along. What would you like, Mom? Chinese?"

She nodded.

"Then we'll be right back."

Bethany couldn't get over how different John seemed out of the office as he accompanied her to order lunch. Something about him heightened her senses, and it was hard to concentrate on the selections of Oriental cuisine when he stood so near. She forced herself to relax and choose the food and beverages for her and her mom, then returned to the table while he picked up his own order and joined the group.

When all of their meals had been distributed, he took Jessica's hand, looking a touch awkward as he offered his other hand to Bethany. "We always make a circle for grace. Hope you don't mind."

"Not at all." She swallowed her nerves and placed her hand in his. Sure the tingle that surged through her at his touch was her overactive imagination, she bowed her head.

"Dear Lord," he prayed, "we thank You for this wonderful day and the opportunity to enjoy Your bountiful blessings with friends. Please bless our food and our conversation as we visit. In the name of Your Son, Jesus, amen."

"Amen," the others echoed.

"So, Mrs. Prescott," John said, unwrapping his cheese-burger. "How'd you get along with my daughter while Bethany and I were making the rounds of the court?" He took a healthy bite.

"Famously," she said without hesitation. "Little Jessica and I are already friends, aren't we, honey? I was just admiring her pretty new shoes."

"Uh-huh," she said, ponytails dancing as she nodded to her dad. "She used to fix Bethany's hair like mine." She bit into a French fry.

"Is that right?" John flicked a glance at Bethany. "I bet it was real cute that way. Maybe she'll wear ponytails to work sometime." A teasing grin broke across his lips.

She looked from him to her mom and back again. "Right. That would be real. . .cute. Maybe I'd start a new fad."

He just chuckled.

"Well, well." Cynthia Hargrove sidled over to the table, her perfect eyebrows arched high. "Imagine meeting you two here." Dark eyes that resembled melted chocolate when they drifted over John and Jessica hardened to the solid variety when they swept on to Bethany and her mother.

"Hello, Cynthia," John replied, reverting to his more reserved persona in her presence. "Jess and I ran into Bethany and her mom at Penney's. Would you care to join us? We can always pull up another chair."

"Thank you, no. I've already eaten. I wouldn't dream of intruding on your little. . .tête-à-tête."

"Well, another time, then."

"Maybe. Meanwhile, I'll see you at work. You all have a nice day." With a last cool glance encompassing the foursome, she stalked away.

Despite a definite easing of tension as the sales agent took her leave, Bethany couldn't help but notice the cloud the woman's intrusion cast over their joviality. When their conversation resumed momentarily, it was more general, bordering on stilted. Gone were the flashes of humor and the camaraderie they'd been enjoying. Even Jessica was less bubbly, as if picking up on her dad's mood.

Bethany already missed the relaxed John she'd glimpsed for that short period of time. Somehow she sensed that was the real one.

John took the elastic bands out of his daughter's hair and began brushing out her silky curls for bedtime.

"Today was fun," she said, toying with the ribbon on the front of her nightie.

"It was. What was your favorite part? Story hour at the library? Shopping for shoes?"

"The food court. The corn dog and ice cream cone."

"Figured you'd like those."

"And the nice lady."

"Mrs. Prescott? Yeah, she seems real nice, doesn't she?"

"Uh-huh. But I mean the other one. Bethany. I like her. A lot."

"You do, huh?" A charming mental picture of his secretary and her kind ways surfaced. Even her easy manner with Jessica had impressed him. In fact, he'd noticed thoughts of Bethany coming often to his mind lately. It was getting difficult to dismiss them. He liked the pleasant timbre of her voice, her dazzling smile, those expressive eyes—even the perfume she wore lingered in his mind. He let out a deep breath. "Yeah, she is pretty nice. Grandpa and I are both glad she works for us."

"I didn't like that other one. The one who stopped at the table. She has a mean face."

John stopped brushing and turned her around, placing his hands on her shoulders. He spoke gently as he met her gaze straight on. "I don't like it when you say unkind things about people. Cynthia Hargrove may not have a kind face, but that's because she has lots of problems. And they make her sad."

His daughter's eyes shimmered with tears, one of which traced a path down to her chin. "S—sorry for saying a bad thing."

He drew her into a hug. "It wasn't bad, princess. There's no need to cry. I just want you to always look for something nice to say about people. That makes God smile. He loves Cynthia just as much as He loves you and me. It's like that line in *Bambi*, where Thumper's mommy had him repeat, 'If you can't say somethin' nice, don't say nothin' at all.'"

"Oh yeah." A tremulous smile twitched on Jessica's rosebud lips as she scrunched her face in thought. "She had a pretty skirt."

John had to chuckle. "See? That's more like my girl."

"I love you, Daddy." She leaned close for another hug.

"Love you, too. Now we'd better make quick work of your bedtime story so you can get to sleep. We want you bright and happy for Sunday school tomorrow."

The busy day had taken its toll. Before he reached "happily ever after," Jessica's eyelids drifted closed. John closed the book and put it on her nightstand, then bent and kissed her soft cheek. He lingered for an extra few minutes just feasting his eyes on her cherubic face, all innocence and sweetness.

After his own prayer time, he climbed into bed and flicked off the bedside lamp. He'd enjoyed the day, too, beginning with the library. Today's note seemed to have a personal ring to it:

There's something so beautiful in coming on one's very own inmost thoughts in another. In one way it's one of the greatest pleasures one has.

—*Olive Schreiner*

He had no argument with a statement like that—which is why he'd searched for another quote to add to it. He was beginning to enjoy this.

❧

"Good night, dear," Mother called from the hallway outside Bethany's room.

Propped up on pillows in bed as she finished her nightly devotions, Bethany closed her Bible. " 'Night, Mom. Hope I didn't wear you out today."

She poked her head in the open doorway. Her face glowed pink, the way it had when she was in the pink of health. Still damp from bathing, stray hairs formed little ringlets around her face. "Not at all. A soak in the tub did wonders. I'll probably sleep like a log."

"Good. I enjoyed the day, too."

"I like that boss of yours. And that dear, sweet child. Tsk-tsk." She wagged her head. "What a pity, a little angel like that, motherless. I'll definitely be keeping them both in my prayers."

"I'm sure they'll appreciate it. But he *is* quite nice, isn't he? He and his dad are both easy to work for."

A look of puzzlement crimped her mom's features. "What did he mean about you redesigning the office?"

235

Bethany smirked. "He was just joshing. I was fooling around one day at lunchtime and did a couple of sketches, revamping the company logo and stationery. I didn't actually intend for anyone to see them, but John did, and he liked my designs. Now they want me to call a sign company on Monday and order a whole batch of new signs. I was a bit shocked."

Her mom cocked her head back and forth. "Oh, I don't know. You have a way with artistic things. Always have. I'm glad to hear that talent is finally being used."

"Me, too. It was the most enjoyable thing I've done since I started working there."

"Well," she said on a yawn, "I guess I'll go get some beauty sleep. See you in the morning."

"Right. Sleep well, Mom."

Her mother's footsteps faded away, followed by the faint click of her bedroom door's latch. As Bethany set her Bible on the nightstand, her gaze fell on the note she'd brought home from the library bulletin board. Her new pen pal had added a line:

They are never alone that are accompanied with noble thoughts.

—*Sir Philip Sidney*

Bethany smiled. She'd never considered herself as having "noble thoughts," but if someone else thought of her that way, she didn't mind. She mulled over the rest of the afternoon's pleasures—meeting John out of the blue. And his darling little girl—what a sweetheart. It had been a pleasant interlude until

Cynthia came along. Heaven only knew what she must have thought, seeing the handsome widower and his daughter out with her and her mom as if it had been a planned outing. Oh well, nothing could be done about that. *Dear Lord, please continue to work Your healing wonders in John's heart. And look after his sweet Jessica. Help them both to feel Your loving presence in their lives day by day.*

◌◈◌

A loud guffaw sounded from the break room. At her desk, sorting stacks of new forms from the Bakersfield Association of Realtors office, Bethany paused in her work.

"As the saying goes," she heard Rick say, " 'Don't borrow trouble. Be patient and you'll have enough of your own.' "

Craig snorted. "That's a winner. Where'd you come up with that gem?"

"Oddly enough, it was on one of those sticky notes I happened to see at a burger joint."

"Sticky note? Now that you mention it, I came across one of those the other day, too. Had something like, 'Better to be happy than wise,' or some such nonsense. Can't remember where I saw it."

"You guys talking about those sticky notes?" Cynthia chimed in. "Strange, how those things have been popping up around town. I saw one stuck to the restroom mirror at Don Pepe's not too long ago. As I recall, it said, 'What you possess in this world will go to someone else when you die, but what you are will be yours forever.' Sounds like some holier-than-thou has a deep desire to preach to the rest of us poor lost souls or something."

Bethany cringed. She bit down on the inside corner of her lip to stem the tears threatening to gather. She hadn't been trying to preach to anyone. She'd just wanted to pass along things for people to think about. But if that was the reception her quotes were getting, maybe it was time to keep them to herself. That resolve intensified when she heard John enter the conversation. *Don't tell me even* he *has read some of those sayings!*

"Oh, I wouldn't be so hard on the person who wrote those notes," he said.

Her spirits perked up a notch.

"I don't think preaching is what the writer's aiming for. It's more like encouraging. The last note I saw said, 'We have not been put on this earth primarily to see through one another but to see one another through.' Sounded sensible to me."

Bethany remembered posting that one at the library. She frowned. Hadn't he mentioned going to the library with Jessica when they'd crossed paths at the mall last weekend? Well, no matter. He had no clue that she went there regularly. Now that she and her little hobby had become the talk of the office, the time had definitely come to quit spreading the notes around. Period. Before her identity came to light.

But for some strange reason, her spirit felt deflated. Now she would lose her anonymous pen pal.

Chapter 7

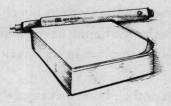

Leaning against the doorjamb of the break room, John had a clear view of Bethany at her desk. Her yellow blouse and russet skirt complemented her light auburn waves, gilded with a silver outline of light from the office's window. As it happened quite often of late, his gaze settled on the pleasant picture she made as she sorted forms into piles.

She hadn't appeared to be paying any mind to the banter taking place between the agents, until their joking focused on the sayings they'd been finding around town. That was when John watched her visibly deflate. She stopped working momentarily, and her shoulders sagged. Ignoring the chatter and laughter of the others, he took a last gulp of his coffee, moved to the machine, and dispensed a cup for her.

When she looked up as he neared the desk, her eyes lacked their normal sparkle.

"Thought maybe you could use a break," he said, offering her the disposable cup. "I didn't know if you take cream or sugar."

"Thanks." Even her smile seemed forced as she accepted it. "I usually do, but this is fine."

"You sure? I could—"

Her raised hand cut off his words. "It's okay. Really." As if to prove it, she took a sip.

He gave a nod. Then, not knowing what else to say, he retreated to his office and sank onto his chair. There was no reason on earth Bethany should have been bothered by the discussion that had taken place in the break room. No reason at all, unless. . .

Shuffling through the phone messages she'd taken for him, he frowned. They'd all been neatly printed. None was written in the small script he'd have easily recognized. Yet for some reason he could not define, John suspected that his pleasant, talented, sensitive young secretary just might be the author of the mystery notes. But how to be sure? That was the question.

🙾

Alone in her room, Bethany made yet another attempt to convey her feelings to her friend and confidant on paper. Her wastebasket brimmed with a number of discards.

> *Dear Jill,*
>
> *This has been the absolute worst week of my life. You won't believe this, but suddenly my notes and I have become the talk of the office—like the whole thing's a big joke! I'm sure the guys didn't know they were talking about me, but it still hurt to hear everyone making light of those sayings. The only one who didn't make snide remarks about them was John. I don't think it's in his nature to say unkind things about anyone or anything.*

Reading over the lines she'd scribbled in frustration, Bethany let out a ragged breath and wadded up the stationery. She was making too much of this. It wasn't the end of the world, just the end of her hobby. From now on she'd keep the touching sentiments to herself. *All* of them. In fact, for the last couple of days, she'd driven around town in a frenzy after work, removing notes from all of the places where she tended to leave them. She'd even returned her library books early just to retrieve the one from that board before her anonymous friend had a chance to add a comment. From now on, she'd let people look up their own thought for the day. Why should she care?

Still, knowing that at least John hadn't said anything to add to her angst, she smiled as an indescribable warmth flowed through her being. Heaven help her, she was having a hard time keeping thoughts of him on a business level. This was not good.

◌

John made three trips to the library board while he waited for Jessica, but he found only standard notices posted. No yellow sticky note. Accustomed to finding an inspirational quote nearly every Saturday and then coming up with a suitable reply, he realized how that small activity brightened his week. Now the conviction that the mystery writer was Bethany became even more certain. Maybe it would raise her spirits to be on the receiving end of a message herself for a change. Already having copied several neat sayings onto index cards for possible use, he smiled and tacked one up in the usual spot:

Thy life which looks to thee so comfortless!
This is the word: "Some one hath need of thee."
—*Emma C. Dowd*

Realizing how true that sentiment actually was becoming, John had to fight a silly grin determined to spread from ear to ear. He took Jess for a Happy Meal, then dropped her off at his mom's so she could swim in the pool. There he phoned his friend Steve and suggested they go biking after the worst of the day's heat was past.

Early that evening, the wind whipped through his hair as he and Steve pedaled side by side on the bike path bordering the Truxton Extension. But all too soon his thighs and calves protested as if they were on fire. "Let's stop for a breather. There's a cool spot right over there." Veering off the paved strip, he tipped his ten-speed on its side.

Steve followed suit, and the two of them flopped down onto the grassy knoll near one of the twin charging ponds. "Man, I haven't seen you with such a sappy expression for ages."

Watching a pair of long-legged blue herons wading in the rippled pond, John took some gulps from his water bottle. "What do you mean?"

Steve tucked his chin. "You're kidding, right? I mean, look at you. I'm used to seeing you all down in the dumps, not interested in much of anything. Now all of a sudden you're eager to hit the trail again. Is there something you're not telling me, pal? Or maybe some*one* you're not telling me about?"

Not quite ready to admit his growing attraction to Bethany—even to himself—John kept his tone casual. He'd been doing some serious praying about the situation and truly felt the Lord was leading him toward her. Still, there was no point in jumping the gun. He would never completely forget his first love. But now he could understand a heart's capacity to love again, when given the chance. "Nope. None of the above. I've just decided to get back to life, that's all. Dwelling in the past never does anybody any good." He averted his gaze to the distance, where the hills were obscured by summer smog, then looked back at his friend in all seriousness. "Actually, I was feeling a bit jealous, being this lily white, when you've been baked to a crisp in the hot sun. Thought it was time to revive my California tan again."

"Yeah. Right. And I've just been elected mayor of Bakersfield." Steve shook his head.

"Well, you know what they say."

"What's that?"

" 'All things have an end.' " Grinning, John lumbered to his feet. "Whoa. I had no idea I was this out of shape. I think we should've packed it in half an hour ago."

Steve got up and clamped an empathetic hand on his shoulder. "Never fear, buddy. This is just a hint of how you're gonna feel tomorrow." Snickering, he grabbed hold of his bike and pulled it upright. "Come on. Our cars are probably only six or seven miles away."

John groaned and reached for his ten-speed.

❦

"So how's it going, *Bethany*?" Rick crooned at Bethany's elbow, his voice taunting and seductive. "How about you 'n' me going out for lunch?"

In the middle of typing Mr. Granger's property ads to fax to the newspaper, Bethany was in no mood for needless interruptions, let alone needless *passes* when the office was all but deserted. This was not the first time he'd sidled up to her when no one was around, making offensive, suggestive remarks. She stopped typing, gave a slow blink, and glared up at him. "No thanks. I have too much to do."

"You already have a boyfriend?"

Bethany didn't dignify the question by responding.

"Nobody'd be the wiser. What do you say? No point in hanging around this dump at mealtime. We could catch a quick bite, talk a little. What's the harm? You might even enjoy yourself. I know I would."

She sat back and crossed her arms. "I said no. I meant no. Thanks."

"You heard the lady," John said, exiting his office. "She's not interested."

Rick smirked. "I was only trying to be friendly—unlike some people around here." He shrugged and blew out a disgusted breath before skulking away.

"I suppose the guy's really harmless," Bethany said, fighting an irritating blush as the door slammed. "But thanks for coming to my rescue."

"Anytime. I mean that." He peered down at her work. "Looks like Dad has you quite busy this morning."

"I prefer being busy. It makes the day go faster."

He nodded. "Same here. Oh. I almost forgot." He reached into his pocket and withdrew a few stylized ballpoint pens in red, white, and blue, featuring the new logo. "We just got these in yesterday. From your design, you'll notice. Thought you might like some for your desk."

"Thank you." Her fingers brushed his as she took them from him, and Bethany immediately concentrated on perusing the company name and the contemporary style of the pens. "They turned out really nice, didn't they?"

"We like them."

She nodded, not knowing whether to pursue further conversation.

John saved her from making the decision by turning and going back to his office.

Strange how *quiet* the whole place seemed now, Bethany mused, yet how *full* it seemed with only the two of them. The deserted office somehow magnified his presence. She opened her drawer to put the new pens away.

That's when she saw it.

An index card with a printed quote:

> *The greatest and perhaps the only perfect gift that we can give to the world is the gift of ourselves at our best, and that means not just the skill of our hands and the cunning of our brains, but our dreams, our finest resolutions and most solemn promises to ourselves.*
>
> —*William N. Thomas*

Bethany's heart forgot how to beat.

He knows. She swallowed.

But so do I, now. The realization lingered on the edges of her mind, gradually instilling her with courage she didn't know she possessed.

Nibbling her lower lip to contain a delighted smile, she scooted her chair back from the typewriter and got up. She was suddenly glad no one else was around as she walked quietly to John's office and stood in the open doorway. "So it was you."

A lazy grin spread across his lips. "Guilty as charged. I kind of suspected you were the mystery writer whose inspiring sayings brightened many a day for me."

"Did they really?" Her insides began to quiver. She laced her fingers together and twisted them nervously, struggling to still the flutters, trying to stay calm as she studied the pattern in the carpet.

"More than you know, Bethany."

Something in the way he said her name, softly, like a summer breeze, made her breath catch in her throat as she raised her gaze to his.

"For quite a while now," he went on candidly, "I've been wallowing in self-pity, bemoaning fate's cruelties. If not for Jessica, I'd have probably cast off my faith a couple of years ago and started down the infamous Road to Perdition. Or more correctly, if not for Jessica and you. You might say you've helped bring me back to life."

She smiled. "I don't know what to say. I'm. . .humbled. I've been praying for you and that little sweetheart of yours since the first time I met her."

"You made quite a good impression on her, too. And we both appreciate your prayers."

"I'm really glad the quotations brought you enjoyment."

She paused. "As your comments did me."

His light brown eyes, filled with unspoken words, locked with hers. He tipped his head. "Then it seems we're on the verge of something, you and I."

"So it would seem."

For a timeless minute, as if they were poised on the edge of a precipice, one with a fragile bridge over the gaping emptiness, a breathless silence hovered poignantly around them. Then John got up and came around the desk to stand before her—close enough to touch her, only he did not. His gaze roamed her features, briefly lingering here and there, finally stopping on her lips. His expression was vulnerable. Earnest. Hopeful. And a gentle smile took up residence in his eyes.

It was hard to breathe with him towering over her. Bethany felt her pulse rushing in her ears. Yet she felt no fear. She trusted him instinctively.

"Tell me, if your boss were to ask you out, what would you say?"

"I would say yes," she whispered.

A grin widened his mouth, crinkling the corners of his eyes in a most endearing way. "That's what I was hoping."

⌘

Bethany tried on everything in her closet before settling on her basic "little black dress," accenting its classic simplicity with pearls that once belonged to her grandmother. She spritzed on a light mist of her favorite floral perfume and slipped into strappy heels. Then she stepped back to assess her reflection, pleased at the way the hint of blush and taupe eye shadow enhanced her features. She hoped John would like what he saw. Picking up her evening bag and hairpin lace shawl from her bed, she headed for the living room to await her escort.

At the piano, her mother stopped playing and turned as Bethany entered the room. "My, don't you look lovely. I haven't seen you in that dress for ages."

"I hope it's suitable. We're only going to dinner."

"It's perfect. I'm glad John's taking you out. He seems to be a decent young man. It's time he put his sadness behind and reached out for some happiness in his life again. Time for *you* to find happiness, too."

Bethany smiled. "I think you're making more of this than there is, Mom. We're only going on a date, not making a commitment." But inside, she had to admit that for the first time in her life, she yearned for something lasting, for a loving relationship like Jillian had found. No longer did mere friendship satisfy the longings of her heart. Maybe things wouldn't work out between her and John, but she sensed that the Lord was showing her that her future might include love, one day, when the time was right.

"We'll see. It may be a date now, but one never knows what may come of it."

Before Bethany could respond, the doorbell chimed. She swallowed against the swarm of butterflies in her stomach and went to answer the summons.

John's mesmerizing smile met her as she opened the door. Tall and heart-stoppingly handsome in a navy blazer and charcoal gray slacks, he held out a long white box tied with a silver bow. "Flowers for the lady."

"Oh," she breathed, surprised by his thoughtful gesture. "Thank you. Won't you come in? I'll put these in water."

"Don't worry yourself about them, dear," her mom said, coming to her side. "I'll look after them for you. Nice to see you again, John."

"Same here, Mrs. Prescott," he said with a gallant tip of his dark head as his form filled the door frame. "I'll take good care of your lovely daughter."

"I've no doubt of that. Have a great time, both of you."

"We'll do our best." He offered his arm to Bethany and ushered her to his car. "Mexicali okay with you? Or would you prefer something other than Mexican?" he asked after coming around to the driver's side and climbing in.

"That's fine. I like just about anything."

"Then Mexicali it is." Soft classical guitar music from the tape deck started up along with the engine, and after a short drive they pulled into a slot at the popular Spanish-style restaurant.

Once they'd been seated in a booth and given menus, an attractive young Hispanic girl brought a basket of warm tortilla chips and a bowl of salsa and took their orders. A blend of quiet instrumentals and mariachi music played in the background, muting the voices of the other patrons and creating an intimate atmosphere.

"So." John scooped salsa onto a chip. "I can't help wondering. How did you get started on that sideline of yours, tacking up notes on bulletin boards?" He popped the chip into his mouth.

Bethany smiled and felt her cheeks grow warm. "It all started with my dad, actually. Him and his fortune cookies."

"Your father made fortune cookies? Actually baked them?"

She nodded. "It's a long story. But that's how he caught Mom's attention. He put touching scripture verses into hers. He used to make me special cookies, too, with sweet sayings inside. I've been fascinated with thoughtful sentiments ever since. I hoped other people might enjoy reading a neat thought for the day. Or at least that was my intent. I suppose it sounds silly."

"Not to me, it doesn't," John assured her. "They got me to thinking about something besides myself and my problems. They really did brighten my days. I got so I looked for notes wherever I went. I enjoyed pondering the messages—and thinking up suitable replies."

"It's good to know someone appreciated them." She paused, toying with a broken chip. "You know, I was really close to my dad. It was hard to part with him. I can't imagine how difficult it must have been for you to lose your wife, to say nothing of having a darling little girl to raise without her mom."

"Yes, it was. . .rough."

"Well, if you ever need somebody to talk to sometime, I hope you'll think of me. I'd like to hear about her."

His gaze softened as it met hers. "Thank you, Bethany. Maybe I'll do that—someday."

The waitress arrived with their meals at that moment, placing Bethany's chicken chimichanga and John's *carne esada* before them. "Is there anything else?"

"This is great for now," John told her. He reached for Bethany's hand and bowed his head. "Thank You, Father, for this food. We ask Your blessing upon it and on our conversation

as we enjoy Your provision. May we be conscious of Your leading in our lives day by day. In Jesus' name, amen."

By the end of the evening, after hearing how John had
gotten into real estate and having him share cute stories about
Jessica and some of his life's dreams, Bethany no longer was
conscious of butterflies in her stomach. She felt as comfortable
and at ease with him as if they'd been friends for years. He was
easy to talk to, and she had no qualms about sharing some of
her own private hopes. Maybe that was how it was with kindred spirits, she conceded, wondering if perhaps the Lord had
brought them together for a reason.

"Well," John said as he escorted her to her door after the
drive home, "thanks for coming to dinner with me. I enjoyed
getting to know you a little."

"Thank *you*, John," she said, wondering why her voice
sounded so breathless. "I had a very nice time."

The warm evening breeze toyed with a few strands of
Bethany's hair, tossing them across her eyes, and as he gazed
down at her, he brushed them gently away with the backs of
his fingers. "Does that mean you'd do it again?"

A shivering sensation tingled through her. She smiled.
"Anytime."

"I was hoping you'd say that." He hesitated for a heartbeat,
then raised her chin with the edge of his finger and placed a
feather-light kiss on her lips. "Good night, Bethany."

"Good night," she whispered. Somehow, with her knees
feeling like gelatin, she managed to go inside. *Oh, Jilli. . .I think
I know how love feels. . . .*

Chapter 8

Six months later

Bethany stood before the full-length mirror, awed by the reflection staring back at her in white Chantilly lace enhanced by sequins and pearls. She let out a nervous breath and turned. "How do I look?"

"You look gorgeous," dark-haired Jillian said, fluffing out Bethany's veil. "Positively gorgeous. I always knew you'd make a beautiful bride."

Bethany fought tears as she leaned to hug her slender friend, a vision herself in a long gown of emerald satin accented by a white faux fur stole. "Who'd have believed it, Jilli? Me, a bride. I never thought anything could surpass friendship—until I grew to love John."

"Love does have a way of changing our priorities, doesn't it?" Jill teased. "I prayed that God would bring someone very special into your life. I like John a lot."

"We all think the world of that man," Mom said, crossing the room with their beribboned bouquets of red and white roses. "And his sweet little daughter." She handed one to each of them, then hugged both girls, unmindful of the crush of tulle and satin beneath her fingers. Her eyes misted over as she eased away from Bethany. "I only wish your father could have been here to give you away. It was his grandest hope."

Bethany swallowed a lump in her throat. "I feel him here, Mom. I think he's looking down on us with joy."

She nodded, blinking away the tears. "Well, I do believe I hear our cue. Time for us to go, my beautiful girls." Mom led the way from the bridal room to the broad foyer of the wedding chapel, where an usher escorted her to her place of honor for the ceremony.

Banks of crimson poinsettias and lighted garlands from the worship center's annual Hanging of the Green production turned the spacious sanctuary into a glorious red and green bower glistening in the soft flickering light from twin candelabra and miniature lights. Bethany smiled down at her soon-to-be daughter, their little flower girl, all copper ringlets and ribbons and tulle. In her filmy white gown and trailing emerald sash, she resembled a Christmas angel as she stepped onto the runner, sprinkling red rose petals in her wake as the smiling audience looked on.

Glowing with pride as he watched after Jessica, John stepped up to Bethany and offered his arm, resplendent in a black tux with emerald accents. "You look beautiful," he murmured, his adoring gaze enveloping her.

The radiant love in his eyes nearly rendered Bethany speechless. She was barely aware when Jillian and John's best man, Steve Cochran, started down the aisle in measured steps to take their places. All she could do was smile as she took John's arm and accompanied him to the front, where John's silver-haired pastor awaited them, a small black book open in his hands.

"Dearly beloved, we are gathered here. . ." the minister began.

Intensely conscious of John's nearness and his strength, which kept her knees from buckling, Bethany drew a rose-scented breath and concentrated on the pastor's words, hoping she responded correctly in all of the appropriate places—a considerable feat, with John's light brown eyes locked on hers the entire time.

At last came the words she'd been waiting for.

"You may kiss your bride."

John smiled and lowered his head, and his lips met Bethany's in a tender, passionate promise. "I'll love you forever, Bethany," he whispered on their release.

She smiled into his eyes. "I'll make a note of that."

A soft chuckle rumbled from deep inside him, and he kissed her again as the audience applauded.

Jessica tiptoed over to them both. "Are we married now, Daddy? Is Bethany my mommy?"

"Yes, sweetheart," he said. "Yes, she is."

The pastor grinned. "Ladies and gentlemen, it is my great honor to introduce to you Mr. and Mrs. John Granger—and daughter."

Exchanging an understanding smile, John and Bethany each took one of the little redhead's hands and strolled with her up the aisle.

SALLY LAITY

The tender stories of love and faith penned by Grace Livingston Hill and Janette Oke were the inspiration that started Sally on her writing career. Her first two novels were released by Barbour Publishing in 1991, and she was also given the honor of helping to launch their new Heartsong Presents Book Club. Now with an assortment of over thirty novels and novellas to her credit, Sally hopes that her stories of God's mercy and faithfulness will bless readers' hearts. In her spare time, she enjoys scrapbooking family photos and watching her grandchildren growing in the Lord. She and her husband of forty-four years make their home in sunny southern California.

eBay Encounter

by Jeri Odell

Dedication

For Rob and Kelsy:
I'm glad you waited for God's perfect gift in each other.
May all the dreams He's placed in your heart bear fruit.
I love you both.
Mom

Every good and perfect gift is from above,
coming down from the Father. . . .
JAMES 1:17

Chapter 1

You did it, honey, you did it!" Jonica Granger's mom hugged her a little too tightly, knocking her graduation cap to the floor.

"Of course she did it, Bethany. Did you ever doubt for a minute that she would?" John Granger swooped over and plucked his daughter's cap off the floor of the McKale Memorial Center just as someone nearly tromped on it. He placed it atop her curls, and she adjusted it. His light brown eyes beamed with pride as he hugged her close. "This girl of ours hasn't missed a beat since she started setting goals in fifth grade." His wide grin only reaffirmed his obvious pleasure in her focused plans and successes. "A master's degree in business!" He tenderly rubbed his hand across the leather folder in which her diploma resided.

Oh, how she loved this family of hers. The last few years, since she'd lived out of state, she'd noticed that both her mom and her dad had begun to show the wear of years. Gray wove itself throughout Dad's glossy mink-brown hair, and Mom's hazel eyes now sported permanent laugh lines. Still, they made a striking couple, and growing up, she never doubted her parents' love—for her or each other.

While her parents gushed over all of her accomplishments, doubt ate at Jonica. *Have I made the biggest mistake of my life?* She glanced around the crowded basketball court and wondered if any of the other master's recipients battled the uncertainties she faced.

At first goal setting had been a game—win the spelling bee in fifth grade, get straight A's in junior high, become student body president, graduate valedictorian from high school, earn a BA in music, get her master's in business from the University of Arizona. . . The more goals she'd set, the more excited her parents had become. Her dad displayed her list on the fridge like a prized trophy and checked off each goal as she completed it. Though she thanked God for her successes, she wondered if she'd lost sight of His plans for her.

"Thanks for setting the bar so high, Joni," her younger brother, Jack, complained. "I'm only in my freshman year, and do you know the expectations they have for my college career? All thanks to you, I might add." He, too, gave her the Granger hug, so tightly she could barely breathe. She wondered when he'd gotten so tall; he now towered over her five-five frame. His curly mop of honey-colored hair matched hers exactly.

When he loosened his hold, Jonica quipped, "You know my number one goal has always been to make your life difficult."

"And of course you succeeded with that objective, too." Jessica added an eye roll to her statement as she bounced Jonica's chubby, dark-haired nephew on her hip. Her smile and wink let Jonica know how proud she was, as well. Everyone said they shared the same wide smile—dimples and all.

Jonica reached for her older sister's son, and Tristyn plunged toward her. She nestled the toddler close and rubbed her cheek against his velvet-soft one. Used to both family and friends teasing her about being the goal-settingest girl in the entire world, she didn't let their jokes faze her. Planning obviously worked for her.

Then the doubts resurfaced—*I just wonder if I made the wrong plans.* She really didn't want to run a business—she desired to write music. Her mother and grandparents had given her a deep love for words and music—how she yearned to put the two together. But the logical, left side of her brain always shot down her creative longings. First you find a way to make a living—then you follow your dreams.

"An upscale antique store and art gallery is just the ticket to a dream come true." Her mother kissed Tristyn's pudgy cheek.

Jonica bit her lip. *It is a dream come true—just not my dream.* Her mom loved antiques, but Jonica, not so much. When Jonica decided she wanted to be an entrepreneur, her mom suggested an antique store. Since she lacked a better idea, she went with it.

Jonica lifted her chin and sucked in a determined breath. She could string words together by night and sell antiques by day. Someday, when her songs began to sell, her parents could retire, move to Tucson, and run her antique store, because she'd be in Nashville or somewhere similar writing songs that moved people and changed lives.

In the meantime, Jonica needed to hunt for some retail space, preferably up in the Campbell-Skyline area, and she'd have to start amassing antiques. She had her business plan in place and in six months would have her store up and running. Thank heaven for the inheritance she'd received from Grandfather Granger. Yes—this was the right thing to do. Songwriting could be a wonderful hobby, but not an easy or lucrative way to pay the rent. Running a business would provide a nice living and give her parents peace of mind that she'd chosen well.

∽

"eBay seems like the perfect place to find some steals for your store," Sheryl assured Jonica as she raised a forkful of pasta to her lips. She and her two roommates sat around Ana's retro table eating dinner. Their shared kitchen resembled a 1950s diner.

Ana nodded her agreement while she chomped on a breadstick. After swallowing, she added, "Lots of people know nothing about antiques, so they practically give away valuable treasures. Treasures you need for your store."

Jonica weighed their words, studying her friends. Both were brunettes, though Ana's hair was a few shades darker than Sheryl's.

She shrugged. "Maybe you're right. I was thinking more along the lines of estate sales, but I've discovered there aren't too many of those in Tucson. Yet I *so* dislike the Internet," Jonica reminded them. She took another bite of her salad.

"We'll help you," the twosome chimed in unison.

"Can't. I'm busy. It's my night for dishes," Jonica said. She didn't enjoy surfing the Net or shopping on the Net—even e-mail was nothing more than a necessary evil.

"As soon as the kitchen is cleaned up, we'll sign you on,"

Sheryl assured her as she finished her pasta. "I'll even help so you'll get done quicker."

She wasn't sure she wanted to get done quicker. "Have either of you ever used eBay?" Jonica asked, rising from the table and carrying her plate and milk glass to the sink.

"I have." Sheryl nodded her head, her long straight hair brushing against her cheeks. "I sometimes find things for my classroom on there for a steal."

"I've browsed but never purchased." Ana joined her at the sink.

"You'll need a name to sign in under." Sheryl handed Jonica her plate.

Jonica rinsed the three red stoneware dishes. "How about Tucson's Antique Queen?"

"No way. You don't want people to know where you live," Ana assured her.

"Or that you're interested or knowledgeable about antiques," Sheryl chimed in.

"Incognito, huh?" Jonica closed the dishwasher and turned the dial to START. "Why?"

"There are a lot of nuts out there. Anonymity is best." Ana headed to the computer nestled in the corner of their living room with Jonica following.

Ana settled onto the padded chair and rolled forward toward the computer desk. Her nimble fingers typed in "www.ebay.com," and up popped the bright letters signifying they'd arrived at the hottest shopping spot on the Net—the site with 135 million customers and 1.8 billion items. Ana clicked the mouse on REGISTER, and they were off. After typing in Jonica's name, address, city, state, zip code, and phone number, Ana entered Jonica's e-mail address. Next came the dreadful task of choosing an eBay user ID. After several attempts, Jonica settled on "Shoppingirl007."

Ana slid out of the seat, and Jonica took the chair. She found the antique section and checked out what the world of technology offered. Scrolling through the items, she was overwhelmed by how little she knew and how far she had to go. Could she possibly open a store in five months and three weeks? Was she nuts to try? Then she thought of the list hanging on the fridge back home in Bakersfield. It was the last box her dad had to check off. Could she steal that pleasure from him?

❦

Houston James studied his antique store's numbers in Quicken and rechecked each column—just to be certain he hadn't forgotten to enter something. His heart raced faster. Sure enough—the numbers didn't lie. They'd had a good year—a very good year, to be exact.

"Dad, we did it! We sure enough did." When Houston was excited, his Texas accent thickened.

His dad looked up from the counter, where he stood near the cash register. "What'd we do, son?" A gray eyebrow lifted over a bright blue eye—eyes that were said to match Houston's exactly.

"We have enough profit to start our Tucson store without touching our reserves." Certain his dad's grin mirrored his own, Houston rose from the computer, and they exuberantly gave each other pats on the back.

"That's wonderful, son. A job well done—and in only five years." The elder Houston James shook his head. "Teach all those naysayers not to mess with my boy." His tone filled with parental pride.

Houston knew his dad was remembering the man at the bank who didn't feel they were a safe bet to open an antique store in the Scottsdale area. He'd quoted the statistics on failed businesses. So his dad put all of his rodeo savings into the pot and risked everything on Houston's dream. He'd more than paid his dad back, and now they were ready to expand! He couldn't quit grinning.

He glanced around the small but well-stocked store. He bought the antiques, and his dad refurbished them. Together they made a great team. After much marketing research, Houston discovered a large hole in the Tucson market. The city, 120 miles to the south, had many low-end stores—with a lot of junk to sift through before you found the true treasures—but nothing like what he and his dad offered at their shop. Most people nowadays didn't have the time to redo; they wanted their antiques in tip-top shape—a service they provided.

"Whoever thought at the ripe old age of thirty you'd be livin' your dream?" His dad's Texas drawl accentuated each word.

"Almost." *Almost—except the wife and kids.* Invariably the sadness hit when the subject arose. He'd never imagined his life would turn out this way. Very, very single. He'd hoped to meet Miss Right in college, marry shortly thereafter, and have two or three kids by now. But for some reason, that wasn't to be.

"You'll meet someone someday, son. It's not like you don't date."

Houston nodded but was no longer sure. He did date—frequently. But rarely did one date lead to a second. Not wanting to waste his time or the lady's, he figured why bother if nothing clicked?

"Any number of women at church would date you in a heartbeat."

"Yeah, but most of them want to lasso a guy and drag him to the altar—almost sight unseen. As long as a fellow's breathing, that's all that matters. I want more than that. Why do they all seem so desperate and ready to settle? And why is Miss Right so hard to find?" Houston paced across the width of the store.

"I don't think you'll ever find Miss Right in one date. Why don't you give some poor girl a fighting chance? Maybe three dates?" His dad dusted off a prize Joerns mahogany gentleman's dresser. The chest had red leather trim—a stunning, rare style with a full-size cedar drawer.

"By date three, they're talking china patterns, and I still can't decide if I'd even want to kiss them. So if I don't feel at least interested, why move on to that point?"

Houston returned to his computer, and Froglips1977 signed in to eBay to do his daily search for affordable antiques. No, instead of this continuous never-ending dating ritual, he'd decided about a month ago to let God bring the girl to him. He'd been at a singles' conference at the large church he attended in Scottsdale, and he'd laid his desire for a wife on the altar. He gave up the search and vowed to trust God—whether Miss Right ever showed up or not.

In any case, he'd continue to throw himself into his business and his church. He'd pray to be content whatever the circumstance. After all, if Paul found contentment in chains, surely Houston could find it in singleness. Now on to finding those extraordinary pieces at ordinary prices. . .

"If only this new eBay princess, Shoppingirl, would find another place to shop. Newbies always run up the prices and cause more headaches than they're worth."

"Huh?" his dad asked.

"I'm just complaining about some new girl who's been shopping eBay this past week. My personal pet peeve is inexperienced shoppers who force me to spend more money than is necessary. Maybe I'll just e-mail her and give her a piece of my mind."

"In a nice, Christian way, of course." His dad's reminder checked him.

"Of course." He'd never actually chew anyone out, but he'd at least let her know—in a nice way—what a pain in his side she'd become.

Chapter 2

Jonica's frustration level climbed hourly. For the past week, she'd spent a large portion of each day on her computer scanning the eBay site. She'd found countless items she'd loved to have purchased but unfortunately always got outbid. "This is the most frustrating thing I've ever done." She let out a long, loud sigh. "There must be some secret to all of this that I've yet to discover. I've bid on over four hundred items, and not one of them was awarded to me. Not one! Some guy named Froglips seems to want everything I want—only he gets it."

"Is there someone you can ask for help?" Ana hollered from the kitchen. "Maybe some eBay guru somewhere?"

Jonica stretched her neck from side to side and exited eBay. "No one that I know of." She went to her e-mail account. Her heart dropped to her knees. She had an unopened message from none other than Froglips. With a nervous stomach, she clicked on the envelope and opened his letter.

Darlin',

If you're going to play the eBay game, at least do us all

a favor and learn the rules. You're driving up the prices for everyone and not benefiting yourself or anyone else.

Yours,
Froglips

"How dare he! He called me *darlin'*!" Indignation laced each of her words. She wrinkled her nose.

"Who?" Sheryl asked. Now both she and Ana were hovering behind the computer chair, apparently reading over her shoulder.

"Maybe Mr. Froglips is the answer to your prayers."

Ana's statement perplexed Jonica. "As if!"

"He sounds like the guru you're in need of," Sheryl gently reminded.

"I'm not responding to some jerk who calls me darlin' and thinks he's the ultimate authority on eBay etiquette." Jonica rose from the computer chair and walked toward her bedroom. She paused in the hall and faced her roommates, hands on her hips. "I mean, how dare this guy write me and critique me. Did I ask for his advice? I don't *think* so."

"Maybe he's as frustrated as you are," Sheryl suggested. "If I were you, I'd write and ask him for some pointers. He suggested you learn the rules, so why don't you ask him to teach you?"

"Because he's arrogant and pompous. I will not give him the satisfaction." Jonica closed her bedroom door behind her—fighting the urge to slam it.

☙

Jonica spent the next week in the same cycle. Bidding, rebidding, and in the end, always losing the item to someone else—often Froglips. "That guy infuriates me. He's as annoying as fingernails on a blackboard," she told Ana and Sheryl at dinner. "He puts in his last-second bid and always takes the stuff I want. Stuff I would have paid more for—if he hadn't run the clock out."

"We told you what to do," Sheryl reminded her.

"I know—but unfortunately, I don't think I could write him and be civil at the same time."

"Let one of us write to him," Ana said. Her almost-black eyes sparkled with mischief.

"No way! You two would get me in some sort of mess."

They both snickered.

"Like the time we e-mailed Professor Smyth on your behalf to ask for help and you ended up on a date with the man?"

She glared into Sheryl's green eyes, rolled her own eyes, and shook her head. "Precisely."

"Well then, we'll censor your e-mail," Ana suggested.

"Good idea," Sheryl said. "You write it, and we'll have editorial control. No one hits SEND unless the three of us agree that it's appropriate."

Jonica pondered the suggestion. She did need to do something. She'd lost almost a month and had no store and no antiques. Her final goal of opening a store within six months slipped further out of reach. They were right—she must act.

"Okay—I'll do it. I'll write Mr. Froglips, and then we'll all pull together to shape the letter into something polite but pointed."

Jonica rose from the table, leaving her dinner mostly un-eaten. This guy had gotten under her skin. She settled at the computer desk, elbow on the work surface, head resting on her hand, and played with the Shirley Temple curls she'd been born with, contemplating where and how to start. "Lord, show me the best way to handle this guy." She remembered a sermon from a couple of weeks ago. *Laughter is good medicine, and humor can defuse most any situation.* "The only problem is, I'm not that funny."

Jonica reread the e-mail.

Darlin',

> *If you're going to play the eBay game, at least do us all a favor and learn the rules. You're driving up the prices for everyone and not benefiting yourself or anyone else.*

Yours,
Froglips

She again cringed at the use of *darlin'*. Then she typed:

Dear Mr. Lips,

> *I wasn't sure if I should be bold and just call you Frog, but settled on the more formal approach and used your surname. When I first received your e-mail, I wasn't certain it was meant for me—after all, my name isn't* Darlin', *now, is it? But after reading it several times, I decided it was meant for me, and you just had my name confused with someone else's. So to clear up any future confusion, you may call me Miss Girl, Shoppin', or SG for short. Please feel free to use whichever of those you choose, but I'd appreciate no further use of the term* darlin'—*if you please.*

I do plan to play the eBay game and would love for someone to teach me. Were you volunteering?

And my apologies for driving up the prices. I was only hoping to nab a few antique pieces, and apparently, you and I have similar tastes.

Yours truly,
Shoppin' Girl

Jonica knew she'd failed to be funny, but at least maybe she'd hit the right note—she hoped so. After Ana's and Sheryl's approval and with the mere touch of a button, her e-mail floated out into cyberspace, headed for Froglips's computer.

∞

An e-mail from Shoppingirl was the last thing Houston expected to find in his inbox. After all, he'd sent his a week ago to no avail. She'd continued to run prices up, so he'd accepted her as a competitor—an inexperienced, unwanted competitor, but a competitor nonetheless.

He opened the e-mail and chuckled at her salutation— Dear Mr. Lips. He finished reading her note, admiring her spunk but wondering if he should be teaching her the tricks he'd learned over the years. After all, she was in all honesty his opponent. If he taught her well, would he ever win a bid again? The inner battle began, but he'd always been a sap for damsels in distress.

Houston was just closing up shop for the evening. He'd planned to hit the midweek service at church on his way home. But how could he ignore her honest, open plea to learn? Tapping a pencil on his desk, he had an internal argument with himself. WWJD—that had been the big catchphrase when he was in high school. What would Jesus do? Sometimes he had no idea, but this evening he felt fairly certain. He'd grab a bite, stop for the church service, and write to SG first thing tomorrow. Do unto others—it was the golden rule in Texas.

About eight o'clock the next morning, Houston booted up his computer. It took up most of his entire desk in his bedroom where it resided. He didn't have any space for it elsewhere in his tiny apartment, though. He'd always thought he'd get something bigger but just never had. He pulled up his e-mail and composed a reply to the message from Shoppingirl.

Hello, Shoppingirl,

I want to start with a heartfelt apology from this Texas boy. Where I hail from, darlin' is a term of endearment—not a derogatory name in the least. I, in all honesty, meant no harm or foul by addressing you as such. Please forgive the offense and know none was intended.

Second, there will be no further use of darlin'—not now, not ever.

I wasn't volunteering to teach you, but if you'd like me to, I can. However, I'd rather do it by phone. It's just easier to communicate clearly that way. If you are comfortable with that arrangement, I'll give you my cell number. If not, I understand. We live in a world where trust— especially with strangers—is hard earned.

Yours,
Mr. Lips

Clicking the SEND button, Houston stood and headed for the shower. He was running late for work.

∞

The following night right before he crawled into bed, he checked his e-mail one last time to see if Shoppingirl had responded. To his surprise, she had.

Hi,

> *Thanks for the apology and for clearing the air about the dreaded D word that we'll never mention again. I realize I've never actually known anyone from Texas before. I come from California, and some people can somehow misconstrue almost every word used for a woman and make it disrespectful.*

> *I'm sorry if I put you on the spot, asking you to teach me how to use eBay. I don't like computers in general, I like the Net even less, and I absolutely abhor e-mail, so I ask myself: Why am I spending time writing to a complete stranger? And I don't even know. I guess you sort of felt like a lifeline. You've obviously figured out this whole world of Internet trade and antiques. Will I ever?*

> *I'd like to call you. I really would. I'd like for you to teach me everything you know about eBay and antiques, but my roommates say no way. I promised I wouldn't. So thanks but no thanks.*

> *SG*

Her e-mail sounded slightly melancholy, and somehow

through words she managed to convey her mood to him. He shot off a quick note.

Hey, California Girl,
   Isn't California the place for dreamin'? Don't give up. Just don't bid so early. Wait until right before the close. That will at least give you a fighting chance.
   So I'm curious—why the sudden interest in eBay and antiques?

Texas

❦

It was three days before he heard back from her.

Hi, Texas,
   I'm opening an antique store. I just received my MBA a month ago and am trying to gather enough merchandise to fill a store. So far, I'm batting zero. How about you? Are you a collector?

California

Houston smiled. No wonder the immediate connection with her; she was a kindred spirit.

Hello again,
   Now I know why we're connecting. I, too, run an antique store. Thus all the purchases on eBay. So you are a California dreamer—and your dream is your own store.

Texas

This time her reply was slower in coming. Houston figured he wouldn't hear from her again when her reply arrived almost a week later.

> *Texas,*
>
> *Can I tell you something? Something I've never told another living soul. I guess you're safe because I don't know you and we'll never meet face-to-face. I am a California dreamer, but this isn't my dream. I want to write music. An antique store is a goal, nothing more. What is your dream?*
>
>

SG

Houston felt saddened by her announcement. He waited a couple of days to reply, pondering and praying for wisdom.

> *Cali,*
>
> *Don't settle. Chase your dream, not your goal. One may bring you satisfaction, but the other will ignite your soul with passion. Only your dream can fulfill you. I believe God puts the dreams in our hearts. Our job is to bring them to fruition.*
>
> *I'm thirty years old and living my dream—at least most of it.*

He decided to forgo mentioning the missing wife and kids from his dream lest she misconstrue the comment. All he needed was this cyberspace girl to get the wrong idea and think he was an eligible, marriage-minded man.

My grandparents raised me, and because of them I have a deep love and respect for all things old. Nothing thrills my heart like finding a beautiful antique and restoring it to its original glory. Then finding the perfect home and knowing the piece will be loved and cherished forever—like a part of the family. That, my friend, brings incredible satisfaction—a satisfaction I hope you find, doing whatever the good Lord leads you to do.

Tomorrow I'll be away all day, but would love to meet you here in cyberspace about the same time.

Until then—dream a sweet dream.

Texas

Tomorrow he was driving to Tucson, meeting with a commercial broker, and looking at some available retail space. But there was something about Shoppingirl that intrigued him, and he looked forward to their next visit.

Chapter 3

Jonica reread the e-mail from Texas about a dozen times. His message evoked many emotions, but most of all she just wanted to feel as deeply as he felt. She'd always loved words, and this man had a way with them. He was tender and deep and sincere. She didn't share his note with her roommates—she just wanted to ponder it and cherish it.

Jonica printed out his message and carried it with her through the day. While at a stoplight on the way to Starbucks to meet her commercial broker, she once again read his first line. *"Don't settle. Chase your dream, not your goal."* The statement placed such a yearning within her heart that it literally ached.

"Am I settling, God? Is that what I'm doing? I mean, You tell me in Your Word that I need to work hard. Opening a store is working hard. Writing music probably won't even pay the bills." She shifted her Civic into first gear and let out the clutch. "Texas, you've made me feel more confused than ever." The only thing she knew for sure was that she would meet him in cyberspace tonight. She wanted to know more about him and read more of his passionate prose.

Jonica turned her car into the Starbucks parking lot off River and Campbell. This upscale coffee shop was nicer than the one near her house in midtown. She ran her fingers through her collarbone-length hair and fluffed out the curls. Walking from her car, she admired the bird-of-paradise plants, most covered in red and orange blossoms. They were one of her favorite things about the Southwest.

Since she'd arrived a few minutes ahead of the scheduled meeting, she got in line and purchased a tall vanilla latte. Then she straightened her skirt and settled into one of the light oak chairs at a small table for two. Gazing around the room at the other patrons, she wondered what Texas might look like. Was he tall, dark, and handsome? Was his tone husky with a slow Texas drawl?

"Jonica?" A woman's voice drew her out of her reverie.

Jonica nodded and stood.

The woman wearing a conservative navy business suit held out her right hand. "I'm Sherrie with Brown Brothers."

Jonica shook Sherrie's hand. "Nice to meet you."

"And it's wonderful to meet you." Sherrie took the chair across from Jonica. "Thanks for calling our firm. After our initial conversation, I've found two properties that I thought might suit your needs, as well as your wants. Shall we head up Campbell to Skyline to view the first one?"

Jonica agreed, following Sherrie to her white Expedition. She opened the passenger door, revealing the SUV's tan leather interior, and slid into the kidskin-soft seat, and they pulled out of the parking lot. After a quick left, they drove north on Campbell toward an elite section of town. The Santa Catalina

Mountains stood majestically before them proclaiming God's glory. Exhilaration swept through Jonica at the sight. Ascending into the foothills, they followed the winding road.

"I don't think I could ever grow tired of this view—it's gorgeous." Awe filled Jonica's words.

Sherrie glanced at her and smiled. "This would be a wonderful drive to work every day, wouldn't it? Not only the mountains, but the foothills are quite beautiful, too."

Jonica nodded, admiring the saguaro-laden hills; the cacti raising their arms in praise to their Creator. The Palo Verde trees were covered in yellow blossoms. "The desert has definitely stolen my heart, and I never could have guessed it would." She admired the scene before her. "You know, the houses along here are none too shabby, either."

They both laughed, knowing most of the homes along this drive were probably in the million-dollar range.

"I love the red tile roofs," Sherrie said.

"Me, too. Who knows? Maybe someday. . ." Jonica would love to own a southwestern home, and here in the foothills would be the perfect spot.

"So tell me a little about yourself," Sherrie encouraged.

"I grew up in Bakersfield, California, wanted a change, and was offered a full ride at ASU, so I did my undergrad up in Phoenix. My roommate in the dorm was from Tucson, so I came down here with her fairly often and fell in love with the place—everything, that is, but the traffic and lack of freeways."

Sherrie laughed. "I think we're still hoping to be small town, but that's tough with three-quarters of a million people trying to share the road systems."

The Catalinas grew ever closer, looming before them. Sherrie turned just before Skyline into the Paloma Village Center. Jonica breathed in her surroundings, her eyes hungry to see every detail. She loved the architecture of the flat-roofed terra-cotta building. This was it—this was where she wanted her shop to reside. Everything about the place seemed perfect—the view, the ambience. She loved it all.

"I'm convinced this will be your favorite, and I think this one will best suit your needs and, more important, your goals."

They exited the SUV, and Sherrie unlocked the door to the vacant shop. Jonica noticed there was a gallery right down the sidewalk. Perfect. Hopefully they would draw clientele for each other. She swept through the door, the large room beckoning her.

"Sherrie—this is the spot. I really want this place. It's quaint with a definite Southwest flair." Jonica began making plans in her head. "I could put the larger pieces over here." She pointed to a sidewall. "And the cash register back here out of the way."

Sherrie grinned and nodded, encouraging her to dream and see the place with all its potential. "Make it your own."

Jonica spun around, arms thrown open. Even if she didn't feel passionate about owning an antique store, she did feel passionate about this perfect little shop. "I love it. I absolutely love it!"

Sometime during her ardent proclamations, two gentlemen had entered the building, and both seemed transfixed by her enthusiastic display. Jonica's cheeks grew warm. Sherrie stepped forward and introduced herself. Jonica was grateful Sherrie was taking the attention off her. The older man of the two shook

Sherrie's hand. He was a broker, too, and he and Sherrie got involved in shoptalk.

It was the younger fellow who'd caught Jonica's attention. Something about his penetrating, bright blue eyes drew her. "Hello," he said while extending his right hand. The one word was spoken with a Southern drawl. She grasped his hand, and his grip warmed her.

"Hi." She tried not to gape, but he looked nothing like her idea of a Southern boy. He reminded her of a Californian with his golden hair and skin, a surfer boy with muscles peeking out from under the sleeves of his T-shirt. He had a scruffy face—about three days' growth, but not enough to qualify as a beard and mustache.

But when he smiled, there was nothing scruffy about him. He had two of the biggest dimples she'd ever seen. Man, was he good-looking, and she never thought of golden boys that way. She normally liked the tall, dark, and handsome type. This guy was only one for three. He was tall, and though very attractive, he wasn't handsome in the conventional suit-and-tie kind of way.

⚬❧

Houston tried to check out the building he'd just leased, but his eyes kept wandering to the beauty before him. Everything about her spelled adorable, from her nose that turned up at the end to her honey-hued curly mop. Her enthusiasm first caught his attention, but her embarrassed smile held it. The strangest thought hit him—*Is she the one God's dropping in my lap?* He'd never had that sort of immediate attraction to a woman before.

But sadly, in only moments, he'd break her heart, because she loved this place, and he'd just unknowingly snatched it out from under her. Then she'd probably want nothing to do with him.

"Out lookin' for retail space?"

Jonica nodded and eyed him warily.

"Me, too." He didn't want to break the news before he had a chance to know her a bit better. "Do you live in Tucson?"

"Yes." She glanced over to where her Realtor and his discussed business in low tones.

"I'm going to be a newcomer. Moving down from Phoenix. Do you know any good churches?"

The question thawed her a degree or two. "I attend Casas. It's a large church and definitely teaches the Word."

Sounds like she might be a Christian.

"You can get directions off their Web site."

She's keeping solid boundaries in place.

"Any chance you'd meet a stranger for dinner and fill him in on the do's and don'ts of Tucson living?" he asked, flashing her a sincere smile.

"You know, I haven't been here that long myself—only a couple of years. I'm probably not the right person for the job." But something in her eyes belied her words. A part of her wanted to, of that he was sure.

"You ready?" her Realtor asked.

She nodded. "Nice meeting you." And she was out the door. Well, so much for that one God may have placed in his path. She was long gone, and he'd never even discovered her name.

"What do you think?" Bill asked. "Does she look as good in person as she did in the online virtual tour?" He meant the shop, of course, but for a moment Houston related the question to the mystery girl. *If it's meant to be, Lord, You'll have to make it happen.*

"She's perfect. Just what I was looking for. Sounds like the space was just what those two were searching for, as well." Houston glanced at the door through which the two women had exited moments before.

"I think she would have taken it. Good thing we got here first."

"What sort of shop did she plan to open?" Houston wondered aloud.

Bill shrugged. "Her agent said something about a gallery of some sort. I didn't catch the details."

Houston shrugged. *Easy come, easy go. At least that's what they say.* He did some measuring and wrote down some figures. Then he and his dad would put their heads together and figure out how to best utilize the space. As they left the complex, he marveled at the incredible views. To the north stood mountains draped in purple majesty, reminding him of God and His majesty. To the south the Tucson valley spread far and wide. He'd bet the night view was even more spectacular with lights dancing across the city. There was something about Tucson he really liked. Maybe it was the simplicity in comparison to Phoenix.

Chapter 4

I'm sorry, Jonica. I know you really loved that spot, but this one will be nice, too," Sherrie assured her.

Jonica wasn't convinced. Nothing could beat where they'd just been. "Where do you think that guy was from?"

"Huh?" Sherrie raised her eyebrow. "Oh, you mean the good-looking client?"

"Yeah."

"Texas. I have family there, and he definitely had the same twang."

Jonica thought of Froglips. "Texas, huh? Do they all look like that down there?"

Sherrie giggled. "No, sadly, they don't; but if they did, I'd be moving."

"Mmm."

Sherrie turned right into Campbell Village, stopping at the putty-colored building. Jonica did like the look of it.

"There was a gallery in here at one time, but they closed up shop a few months ago. I think that might draw people who come by looking for the old place to your new place. I feel it's ripe for another artsy type shop. And compared to the low-rent antique district over on Country Club, this is an upscale site, yet only a couple of miles away." Sherrie paused. "What do you think?"

"It's not Skyline and Campbell, but it is charming. Let's check out the interior." Jonica unbuckled her seat belt and hopped out.

They toured the inside. The square footage was comparable; however, the views were sadly lacking. But all in all, Jonica felt it was the next best thing. Sherrie agreed. They moved out to the porch.

"You ready to sign the lease?"

"I don't know." Jonica gazed around the area, noting the other occupants. "It's mere blocks from my house, but there's no Starbucks in the same complex." She referred to the already-leased shop they'd just visited. "The drive won't be nearly as much fun, but gas will cost me next to nothing." Jonica verbally processed the pros and cons. "I think I'd like to think on it overnight. Can I let you know in the morning?"

"Sure."

Jonica appreciated the fact that Sherrie didn't remind her that another guy like Mr. Texas could come along and snag it out from under her. She already knew that and didn't want the reminder. She had to pray about this decision and make certain she should move forward.

Sherrie drove her back to her car. They bid each other good-bye, and Jonica drove home. Both of her roomies were gone, so she had the house to herself. She paced through it, talking aloud to God. "Do You keep closing doors because I'm on the wrong path?" It sort of seemed that way. So far she had not one antique to stock her store with, and the storefront she wanted was taken just minutes before her arrival. She didn't know whether God was closing doors or she just needed to learn perseverance.

Jonica spent the evening in her room with her Bible and prayer journal. She skipped dinner, knowing sometimes in fasting the voice of God was louder and clearer. At nine o'clock she headed for the computer, looking forward to a visit with Texas. When she signed on, he'd already sent her an e-mail.

> *Hey, Cali,*
> *Did you dream a sweet dream last night?*
>
> > *T*

Jonica smiled and typed her reply. She loved his pet phrase—dream a sweet dream.

> *Texas,*
> *I did dream a sweet dream today, but sadly, not all dreams come true.*
>
> > *SG*

She wondered what words of wisdom he'd offer. Something about him calmed her and centered her.

> *Cali,*
> *Sometimes life is funny that way. Amazingly enough, I had a dream come true today but I don't feel good about it, because sometimes when we win, others lose.*

Boy, did she know that story firsthand. Maybe that big, tall Texan who'd stolen her store out from under her had some remorse, as well.

> *Have you been on eBay today? There are some antiques on there that close out tomorrow. Put in a bid about five minutes before the close. That way you're not competing against yourself. Timing is everything.*
>
> *T*

"He is the nicest guy." She sighed.

> *Texas,*
> *Thanks for the advice. I'll give it a shot.*
> *Can I ask you a personal question? Sure, you say. Are you a Christian, and if so, what does that mean to you? (Feel free not to answer.)*
>
> *SG*

She hit SEND with reluctance and waited for his reply.

> *Cali,*
> *I am a Christian, and what that means to me is everything.*

Upon reading his first line, Jonica breathed a huge sigh of relief. He was a kindred spirit. A friend in the Lord. "Thank You, Jesus." She read on.

*As a young boy I invited Jesus into my heart because
I knew I wanted to be in heaven someday with my mom.
Later, I also understood I couldn't meet God's standard of
holiness without Jesus and His sacrifice for my sin.*

*Now walking with the Lord is a daily reality in my
life. I try to always be involved in some sort of Bible study,
but I also just like hanging with Him—you know, talking,
praising, singing. I go to church on Sundays and also try to
catch a midweek service—not because I have to, but because
I enjoy being with other believers. Also, because in God's
Word, He encourages us not to give up meeting together. He
wants us getting together with other Christians.*

Somehow without even hearing his voice, she could perceive
his Texas twang, as Sherrie called it.

Did I answer your question? How about you?

Something in Jonica's heart changed as she read his e-mail.
Was it possible to fall for someone she didn't know? Her grandfather had—head over heels, as a matter of fact. Was she?

Texas,

*You did answer my questions, and quite eloquently, I
might add. I like the way you string words together, and
I like that your beliefs match mine.*

*I'm very sorry you lost your mom at a young age. That
explains why your grandparents raised you. What about
your dad?*

*Anyway, back to the being a Christian topic. I come
from a rich heritage of godly people—people who loved
the Lord and lived for Him. He's been a part of my life
always; even before I realized or recognized Him, He was
there. I, like you, gave my heart to Jesus at a young age and
have always tried to live according to His Word.*

*But my real question, now that I know we are coming
from the same place: How do you discern His will? What
if you're heading toward what you believe is His plan
and suddenly the door slams in your face? If this happens
several times in a row, do I assume God is closing the doors,
or do I assume He is testing me and wants me to practice
perseverance? I'm not very good at this—as you can tell.*

Thanks,
SG

Man, oh man, did Cali ask the hard questions. Houston
got up and walked to the kitchen—just mere steps away from
his bedroom. He rubbed the back of his neck. "Lord, what do I
say? I need You to guide my answer." He opened the tiny fridge
and poured himself a cold drink of water.

He sauntered over to the bookshelf in his miniscule living
room. He pulled his old *Experiencing God* workbook from the
dusty shelf and sank down on the blue plaid love seat—there
wasn't enough space for a full-size couch—and perused
the Bible study he'd done more than once. After finding
the information he searched for, he carried the dog-eared
workbook and his water back to his computer desk. Settling
onto a padded stool, he clicked REPLY.

Cal,

Sorry for the delayed response. I went to search for one of my favorite tools. Did you ever do the Experiencing God workbook by Henry Blackaby? Anyway, it's been a great resource in my life.

One of the things he addresses is the way God speaks to His people, which I think helps discern His will. Blackaby says, "God speaks by the Holy Spirit through the Bible, prayer, circumstances, and the church to reveal Himself, His purposes and His ways." Yes, one of the ways God speaks is through the circumstances in our lives; however, He normally uses more than just circumstances. What are you hearing as you read His Word? What's on your heart in prayer? What is your pastor saying that speaks to you from his sermons? Is it all lining up and pointing in one direction?

The bottom line, Cali, is God wants us to know Him and spend time in His presence. Answers often don't come easy or quick, because He's more interested in us sitting at His feet than sending us off on the right path where most of us would probably barrel ahead on our own.

So my best advice is sit, wait, listen. And I hear you groaning as you read these words. Patience, my friend. Patience.

Houston yawned and glanced at his watch. They'd been visiting for almost an hour.

As for my dad—he's alive and kickin', and that says a lot since he followed the rodeo circuit for more years than a *sane man would have. He's had just about every bone in his body broken or cracked. Thank the good Lord he finally retired. He and I are the best of buddies.*

Well, I've enjoyed talking with you, California Girl, but I'm beat. Long day. You dream a sweet dream.

T

Disappointment hit Jonica, and the letdown surprised her. She wasn't ready for her time with Texas to end. Worse, he didn't mention getting together for another cyberspace conversation. To her, his farewell sounded too final. She'd thoroughly enjoyed the time spent with him. "All good things must end," she reminded herself in a whisper.

She wrote her last e-mail to Texas.

Texas,

Thanks for sharing with me about knowing God's will. What you said makes lots of sense.

You dream a sweet dream, too.

SG

Both Sheryl and Ana had dates tonight, so Jonica was home alone. "What is wrong with me?" she asked her reflection in the entry hall mirror. Everything had gone downhill today—from finding the perfect space for her store to losing her new e-mail pal. Jonica decided the house needed a good cleaning. *What a way to spend a Friday night.* She threw herself into the task with a vengeance. Sometime after midnight, she fell into bed—good and tired.

The following morning Jonica spent a solid chunk of time with the Lord. She reviewed her journal to see what had been on her heart recently. She reviewed her sermon notes from the past couple of Sundays. Everything seemed to be saying, "Be wise and prudent." *Hmm?*

Jonica wandered through the living room and into the kitchen. Both Sheryl and Ana were at the table, drinking coffee and discussing their dates. Jonica poured herself a cup and joined them. "We make a pretty picture," she joked. All three appeared quite disheveled in bathrobes or jammies with hair sticking out in all directions.

"Wonder what Don and Tom would think of us now?" Ana raised an eyebrow in a questioning expression.

All three giggled.

"Hey, Jon, how did the shop hunt go?"

Jonica filled her roommates in on the previous day. Her voice sounded flat and discouraged in her own ears. She shared with them her spiritual struggles and her questions about the next step in her life. "I don't even know if I want to open a store. Am I chasing the wrong dream?"

Sheryl's brows drew together, and two parallel lines formed above the bridge of her nose. "When I finished college and got my first teaching job, I nearly freaked. I went through exactly what you're going through: panic, doubt, uncertainty. The list is endless. It's fear, Jonica. Fear of stepping out and failing. Fear of hating it once you've spent years preparing for it. And we know fear is never to be our motivation, because fear isn't from God."

Ana chimed in. "You think too much. Stop thinking and

follow your plan. Have your plans misled you so far?"

"No," Jonica admitted. "I'm just so afraid my plans aren't God's."

Sheryl jumped up and pointed at her. "There it is again—fear!"

Ana laughed and tugged on Sheryl's robe. "Settle down. You made your point." Then she rested her dark gaze on Jonica. "She's right, you know."

Jonica nodded her acceptance of the truth. She traipsed over to the microwave and reheated her mug of tepid coffee. "So you think it's fear, and I'm reading too much into the closed door?"

Sheryl had settled back into the red padded kitchen chair. "Okay, let's pull the pieces of the puzzle together. You haven't had much success on eBay, but that could just be your lack of experience—not a closed door. The first storefront was already leased, but the second one is ready, willing, and waiting for you to sign on the dotted line."

"The first was way more expensive," Ana reminded her. "Sure, the place had great views, but honestly, was it the wise, prudent choice? I know when I opened my janitorial service, it took awhile for the monthly total to be in the black instead of the red. Those first months the outgo is always more than the income. You have the MBA. You know the stats on failed businesses."

What they were saying made sense. So much sense that her insides calmed and for the first time since graduation, she felt peaceful, restful. "You two are wise beyond your years." Jonica rose to go call Sherrie.

"And prudent, too," Ana threw out, and both she and Sheryl chuckled.

Jonica returned a few minutes later. "You won't believe this. The second one is no longer coming up on Sherrie's computer. She thinks it may have been leased. She's making some calls."

So much for Jonica's peace. . .

Chapter 5

After puttering around her apartment most of the day, Jonica gave in and checked her e-mail. She so badly wanted a note from Texas but was convinced he'd written his last. She was probably too spiritually immature and insecure for a guy like him. He really seemed to know the Lord.

Her heart did a little dip when she saw his name in her inbox. She grinned and clicked on his mail. The day just got brighter.

> *Good morning,*
>   *I'm headed out the door to meet my dad for breakfast. Though I had several new e-mails in my box, the first one I clicked on was from Shoppingirl.*

She understood. His was the first one she clicked on, too. The knowledge warmed her.

> *Your note was short but sweet. Somehow that is how I imagine you—very sweet with a good heart, but then I*

found myself wondering how old you are. I sort of assumed mid- to late twenties because you recently graduated, but it dawned on me—you could be forty or fifty. So, my friend from California—how old are you? Tell me about yourself.

T

"He wants to know about me," she whispered. Her heart longed to know all about him, as well, but she was somewhat terrified by her fast-moving emotions. Leaning her head back, she closed her eyes and sighed.

"What's going on?" Ana asked as she passed through the living room.

Jonica decided to fess up. She swiveled the chair around to watch Ana's reaction. "I'm falling for the guy on the Internet."

Concern sketched itself across her features. "Are you nuts?"

Her raised voice drew Sheryl out of the kitchen. "Who's nuts?"

Ana pointed her tanned finger at Jonica. "Your roommate. She's fallen for some cyberspace dude."

"Jonica, what in the world are you thinking?"

"She's obviously not," Ana accused.

"You guys are the ones who encouraged me to write to him. When I did, he wrote back."

"And in what—three or four weeks—you've fallen for him?" Sheryl shook her head in exasperation.

"One of the girls who works for me met a guy on the Internet—in a Christian chat room. After corresponding—more than a few days, I might add—she agreed to a date. Being young and not too bright, she had him pick her up at her house."

Ana's face showed disgust. "He raped her." Her voice had taken on a deadly serious tone. "Three times, Jonica. Three times. She was so beaten up, her own mother didn't recognize her."

"But this guy's a Christian," Jonica assured them.

"How do you know?" Sheryl asked. "People can be anyone or anything they want on the Net. They sort of reinvent themselves. A lady I work with met a guy in a singles' chat room. He ended up being a sixty-year-old married pervert instead of the thirty-year-old bachelor he claimed."

"But I didn't meet Texas in a—"

"Texas—his name is Texas?" Ana wore her Doubting Thomas expression. "Get real."

Jonica turned and pulled a folder out of the file drawer designated as hers. "We've never actually exchanged names. Here, just read these." She shoved the file folder toward Ana, but Sheryl intervened and grabbed it first. She headed into the kitchen and plopped down at the table, Ana and Jonica on her heels.

Jonica kept the printed e-mails in chronological order, so after Sheryl read the first one, she passed it to Ana.

After perusing a few, Sheryl said, "He's charming. I suddenly want him to call me darlin'."

Ana piped in, "I think he's smart and cunning. 'Call me—it's easier to communicate by phone.' He's trying too hard to get too friendly too fast."

Jonica's defensive hackles rose. "But when I said no, he never pressed the issue."

They both looked up from their spots at the table with "duh" expressions on their faces. "Predators know just when and how hard to push. We teach our fifth graders that."

Feeling stupid, Jonica hung her head. They'd never believe what she knew in her heart.

"And you—" Ana's accusatory tone made Jonica cringe. "You not only come across as charming, but vulnerable and needy. Easy prey, Jonica. Easy prey."

" 'I guess you sort of felt like a lifeline.' " Sheryl quoted a sentence Jonica had written, shaking her head in disapproval. "And what is this?" She stood and waved one of the e-mails at Jonica. "You told a complete stranger you want to write music. You've never even told us that!"

"Best friends are always the last to know." Sarcasm laced each of Ana's words.

Somehow this plan had backfired. Jonica had counted on their seeing Texas the way she did, but instead they ripped both him and her to shreds.

"He says he's thirty years old and living his dream—at least most of it. I'm sure you're the missing piece to the rest of it." Sheryl rolled her eyes.

"Yeah, and he's probably eighty."

"Maybe he's not even a he," Sheryl said.

"You guys have more than made your point." Jonica left the room. In her bedroom, the message light blinked on her cell phone. It was Sherrie, and she wouldn't know anything until Monday. Jonica lay across her bed thinking about Texas. Somehow, in her heart of hearts, she knew he was the real deal. His testimony and knowledge of God couldn't be faked, could they?

A half hour or so later, there was a knock on her door.

Sheryl and Ana entered upon her bidding them to come in, though they were the last two people on earth she wanted to see right then. Sheryl set the e-mail folder on her dresser, and they both took a spot on the foot of her bed.

Ana started. "Jonica, we're sorry we were so rough on you."

Sheryl jumped in. "We love you and don't want you to end up being another statistic."

"I know." Jonica forced a smile.

"Maybe he is the real deal," Sheryl said.

"The Christian stuff sure seemed authentic," Ana agreed.

"We will give you our permission—like you need it—to move forward with awareness and trepidation." Sheryl chewed on her lower lip.

Jonica knew she wasn't convinced this was the best avenue. "What do you mean?" she questioned.

"Write to him, but don't ever tell him your real name or where you live." Ana tossed out their stipulations. "We get to monitor all e-mails. If anything is a red flag, you will promise to stop all contact."

"You sound like my mother—when I was about ten." Jonica wasn't sure she wanted to follow their "rules."

"It's for your own good," Sheryl assured her. "This could be a dangerous situation. Since you're smitten, you aren't thinking clearly."

Jonica knew that part was true. She saw no danger in Texas at all. Maybe that's what all young women thought, even the ones who ended up dead.

"You need to find out his name so we can check him out," Ana said.

"This feels smarmy." Jonica wasn't sure she wanted any part of their strategy. "And how am I going to learn his name without telling him mine?"

"We've got a plan." Sheryl smiled.

"Somehow I knew you would." Jonica rolled her eyes. This wouldn't be the first plan they'd concocted. And they almost always backfired.

"Use your middle name. Tell him you're Beth," Ana said.

Jonica shook her head. "You want me to lie?"

"It's not a lie," Sheryl assured her. "Your name is Jonica Beth Granger. You can be Beth John. Not at *all* a lie—just a slight rearranging."

"Remind me again why I'm doing this." She was fairly certain God didn't approve of rearranging—slight or not.

"Because it's worth finding out if he's the real deal."

Ana nodded in agreement. "Plus you're already crazy about the guy—and maybe he's crazy about you."

"It's worth the risk as long as we make sure you're protected from danger."

"What about my heart?" Jonica asked. "Who will protect it?"

❦

Houston gave up hope of hearing from Shoppingirl again. It had been almost a week since their last correspondence, and foolish as it sounded, he missed her. As the days passed, he pondered the text they'd shared and faced the fact: He had an old-fashioned crush on her. Then he freaked himself out—what if she was a fifty-year-old woman? The thought scared the very breath out of him.

Still, every time he pulled up his e-mail, like he was doing right now, he scanned for her name. She must be a fraud, because she wasn't willing to reveal anything about herself. But nothing about her seemed phony. What did it matter? She'd disappeared. *Move on, buddy. Life's too short to dwell on—*

"She wrote! She finally replied." He danced a victory dance before pulling up her note.

Hey, Texas,

It's been awhile. I just wasn't sure I was ready to reveal more about myself to you. It's a scary world, and when you can't see someone's expression as you talk or hear the inflections in their voice, how do you know the words are real? Even when they're standing before you, you can't always discern truth from fiction.

I'm twenty-five. A middle child from Bakersfield. Older sister, younger brother. My sister is married and has an adorable son. My parents are still married and still in love. I had a middle-class life—nothing special and yet very, very special, if you know what I mean. To have a family that's intact and seminormal is nothing short of a gift these days.

My name is Beth and my so-called life has always gone according to plan, until this last month. Now nothing is falling into place. I haven't successfully located a spot for my store or any antiques to fill it. I've tried to follow your advice regarding eBay, but antiques seem to be in high demand. I've noticed you've been steering clear of anything I bid on. You might as well not

*bother—at least one of us should be amassing
merchandise.*

Now it's your turn.

Me

"Thanks, Lord." Houston grinned and read her words
again. "I'm pretty gone on this girl. Maybe she's the one You're
dropping in my lap." He sure hoped so. Beth. Nice name. Short
and to the point.

Beth,
It's good to meet you. I'm Houston. Houston James.

He noticed she didn't give her last name, but that was okay.
He'd provide her the time and space she needed. And he'd be
completely honest and open.

*I've wrestled with the same demons you mentioned.
And all I know is that yours is the first e-mail I want to
read when I get up in the morning and yours is the last
e-mail I want to send before I crawl into bed for the night.
You make my dreams sweeter and my mornings brighter,
and you feel like a kindred soul who loves God as much as
I do.*
*From the sound of your note, I'd bet you've been hurt
and lied to—probably by a guy who broke your heart.
Trust is a gift and when broken, hard to repair. I don't
ever want to break the trust you've so graciously bestowed
on me. So thanks for taking a risk on this Texas boy.*

I promise you, I'm as authentic as they come and you can ask me anything. I'll give you nothing but the truth.

I think I already told you about my childhood. I lived with my grandparents while my dad followed the rodeo circuit around the country. I, too, am so grateful for family. All I have left is my dad and some distant relatives I barely know. Someday, when I meet a special lady, I want a half dozen kids to fill the house with noise and laughter.

I don't know what God's doing with your business plans, but He knows. A line from one of my favorite songs says, "When the darkness closes in, Lord, still I will say, 'Blessed be the name of the Lord, blessed be Your name. Blessed be the name of the Lord, blessed be Your glorious name.'"

I'm late for work. So until tonight, my California dreamer, I'll be missing you.

Houston

Chapter 6

"Oh my goodness—I'm in love with the guy," Ana gushed as the three of them read Houston's e-mail together. "I want to clone him."

"If you do, make me one, too," Sheryl joked. "While you guys are at work, I'm going to Google him."

"That's awful." A pang of guilt stabbed Jonica. "I already feel horrible. As much as he stressed honesty, I feel like the biggest fraud on the face of the earth."

"That's why I'm doing the dirty work," Sheryl reminded. "We just need to guarantee he's the real deal before we turn you loose to live your own life."

"No one else would put up with you two," Jonica reminded her roommates.

"We know," they chimed in unison.

Jonica switched topics. "Hey, I found an ad in Sunday's paper for a manager to run a new upscale antique store here in Tucson. I'd do everything but the bookkeeping and buying. And let's face it—buying hasn't been my forte so far. At least not on eBay. What do you guys think?"

"Breakfast—I think I need my cereal before I have to make a life decision for you," Sheryl quipped.

The three of them headed for the kitchen. Sheryl grabbed several cereal boxes while Ana set the milk on the table. Jonica gathered up spoons and bowls. Once they were all seated, Jonica read the newspaper ad aloud while they both filled their bowls.

"What are your long-term goals?" asked Ana, pouring milk over her shredded wheat cereal.

Jonica shrugged, reaching for a box. "For the first time in my life, I have absolutely no idea." And she felt so lost without a plan.

Sheryl studied her a moment. "If you could do anything, what would it be?"

"If I didn't have to eat and pay rent, I'd write music. But since money is required for survival—"

"Jonica, running a business takes an enormous amount of focus and energy. If your heart's not in it, I don't think you should waste your time. Apply for this job, and then in your off hours you can write music." Ana tilted her head to the side. "Just my opinion."

"I agree," Sheryl piped in. "Give yourself a year and reevaluate."

"My dad will be so disappointed." Jonica stared into the half-empty cereal bowl.

"We know your dad," Ana said, "and he'd be more disappointed if you only followed your list to please him."

"Jonica, your parents want you to be happy and fulfilled—not glued to some list. You have to let go of it."

"Maybe God's trying to teach you to follow Him instead of your own goals." Ana shrugged.

"You're right. I'll send in a résumé. That doesn't mean I'll get the job, but I have nothing to lose trying." Jonica emptied the remains of her breakfast down the garbage disposal, loading her bowl and spoon into the dishwasher. "Between updating my résumé and writing to my sweet Texas boy, my day should be full." Jonica grinned and winked on her way out of the kitchen. Just thinking about Houston gave her a delicious feeling in the pit of her stomach.

Her first stop was the computer. She reread his e-mail—this time without an extra four eyes peering over her shoulder. She savored his words, and her heart beat a tad faster when she read "my California dreamer." *I sure hope you're the real deal, because I'm falling.*

Hi, Houston,

Thanks for understanding and empathizing. I've never had an Internet friend before, and my roommates are trying to pound the fear of strangers into my head. I have to tell you, though, I'm having a hard time being afraid of you. You just feel like the safest and best part of my day.

You are right, though; I do have some trust issues. I did have a guy break my heart while I was in college. He wasn't honest, nor was he everything he claimed to be. It was a long time ago, but the residual effects remain. How about you—have you ever been in love?

I'm going to apply for some jobs today. I've decided to hold off opening a store since I'm not even sure that's what

I want to do. If I work for someone else, I'll have time to write music and dream. Thanks for reminding me how important our dreams are.

Have a wonderful day at work. Looking forward to your next e-mail.

Me

Late in the afternoon, Ana brought home a pizza, so the three girls gathered in the kitchen to eat and share tidbits from their day.

"I fine-tuned my résumé and mailed it off to some PO box in Phoenix. There wasn't a name or anything, which makes me a little uneasy." Jonica tore off a slice of Hawaiian pizza.

"Well, I spent my day on the Web hunting down info on Houston James." Sheryl paused to take a drink of her diet soda. "I found nothing except some Pearl Harbor survivor. I did, however, find an Ivan Houston James, better known as the Texas Kid. A rodeo veteran and possibly Houston's dad. He participated in professional rodeo almost longer than anyone, and though never a big winner, he placed consistently in the top ten."

Sheryl paused for a bite. "I couldn't find any info on his family or personal life. Or where he is now or if he's even alive. Seemed like rodeo was his life."

"So how old is this Ivan fellow?" Jonica asked.

"Somewhere around fifty-five now."

"He must be Houston's dad." Jonica was certain.

"Hey, speaking of Houston, let's go see if lover boy wrote us an e-mail," Ana said.

Jonica hated sharing him and their personal correspondence, but she'd promised, so for the time being, she'd endure. As she pulled up her e-mail account, her roommates hovered behind her chair.

> *Hi, Beth,*
>   *Your roommates are wise and you should listen to them.*

"Didn't we say that?" Sheryl asked. "Smart guy."

> *If you were my sister, I'd be throwing a fit about now. I'd be telling you how crazy you are. But I have an idea to put everyone at rest. Why don't you and your roommates hop in the car, and in seven hours and eleven minutes (per MapQuest), you'd be in Phoenix.*

"He lives in Phoenix!" Jonica was shocked and excited. "I thought he lived somewhere in Texas. Do you have any idea how close he is?" The echo of her pounding heart beat in her ears.

> *Or if and when you're ready, I'll make the drive to Bakersfield.*

"He wants to meet us!" Ana was nearly giddy. "I say we go."

> *My store is in Scottsdale—Agape Antiques because they have been loved unconditionally. Maybe it sounds a little corny, but I somehow wanted to convey that I was a Christ follower to other believers. I'm usually there from*

9:00 to 5:00 daily, except Sundays. I can't wait until the day my eyes meet yours for the first time.

"Me either, baby. Me either," Ana joked, but his words melted Jonica's heart into a warm puddle much like melted candle wax.

Ah, Beth, you are the best part of my day, too. When I see your name in my inbox, my heart dances a jig. And though I've never been in love before, I have a feeling it's pretty wonderful. I have a feeling you're pretty wonderful. I'm sorry some guy hurt you, and if you ever give me your heart, I'll protect it with all that I am.

Jonica knew he already had her heart—every ounce of it.

I think holding off on your own store might be the best idea. You deserve to love what you do and do what you love.

Dream a sweet dream,
Houston

She rose from the computer chair and strolled across the room. "He's barely a hundred miles away. I had no idea he was so close, so accessible." Excitement knotted in her gut.

"Do you have any idea what we're doing this weekend?" Sheryl asked.

Jonica's heart beat even faster. She turned and faced them. "No way."

"He invited us," Ana reminded her.

Suddenly, meeting Houston seemed overwhelming. "I'm not ready."

"Are you giving in to the fear thing again?" Sheryl questioned.

"Yes. Yes, I am. What if he's not attracted to me when he sees me?"

"Pretty unlikely, Miss Cute-and-Petite," Ana said. "Are you afraid you might not be attracted to him?"

"I'm afraid of it all. It's a risk. This is safe. I don't want to meet him." She continued pacing back and forth across the living room. "It's too new. I can't do it—not yet."

Sheryl grabbed her arm. "Jonica, think about it. We visit his store incognito, and if there's no attraction, you never introduce yourself."

Ana nodded. "The sooner the better. You're already half in love with the guy. Why let yourself fall deeper if it isn't going to work?"

"I'll think about it—no promises, though."

❧

"Dad, thanks for having dinner with me tonight." Houston shook open his napkin and laid it across his lap.

"I never turn down a free meal, especially Mexican food," the older Houston James joked. "What's up, son? You seem to have a lot on your mind."

His dad knew him well. "There are a couple of things I'd hoped to discuss with you." He laid a copy of Jonica Granger's résumé on the table in front of his dad and let out a long sigh.

"The ad's been out for two weeks, and she's our best applicant. Problem is, she's one of those scholarly types and has little job experience."

His dad perused the résumé while a woman in a bright skirt poured water into their glasses. "But she does have an MBA."

Houston nodded. "What she learned in the classroom, we learned in the real world. Hopefully the classroom was enough."

"How many did you receive total?" His dad's brows drew together.

"Only three."

The same waitress returned with chips and salsa. Then she wrote down their order; both requested the combo plate: taco, enchilada, tamale, beans, and rice. She took the menus and departed.

The elder Houston shook his head. "What sort of work experience do the other two have?"

"Well, they have more work and less schooling. One lady has managed a fast-food restaurant for a decade. The guy who applied was in real estate and is looking for a day job that gives him more time with his wife and kids." Houston dipped a chip into the salsa bowl.

"The younger woman seems the best choice." His dad waved the résumé in the air. "Let's look at our options, son. I could run the Phoenix store, and you could run the Tucson store—or you can hire this girl."

Houston nodded. "But I thought we'd decided on the two of us staying in Phoenix. Remember—church, friends, leases?"

"I remember." His dad took a sip of water and continued.

"Let's hire her. You spend a day each week in Tucson, and we'll reassess in six months."

Their hot plates of spicy Mexican food arrived. Both let talk subside while they enjoyed their meal. Near the end his dad asked, "You said a couple of things. What else is on your mind?"

Houston laid down his fork. "Love."

His dad choked and coughed. "Love?"

Chapter 7

"I met a girl, Dad." Houston filled him in on the Beth journey. "I think I'm falling in love with her. Is that possible? I mean, do you think you can love someone you've never met? Could it happen this quickly? I've only known her a few months."

His dad laid down his fork, his blue eyes smiling. "Yes to both, son. Your grandparents met as pen pals during World War II. Before either had ever laid eyes on the other, your grandpa proposed and your grandma accepted. You know how deep their love ran."

Houston nodded as a busboy picked up their plates.

"When I met your mom, it wasn't two months and I knew I wanted to spend the rest of my life with her." His eyes misted up. "I just didn't know how short the rest of her life would be."

"Dad, after twenty-five years without her, you still wear your wedding ring. Why?"

His dad smiled, and Houston could tell by the look in his eye that he was somewhere far, far away. "I've just never wanted to take it off. I figured someday the time would feel right, but it never has." He twirled the ring on his finger. "Guess I'm a one-woman man, 'cause there's never been another one to catch my eye."

The waitress brought the bill, and Houston slipped his debit card into the folder.

Houston senior picked up his copy of the résumé and switched topics. "Why don't you set up an interview with Ms. Granger down in Tucson for one day next week? I think you'll have a better feel once you meet her."

"I'll do that," Houston agreed.

"And as for the love thing, I have an old shoe box of your grandparents' letters. Would you like to read them?"

"That would be great, Dad."

"You can swing by my place and pick them up on your way home tonight."

Houston knew his grin was ear to ear. "I can only stay a minute." He winked. "I have to get home and send an e-mail to a certain California girl who's stealin' my heart."

His dad gave him a pat on the back. "I'm glad it's finally happening for you, son."

When Houston arrived home that night, he found an e-mail from Beth. He hoped she'd soon be willing to meet face-to-face or at least share phone numbers. Then he thought of his grandparents, half a world apart, waiting endless days for the mail service. No, this really wasn't too bad.

Houston,

Is a part of you terrified to meet in person? What if the attraction isn't there? What if when you see me, I'm

nothing like what you expected? What if you think I'm
ugly? Or too fat? Too thin? My nose is too big? My hair
is too curly? What if I'm a blond and you go for redheads?
What if we meet and there's nothing? Has any of this
crossed your mind? Or am I—as my roommate often
accuses—thinking too much?

Me

Houston chuckled. "Whoa, Nellie." He'd have to do some
reassuring tonight.

Hey, Beth,
    I'm not afraid to meet you, because what really
matters, I already know. You are compassionate, car-
ing, and I'm crazy about you. You love the Lord, and
I believe you're part of His plan for me. If that's true,
what do I have to fear? Every good and perfect gift is
from Him. The love shared by a man and a woman is
from Him, and who knows us more intricately than
our Creator? I'm absolutely sure I'll adore everything
about you.

Yours,
Houston

While waiting for her reply, Houston emptied the box of
his grandparents' letters onto his bed. He started putting them
in chronological order by the postmarks. Then the little beep
sounded, and he knew Beth had responded.

Houston,

*You make me feel ashamed of myself for all the doubts.
I wish I had your faith and your strength in the Lord.
Somehow, though, you always calm my fears and point
me back toward Him. Thank you for that. Thank you
for becoming my still point in this madcap, mixed-up life
I'm suddenly living. I feel as though God is turning me
upside down and inside out. The plans of man are mere
foolishness, as all my plans have certainly proven.*

Me

After Houston read her e-mail, he began to read the words
his grandparents' had shared so long ago. He decided to share
their story with Beth. Maybe that would put her mind at ease.

Beth,

*Tonight my dad gave me a box of letters my
grandparents wrote to one another during the war. They
had never met, yet they formed a strong friendship that
moved quickly to something deeper. The first time they
met was on their wedding day, and not only did their love
endure almost fifty-five years, but it thrived. They were
simply crazy for each other.*

*"I don't know yet what the good Lord has planned for
us, but I know in absolute certainty, whatever it is, it's
good because He is good." My grandfather wrote that to my
grandmother in their third correspondence. Do you see how
quickly their feelings moved forward? They'd never spoken,
never seen one another, yet they couldn't deny what was*

happening inside their hearts. Nor can I—nor can I. I'm falling for you, fast and hard.

Always,
Houston

He knew before hitting SEND that this e-mail would forever change their relationship, but he didn't know which direction Beth would head. Either his words would draw them closer, or she would run as fast and far as she could in the opposite direction. A risk, yes, but he wasn't big on games. What you saw in him was what you got. What he felt, he said.

⧼◌⧽

"He's in love with us!" Ana's voice rang with excitement.

"Sorry to break it to ya, babe—he's not in love with us. He's in love with Jonica." Sheryl was nothing if not matter-of-fact. "We *have* to go to Phoenix this Saturday; otherwise it won't make a difference if he's a serial killer because we'll all be so wild about this guy we won't care."

Jonica knew Sheryl was right.

"How do you feel about his proclamation?" Ana asked.

"Giddy." Jonica sighed. "I'm falling, too, and that scares me to death."

"Not in your plan, huh?" Sheryl said in jest.

"No." Jonica smiled. "Life quit going according to plan the day I got my MBA. I wish I had the faith of Houston's grandfather." She swiveled her chair back toward the computer. "Now, girls, if you'll excuse me, I have an e-mail to answer." She began to type.

Houston,

 I'm crazy about you, too. My heart is experiencing all sorts of feelings it's never felt before. Just thinking about you plants this doofy smile across my face. Are we nuts?

 My own ancestors all had unconventional love stories, so why ours takes my breath away, I'm not sure. My great-grandfather wrote a song for his beloved. My grandfather put tender words into fortune cookies to woo my grandmother. He also believed God told him upon their first meeting that she was the one He'd chosen for his wife. My own dear parents began their relationship on sticky notes, having no idea who the other was. Why I am surprised or doubting? I don't know.

 All I know is you're terrific, and I don't want to spoil these tender feelings but nurture them.

Hugs,
Me

She never referred to herself as Beth—always signing off as "Me." It felt like less of a lie because she truly was "me."

❧

Saturday arrived and the three girls loaded into Sheryl's yellow Nissan Xterra and drove northwest up Interstate 10 to the Phoenix area. Scottsdale was a northeastern suburb and an affluent area. They decided to make a day of it. First they'd take care of business and visit Agape Antiques. From there, the day could play out in several different ways. But all in all, it would include food, friends, shopping, and undoubtedly a new pair of shoes.

Sheryl informed the other two that she'd checked out the store and its owner. All reports indicated that both had an impeccable reputation. The news lessened Jonica's tension a degree or two.

Almost two hours later they parked in front of an upscale shopping area in Scottsdale. Jonica's heart pounded and her mouth went dry. Her insides resembled a bowl of Jell-O, and the possibility of puking lay in the forefront of her mind. Ana gave her an encouraging hug and then a light shove toward the door.

"Will you go in first?" she asked Ana. "I'll follow you. That way I'm safely sandwiched between you two. We'll just act like we're shopping and check out the place and the antiques."

When they entered the store, a balding, middle-aged man greeted them. "Hello, ladies. Can I help you find anything in particular?"

Sheryl responded. "Thanks, but we're just looking. Do you mind if we peruse?"

"Not at all. Take your time and enjoy." He returned to the front of the store—a slight limp shortening his stride.

They headed for the far corner of the store and pretended to admire a Crotch mahogany vanity dresser and chair. Jonica ran her hand across the impeccable finish. "I can't believe this. Do you think that's him?" she asked in a whisper, her stomach whipping around like a blender set on LIQUEFY.

Sheryl shrugged. "Only one way to find out: Ask."

"I can't ask. What if he says yes? You ask."

The three girls sauntered toward the man, trying to act casual and nonchalant. A knot the size of Texas filled Jonica's gut. Sheryl led the pack as they approached the shopkeeper. Near the front door, he lovingly dusted each antique with a big feather duster.

The bell on the door rang, and a UPS man entered with a dolly full of boxes. "Hey, Houston, how's your day?"

All of the fear and trepidation that churned inside Jonica solidified into anger. Not only was his name Houston, but a wedding ring on his hand caught the sunlight as he dusted! She marched past Sheryl and Ana and slapped Houston James across the cheek. She'd never forget the stunned expression on his face or the red handprint across his cheek. She heard the UPS man and her roommates share a unified gasp.

"You are the biggest *jerk* in the entire world." Jonica stormed out the door with Ana and Sheryl on her heels.

They hopped into the SUV and sped away. Jonica's hand stung, and she only hoped his face hurt worse.

"I feel like we're escaping a bank robbery or something," Ana said. "My adrenaline is pumping."

About a block away, Sheryl pulled into a gas station parking lot and began to laugh hysterically. "I can't believe you did that." She choked out the words between peals of laughter. "But, man, did he deserve that slap!"

"What a creep. Did you see he was wearing a wedding ring?" Ana asked.

Sickened by the whole thing, Jonica felt dazed by the events that had unfolded moments before. She'd fallen for a man who wasn't real. A fake. A phony. A married man. "I was duped. I thought you guys were overreacting, but you were right. I will never, ever correspond with anyone over the Net again unless I know them personally." Tears streamed down her cheeks, and she tried to swipe them away, but more quickly replaced the ones she'd erased.

Both Sheryl and Ana hugged her where she sat in the front passenger seat—at least the best they could given the restrictions of the vehicle.

"He fooled all of us," Sheryl admitted. "I honestly thought he was the real deal."

"Me, too," Ana agreed.

Jonica sniffed. "Thanks for making me come up here. Otherwise, who knows what may have happened." She dabbed her wet cheeks with the tissue that Ana handed her. "I hate men."

Chapter 8

"Hey, Dad. How's the morning gone so far?" Houston stepped out from the office/stockroom when he arrived at the store. He always entered through the back door. He'd taken the morning off to golf, as he always did one Saturday a month. Being alone on a golf course gave a man time to think, talk with God, and rid himself of stress.

His dad touched his left cheek. "The most bizarre thing happened. Three young women came into the store—just looking, or so they said. Then while Dave was here dropping off our latest shipment, one of them stormed up and slapped me!"

"You're serious?" Houston couldn't imagine.

"As a heart attack." He rubbed his cheek again. "Said I was the biggest jerk in the entire world."

"Three women? Maybe some sort of sorority initiation." He honestly had no clue.

His dad nodded.

"What did they look like?"

"I don't know, son—didn't pay much attention. I didn't gawk at them or anything."

Houston drew his lips together in a tight line. "So they were in the store and Dave walked in. Start from there."

"I stood about here dusting these vases." His dad reenacted the event. "Dave brought in several big boxes on a dolly and rolled them past me toward the counter. I greeted him, not paying those girls any mind at all."

"Did Dave say anything?" Houston willed his dad to remember.

"Just the usual greeting." His dad frowned, probably wondering about the interrogation. "He gave me an earful after they left. Kidded with me about being a heartbreaker."

It made no sense at all, unless—Beth and her roommates! He'd invited them to drop by just a few days ago. She'd never mentioned anything, but maybe she'd wanted to surprise him. His gut clenched at the possibility. "Do you remember if he used your name at all?"

His dad thought a moment, then nodded. "Yeah, I think he said something like, 'Hey, Houston. How are you today?'"

"It was Beth—had to be. I asked her to come. . .just didn't think it'd be so soon. And without even letting me know."

"What are you mumbling about, son?"

"I think it might have been the girl I told you about. The one I'm crazy for but have never met. The one who is now convinced you're me."

A worried look settled on his dad's features. "If that's the case, son, you got yourself a real spitfire. I'd be careful if I was you."

Houston smiled at the advice. "So was it right after Dave greeted you that this woman slapped you?"

324

"Yep." He shook his head. "Never saw it coming. I was watching Dave, thinking about what surprise each box held. Suddenly, she was right there with fire in her eyes. And *wham*. My face stung like crazy." He once again rubbed his cheek. "She marched out the door with her two friends following." He paused. "We sure do live in a violent world anymore."

Houston nodded. It had to be Beth. Who else?

"I'm sorry, Dad. I think you took one for the team. I'm guessing that slap had my name on it, and your face was in the wrong place at the wrong time."

"If that's true, son, you're going to have to rein in that filly a little bit. She's too wild for my taste."

Houston didn't bother to explain the whole situation. "You're right. I'll be in on the computer." He returned to the office area.

The first thing he did was sign in to his e-mail and search for an e-mail from Beth among the new arrivals. He wasn't surprised when none was there.

Beth,

I just got into the store this morning and my dad told me what happened. I'm guessing you paid a surprise visit and mistook him for me. By the way, he said you have a great right slap.

He hoped the joke would lighten the situation.

I'm so sorry for the confusion. Wish I knew how to get in touch with you and straighten this out. I'm praying

you get this e-mail before you make the long drive back to
Bakersfield so that we can meet and you can see the truth.
Please call ASAP.

> *Still yours,*
> *Houston*

He included his work, home, and cell phone numbers, but he didn't expect her to use them. He tried to catch up on some bookkeeping but spent more time checking and rechecking his e-mail inbox.

Late that night, after Houston had arrived home, he received an e-mail from Beth. There was no salutation; she just jumped right in.

> *Listen, whoever you are, I'm not doing this anymore.*
> *I don't believe you, and I don't trust you. I happen to know*
> *your dad's name is Ivan—if he was indeed the rodeo star*
> *you claim.*
>
> *I'm fairly certain if I looked up jerk in the dictionary,*
> *your picture would be there. Please don't e-mail me again.*
> *I never want to hear from you—EVER!*

Short and direct. Her words stabbed his heart with pain and sorrow. Could it be over before it began? Houston blew out a long, slow breath.

He quoted his favorite song aloud to remind himself God was still there. God was still faithful. " 'When the darkness closes in, Lord, still I will say, Blessed be the name of the Lord, blessed be Your name. Blessed be the name of the Lord, blessed be Your glorious name.'" Then he sat down and typed one final note. He needed closure.

> *Beth,*
>
> *I know you asked me not to contact you, but please read this last correspondence. Then it's up to you. I'll honor your no-contact request, but my heart will ache with the choice.*
>
> *Please don't let this confused identity spoil what we had. I'm so ready to meet you and have nothing to hide. I was planning a trip to Bakersfield to surprise you. I was trying to glean enough info to be able to track you down once I arrived. Now the surprise is on me. I wanted to take you on our first real date, hold your hand, see your smile.*
>
> *I still believe you're the one for me—the one God chose. How can I get back into your good graces? How can I change your mind?*
>
>

I love you,
Houston
>

He hesitated over whether or not to say he loved her, but this might be his last chance. He hit SEND, sensing the futility and finality of their relationship.

◌⑧

When Jonica arose on Sunday morning, she'd received another e-mail from Houston, even though she'd asked him to discontinue communication. The subject line said, "My last e-mail, but please read it." She didn't read it, but she didn't delete it, either.

Sunday passed in a haze of melancholy. Even attending church and her Bible fellowship hadn't lifted her glum spirit.

On Monday morning, both roommates read Houston's latest e-mail. At breakfast, Sheryl said, "I don't know. I just don't know what to think."

"He sounds so sincere." Ana fixed her gaze on Jonica. "Said he loves you."

The news squeezed Jonica's heart with even more pain. Her mind was tired of thinking about it. "If he's lying, would he continue the pursuit?" she wondered aloud.

The phone rang. Jonica picked up the cordless lying on the kitchen counter. "Hello."

"Jonica Granger, please," a rich baritone with a Texas twang requested.

Her heart dropped, and she swallowed hard. "This is she."

"Yes, Ms. Granger." The man's tone was pure business. "This is Houston James."

Jonica leaned against the counter, her legs suddenly weak. "Houston James?" she lamely questioned. "How—" She stumbled over the words. "How did you find me?"

Her roommates sat up straighter and their mouths dropped open.

"You sent me a résumé a couple of weeks back, and you included your phone number."

"A résumé?" She breathed out relief.

"I'd like to set up an interview."

"An interview?" Knowing she sounded like a complete idiot, she tried to redeem herself. "Yes, an interview. Of course."

"Ms. Granger, are you still interested in the job?" His tone had grown slightly exasperated.

"Am I still interested?" She glanced at Ana and Sheryl. She could at least see which guy showed up. "I think so."

"Did you already accept another position?"

"No. No, I don't have another job." Her heart hammered so hard in her chest she could hear it echoing in her ears.

"Could you meet with me sometime this week?"

"Yes. I'm free tomorrow." The sooner the better. Jonica needed to see this man in person, because either his voice was quite different on the phone, or he wasn't the man she'd encountered in the antique store.

"Fine. Why don't we meet for lunch up at La Encantada. Say, Firebirds Rocky Mountain Grill at noon?"

"I'll be there, and thank you." Did he notice the quiver in her voice?

"Until tomorrow, then." A click sounded in her ear.

Jonica laid the phone back on the counter, releasing a huge sigh. "That was him." Her voice still wasn't quite normal. "And I sounded like a total moron."

"Why are you going to meet with him?" Ana questioned.

"I have to be sure. What if he's telling the truth? What if he's just a victim of a huge misunderstanding?" She returned to her soggy bowl of cereal.

"Then we're going with you," Sheryl assured her.

Jonica laughed. "You can't go with me on a job interview."

"Sure we can," Ana interjected. "We're getting pretty good at this spy stuff."

"We'll be there, keeping an eye on you, and he'll never even know."

At Jonica's doubtful expression, Sheryl added, "I promise."

After dumping most of her cereal down the garbage disposal, Jonica gave in and read his e-mail. A part of her believed him or at least desperately wanted to. If he was telling the truth, she'd probably slapped his dad. She both winced and chuckled at the thought.

The next day Jonica dressed with care, choosing a soft, feminine, short-sleeve sweater in baby pink and a black and pink diagonally striped skirt that swirled around her knees. She applied her makeup with light touches. She was pleased with the results. Her hair behaved perfectly, and she felt pretty. Her heart raced in anticipation.

She rode with Ana and Sheryl. They—of course—had concocted a plan but had to arrive early to ensure its success. Upon entering the restaurant, accented by a large fireplace in the waiting area, they gave the hostess the short version of their arrangement. She agreed to seat them first—just as soon as Houston made his appearance. Then she would seat Jonica and Houston nearby. Ana slipped her a twenty to make it worth her while.

The three roommates took a seat in the waiting area. Ana and Sheryl sat together across from Jonica. Every time the door opened, she jumped. She'd already decided if the recipient of her slap showed up, she'd leave immediately.

Then in walked the golden guy she'd met briefly the day she was with Sherrie. *Surely he can't be Houston!* Her heart beat like a tom-tom in anticipation, but her logical left brain kept insisting, "No way."

He approached the hostess.

She held her breath.

"I'm Houston James. I have a noon reservation."

Ana gave her the thumbs-up sign, and Sheryl only grinned. Jonica shook her head in disbelief. The mystery only grew more complex.

The hostess shuffled some papers. "Yes, sir. Here you are." She made a small pencil mark by his name. "The other half of your party is seated in our waiting area."

Houston's blue eyes scanned the section and rested on Jonica. Recognition lit his face.

He remembers. She'd hoped he wouldn't, because it gave him another clue to connect Beth to Jonica. Panic bubbled up inside her. *How will I ever dig my way out of this mess? Why, why did I lie? I knew better.*

"Would that be her in the pink?" he asked in his slow Texas way.

"I believe so, sir."

He made his way straight for her. Jonica's heart doubled its pace, and part of her hoped this was the man she'd fallen for, the man who'd said, "I love you," because not only was he a nice guy; he was a hunk—a gorgeous, gorgeous hunk. The blue shirt that he wore with khaki slacks only accentuated his beautiful eyes.

"Jonica Granger?"

She rose, nodding. Their gazes locked, and something inside her exploded.

"I'm Houston James." He shook her hand, only adding to her feeling of light-headedness. *Are you really? Are you the man who claims to love me?*

She cleared her throat. "Would you mind showing me your ID?"

He shot her a perplexed expression, and she heard a snicker from Ana but didn't dare glance her direction.

"My ID?" He raised an eyebrow in apparent disbelief. "I thought I was the one conducting the interview."

"Of course." Jonica fumbled through her pink purse. "I'll show you mine." She shoved her license toward him.

He studied her a moment before accepting it. His look confirmed that he thought she was some sort of nutcase. He said her name. "Jonica Beth Granger." He seemed to add extra emphasis to *Beth*, and she cringed. *That was a dumb move—a dumb, dumb move.*

Houston handed her license back and reached for his wallet in his back pocket.

"Ana, party of two," the hostess called.

Both Ana and Sheryl gave her an unbelieving stare and followed the hostess to their table.

Houston handed her his license, and she studied it for several seconds. His name was Houston Ivan James, and he was indeed thirty. She returned his license, all sorts of emotions swirling through her. But at the forefront was what a disaster she'd created.

"Are you okay?" he asked. "You look like you've seen a ghost."

"I'm fine—just fine," she said a little too cheerily.

"Houston, party of two," the hostess called.

Houston took Jonica's elbow, and they followed the young woman to the booth just behind Ana and Sheryl. Jonica took the seat facing their booth so that Houston's back would be toward them. Surely that was safest. After Ana's snicker, she wasn't sure they were capable of being as good as they had promised.

Jonica studied Houston. Today his face was scruff free, and amazing dimples accentuated his cheeks when he smiled or talked. *And this man said he loved me.* How would he feel when he learned she'd rearranged the truth along with her name? Should she blurt out the facts or wait until the right moment? Would there ever be a right moment to say, "By the way, I'm also Beth, and other than being a big fat liar, I'm the girl of your dreams"?

Chapter 9

Houston took the proffered menu from the hostess. The woman across from him was lovely, and all he could think of was Beth. As of this morning, she hadn't responded to his last e-mail, and it had been over forty-eight hours. His hope grew dim.

He studied the menu and decided on a sirloin served with a blue cheese sauce. The waitress arrived, and Jonica ordered a salad.

"You sure that's all you want?"

She nodded.

"Well, not this Texas boy." He placed his order and then told Jonica, "I like my meat and potatoes." He studied her a moment. "So, Ms. Granger, tell me what you know about antiques and why I should hire you."

She thought for a moment before speaking. He liked that quality in a person. Too often people rushed forward instead of weighing their words. While waiting, he noted the brown flecks in her otherwise green eyes, and she lowered her gaze under his scrutiny.

"My moth—family loves antiques, so they've always been a big part of my life." She seemed very nervous and chose her words a little too carefully. It seemed as though she was hiding something; either that or she had zero self-confidence.

"How about you—do you love antiques?" he persisted.

Jonica paused and forced a smile. "Not as much as my mother does."

"But you're the one applying for the job. Frankly, I don't care how your mother feels." He'd grown impatient.

"Of course you don't." She finally made eye contact. "*Love* is such a relative term. The point I hoped to make was yes, I suppose you could say I love antiques, but not to the same degree another person might."

This woman actually has an MBA! How in the world did that happen? So far she'd been inept at carrying on a logical conversation. Even on the phone yesterday, she seemed none too bright. Unless she recovered quickly, there would be no way he'd hire her—not ever.

"But in my own way, I do love antiques and feel my education has prepared me for the job you have available." She'd gone from carefully choosing words to rattling them off a mile a minute.

Something about her was familiar. He'd quit listening and tried to place her. "Have we met before?"

"Maybe." She shrugged as though it couldn't possibly matter. "I do think—"

He clicked his fingers and pointed. "You were the one interested in leasing the shop across the street."

She grew silent, fidgeting in her seat.

He frowned. "What were your plans for that building?"

She looked past him and hesitated. "I intended to open my own antique store."

Houston lifted a brow. "I see. And what changed your mind?"

She rearranged her silverware. "Does it matter?"

"It might," he challenged.

"I was having a hard time finding a good location when I ran across your ad."

Wait—this is sounding all too familiar. Jonica Beth *Granger? Mother loves antiques. Never found a spot for her store.* "The right location is of utmost importance when opening a business." His words echoed with sarcasm. *Is it possible, Lord?* He wiped his palms on his khakis and focused on her.

She smiled a tight smile, and her discomfort grew.

His mind whirled. Amazing that she was the one concerned about honesty and trust.

The waitress brought their salads. Jonica spent a lot of time adding the dressing and mixing it up just so. While she was preoccupied, he studied her. She was still adorable, which had been his line of thinking upon meeting her the first time. But was she Beth? His Beth? Couldn't be. Beth lived in California. Didn't she? She glanced up and caught him staring and quickly looked away.

Houston ate a forkful of salad. The day he leased his new Tucson shop, Beth had lost a dream, and Jonica had lost the shop to him. "Do you ever go by Beth?" he asked.

A look of horror crossed her face. "Not really."

Not exactly a solid no.

He nodded, taking another bite. "Where were you born?"

She shifted gears and sat up straighter. "I'm sorry, but what does that have to do with a job interview?" she asked, her tone defensive.

"Plenty. I need that information to run a full background check."

"Oh—a full background check." Then she mumbled, "California." She lay her napkin on the table. "Will you excuse me a moment, please?"

Upon his nod, she nearly ran toward the women's restroom.

Her absence gave Houston time to think about the ramifications of his suspicions. If he were right, neither Beth nor Jonica would ever have to worry about him again. There wasn't much he hated more than dishonesty and duplicity. Disappointment settled into his heart. Beth had turned out to be too good to be true. *I don't understand. Why wouldn't she tell me the truth? What sort of game is she playing?*

ॐ

Ana and Sheryl followed Jonica into the restroom.

"He knows." Jonica paced the width of the bathroom. "He's figured out that I'm Beth."

Sheryl grabbed her arm. "Jonica, calm down and take a deep breath. You were going to tell him anyway, right?"

"I don't know. I didn't expect this and haven't had time to think or come up with a plan."

"Just go back to the table and tell him the truth," Ana encouraged.

"We'll go with you," Sheryl volunteered.

"What if he hates me?"

Sheryl shook her head. "You hated him yesterday. You've apparently worked through it; so will he."

Jonica stared at her pale face in the mirror. Raising her chin, she swallowed her fear. "Of course I have to go out there and tell him the truth. What am I thinking?" She marched out the door, leaving Ana and Sheryl behind.

Upon returning, she noticed Houston's steak had arrived. She slid into her side of the booth.

Clearing her throat, she announced in a no-nonsense tone, "I'm Beth." Heart pounding wildly, she waited—for what seemed like an eternity—for his response.

He stared at her, unblinking. "I figured as much." He kept staring as if she'd just announced the weather or some other nonessential piece of information. Finally, he said, "Jonica *Beth* Granger, so it wasn't really a lie, right?"

Her face warmed with embarrassment. She didn't miss the sarcasm mingled with his every word. "I did lie to you, and I'm sorry. Please forgive me." Her heart splintered into millions of pieces at his hardened expression.

"No wonder you have trust issues." He slid his plate, filled with uneaten food, away as if her deception had caused him to lose his appetite. "It's hard to trust others when you're not honest yourself."

Jonica closed her eyes, her chin dropping to her chest. His accusation cut deep, and tears formed in her throat.

"Wait a minute there, buddy," Sheryl said as she slid in next to Houston.

Houston's mouth gaped.

Jonica shook her head. *This just gets better by the second. If only there were a rock to crawl under.*

Ana slid in next to Jonica. "We told her not to give her real name over the Internet. Do you have any idea how dangerous that is?" She pointed a scolding finger at him.

Houston shook his head in disbelief. "Oh, let me guess—the roommates, right?"

"Sheryl." She held out her right hand. Houston accepted it. "And that's Ana." Sheryl nodded her head in Ana's direction.

Ana also shook his hand.

"So what stopped you from telling the truth today? Or better yet, on the phone yesterday?" One brow rose above Houston's baby blues. His expression challenged Jonica to explain.

"She was getting around to it." Sheryl's frown dared him to dispute those facts.

"Yeah!" Ana threw in her nickel for what it was worth.

"Look. . ." Jonica's voice quaked, and she hated how pathetic and weak she sounded. "This whole ordeal has gone from bad to worse. I have managed to slap whom I assume was your father. I've lied to you about my name and let you assume I still resided in Bakersfield—"

"Also because we threatened her very life," Ana interrupted. "It's us you should be angry with, not Jonica."

His eyes fixed on hers, and the knot in her stomach grew. There was no warmth in his gaze or joy upon learning her identity. She bit her bottom lip and pleaded with her expression for his understanding. "I'm sorry. I'm asking your forgiveness. I can't undo any of this." Nothing in his appearance changed, and she sighed in resignation. Soon the tears gathering would insist on making their debut, and she didn't want him to be a party to that.

"Please excuse me." She nearly knocked Ana out of the booth trying to make her quick escape.

Chapter 10

Sheryl turned in the booth to face him, and instinctively, he knew he was in for an earful. Her green eyes sparked fire, and Ana slid in across from them, preparing for the show.

"Isn't anyone going after her?" He glanced from one to the other, hoping to divert them.

"I believe that would be *your* job," Ana informed him, a disapproving frown highlighting her face.

He looked to Sheryl, foolishly hoping she'd see his side. "How do you think I feel? I bared my soul to her, and she never even told me her real name. When did she plan to?"

"When we were certain you were the real deal." Sheryl's gaze softened the tiniest bit. "This is the most unusual love story ever, but you do love her and she loves you. Isn't that the bottom line?" Her expression pleaded with him to get past his anger.

Ana took the plunge. "If she'd lied to you under normal circumstances, it would be different, but the Net is a wild and crazy place to meet someone. Truly dangerous." She told him a tragic story about a coworker who'd trusted a man she met on the Internet.

"She would have told you on Saturday, but when Houston James turned out to be a middle-aged man wearing a wedding ring, agendas changed," Sheryl reminded him.

Houston chuckled. "My poor dad."

Ana and Sheryl joined him, all three laughing hard.

"You should have seen his face." Ana wiped the tears from her eyes.

"He informed me if I planned to keep that little filly around, she needs some taming."

They shared another round of laughter.

Sheryl's face grew serious. "Jonica asked your forgiveness. Even if nothing comes of this eBay encounter, don't you owe her that?"

The laughter had melted the hardness around his heart, and it ached, knowing he'd hurt her, and all because he let his pride get in the way. "If you'll excuse me, ladies, I have an important engagement to keep."

"Wait one second." Ana pulled out her cell phone and punched in a number. "Jonica, where are you?" She paused. "Over by White House | Black Market? Gotcha. See you soon."

Sheryl gave him directions from the restaurant to where Jonica was. Then she scooted out of the booth so he could exit. A few steps away, he turned back to them. "Thanks, ladies."

Ana gave him the thumbs-up sign. Sheryl just grinned. He heard her say, "Do you think we'll be losing a roommate soon?"

He smiled and sure hoped so.

Leaving Firebirds, his gaze roamed heavenward to the cloud-laden sky. He took a deep breath, savoring the smell of the looming storm. The air had cooled considerably. Thunder roared, and lightning shot across the sky.

"Lord, I failed her, and I failed You. Will You redeem this mess? I'm so sorry."

Houston spotted Jonica sitting on a cement bench. His heart lurched at the sight of her and the defeated slump of her slender shoulders. As he approached, she glanced his direction and their gazes locked. She straightened her posture. He could see that she'd been crying, and his heart broke. He stopped in front of her, hands jammed in his front pockets.

"Mind if I join you?" After his unrelenting anger, he felt almost sheepish.

Her eyes held hope, and she gave him a brief nod. "Please." She patted the bench next to her.

"I'm sorry." They both spoke at the same time and then smiled at each other. He sensed in her the same nervousness he was experiencing. They knew each other so well, yet not at all.

He took her hand—a soft, small, feminine version of his own. And it fit so well inside his. Instinctively he knew this was his other half—the woman God had created to complete and complement only him. He stared for countless minutes, memorizing each nuance of her perfect face. "You are a beautiful woman, Jonica—inside and out."

She smiled, relief reflected in her eyes. "You're not so bad yourself."

"Only not so bad?" He winked. "By the way, I'm Houston James." He gave her hand a little shake. "Would you like to check my ID—just to be sure?" he joked.

"A girl can't be too careful." Her smile sent his heart into orbit.

"No, she can't, and I'm sorry I let your caution make me angry. Now it's my turn to ask for forgiveness."

"Granted," she said without hesitation.

How he wished he'd been as gracious. "What should I call you? Shoppingirl, Cali, California, Beth, or Jonica?"

They laughed at the number of names she'd gone by in their three-month acquaintance. "Your choice."

"Would you have dinner with me tonight—minus the roommates?"

"We're a package deal," Ana informed him, then sat right between them, forcing him to let go of Jonica's hand.

Houston groaned. He'd been so enthralled by Jonica, he'd failed to see them approach. "Not you two again."

Ana placed one arm around Jonica's shoulders and one around Houston's. "Just one big happy family."

"So where are we going for dinner?" Sheryl asked.

"Anywhere you two aren't." Jonica laughed. "I think I'm ready for a solo flight. Time to get rid of the training wheels."

"Training wheels?" Sheryl managed an indignant expression.

"What happened to the three musketeers?" Ana frowned. "Remember—all for one and one for all." She grinned and hugged Jonica. "We can take a hint, so we're heading home."

"It appears you no longer need us," Sheryl said.

"Not much," Houston agreed.

"Fine." She folded her arms across her midsection. "You'll miss us when we're gone."

"Not much," Jonica assured them.

They said their good-byes, leaving Jonica and Houston alone. He stood and held out his hand. "Do you want to walk over to my shop?"

She accepted his extended hand. "First, can we stop by Starbucks?"

"Whatever the little lady wants." Houston exaggerated his accent.

❧

Jonica floated on Houston's arm, barely daring to believe this man was her e-mail infatuation. He was so much better than anything she'd imagined. *Thanks, God. Every good and perfect gift. . .*

"Everything between us has happened very fast." Houston seemed to choose his words with care.

At his statement, dread rose like bile in Jonica's throat. "Look, if you're having doubts. . ."

He placed his index finger against her lips. "No doubts—I promise."

She let out the breath she hadn't realized she'd been holding. "What, then?"

"I believe in the sovereignty of God and the unconventional way He does things."

She nodded her agreement.

"And I believe with all my heart you're the girl God has for me." His gaze searched hers. "Do you believe that?"

"I do."

"How about if I move to Tucson and we take our time

getting to know each other?"

"You'd do that?" The thought pleased her.

"In a New York minute. I want to marry you someday, Jonica, but I want us to know each other well enough to recognize our strengths and weaknesses as a couple. I hope we'll enjoy and savor the days to come as we seek God and fall more deeply in love."

She smiled, her heart warmed by his sensible approach.

"How about if I give you a quick tour of my store, and then we visit at Starbucks until dinnertime?"

"Sounds good. I loved that little shop. It'll be perfect for your antique sales."

"And for my assistant. I hope you'll take the job. Then after we're married, you can work part-time and write music the rest of the day."

This man of hers knew the right words to say. With every minute she loved him more.

Unlocking the store, he stood back and let her enter first. They'd used bold red on one wall. "Wow. The place looks incredible." She admired their handiwork, all very similar to what she'd had in mind.

"My dad did the painting."

"Speaking of your dad—"

Houston laughed, a rich, inviting rumble that stirred her heart. "He's fine—although he informed me you were a bit too wild for his taste. He thought the *little filly* needed reining in!"

"He called me a *filly*? That's worse than *darlin'*! I don't know about you Texas boys."

Houston grew serious. He pulled her around to face him.

Their hands were raised, chest high, palms touching. She threaded her fingers through his. Her eyes searched his face, his expression ever so tender. Her breath caught in her throat.

"My grandpa always called my grandma *darlin'*. I know I promised, but I hope you'll forgive me if I slip once or twice—it's so ingrained in me."

"Darlin'?" She spoke the single word in a breathless tone. "I don't think I'd mind at all—especially now that I *am* your darling."

Houston pulled her into his arms. "I'm dying to kiss you, darlin'."

Did she have the courage to be bold and say what was on her mind? She thought of her grandma Prudie and plowed forward. "And I'm dying to be kissed." She stood on tiptoe and met him halfway. A million emotions melded together into one passionate, toe-curling moment. If any doubts had remained, they'd now vanished.

"Darlin'." Jonica whispered the endearment, liking the sound of it more all the time.

A year later, the Granger family and the senior Houston James gathered together for the uniting of Jonica Beth to Houston Ivan James. It was a simple affair at her home church in Bakersfield. Jonica was still amazed by how well God knew her and how He gave her just what she needed—in a husband and in her dreams. From this day forward, she and Houston would dream a sweet dream together.

JERI ODELL

For Jeri Odell, writing is a privilege and a passion. She loves sharing God and His truths through both the written and spoken word and is humbled and honored that He has allowed her childhood dreams to come to fruition. Her heart for every woman is spiritual growth and an intimate, vibrant relationship with Jesus Christ. Her goal and constant prayer are that her words will bring God glory, challenge women to walk more closely with Him, and point the lost to a Savior. "I have nothing to offer anyone—in and of myself—but He offers more than we can imagine," Jeri says.

Her greatest pleasure, second only to God, is being a wife and mom. She and Dean have been married almost thirty-four years and have three adult children, two of whom are married. Family has filled their lives beyond measure.

eBay Encounter is Jeri's fifth novella. She has also written four novels for Heartsong Presents and a nonfiction book titled *Spiritually Single*. She is the recipient of the Romance Writers of America's 2002 Faith, Hope & Love Inspirational Reader's Choice Award for the Short Historical category. Along with writing, Jeri has spoken at women's events and retreats. You may visit her Web site at www.jeriodell.com.

A Letter to Our Readers

Dear Readers:

In order that we might better contribute to your reading enjoyment, we would appreciate your taking a few minutes to respond to the following questions. When completed, please return to the following: Fiction Editor, Barbour Publishing, Inc., P.O. Box 719, Uhrichsville, OH 44683.

1. Did you enjoy reading *Love Letters*?
   ❑ Very much—I would like to see more books like this.
   ❑ Moderately—I would have enjoyed it more if _____
   _____
   _____

2. What influenced your decision to purchase this book?
   (Check those that apply.)
   ❑ Cover   ❑ Back cover copy   ❑ Title   ❑ Price
   ❑ Friends   ❑ Publicity   ❑ Other

3. Which story was your favorite?
   ❑ *Love Notes*   ❑ *Posted Dreams*
   ❑ *Cookie Schemes*   ❑ *eBay Encounter*

4. Please check your age range:
   ❑ Under 18   ❑ 18–24   ❑ 25–34
   ❑ 35–45   ❑ 46–55   ❑ Over 55

5. How many hours per week do you read? _____

Name _____

Occupation _____

Address _____

City_____ State_____ Zip_____

E-mail_____